GETTING THERE

JOE VANDERHEIDEN

eLectio Publishing
Little Elm, TX
www.eLectioPublishing.com

TRIO: Getting There
By Joe Vanderheiden

Copyright 2015 by Joe Vanderheiden
Cover Design by eLectio Publishing

ISBN-13: 978-1-63213-166-9
Published by eLectio Publishing, LLC
Little Elm, Texas
http://www.eLectioPublishing.com

Printed in the United States of America

5 4 3 2 1   eLP   20 19 18 17 16 15

The eLectio Publishing editing team is comprised of: Christine LePorte, Lori Draft, Sheldon James, Court Dudek, and Jim Eccles.

Without limiting the rights under copyright reserved above, no part of this publication may be reproduced, stored in or introduced into a retrieval system, or transmitted, in any form, or by any means (electronic, mechanical, photocopying, recording, or otherwise), without the prior written permission of both the copyright owner and the above publisher of this book.

If you purchased this book without a cover, you should be aware that this book is stolen property. It was reported as "unsold and destroyed" to the publisher and neither the author nor the publisher has received any payment for the "stripped book."

The scanning, uploading, and distribution of this book via the Internet or via any other means without the permission of the publisher is illegal and punishable by law. Please purchase only authorized electronic editions, and do not participate in or encourage electronic piracy of copyrighted materials. Your support of the author's rights is appreciated.

Publisher's Note
The publisher does not have any control over and does not assume any responsibility for author or third-party websites or their content.

This is a work of fiction. Names, characters, places, and incidents either are the product of the author's imagination or are used fictitiously, and any resemblance to actual persons, living or dead, business establishments, events, or locales is entirely coincidental.

This book is dedicated to my loving mother
Dorothy Rose Vanderheiden
*My hope is that this book is something
that you would have enjoyed*

TRIO
GETTING THERE

PROLOGUE

NDAA – National Defense Authorization Act

SEC. 1021. AFFIRMATION OF AUTHORITY OF THE ARMED FORCES OF THE UNITED STATES TO DETAIN COVERED PERSONS PURSUANT TO THE AUTHORIZATION FOR USE OF MILITARY FORCE.

(a) IN GENERAL.—Congress affirms that the authority of the President to use all necessary and appropriate force pursuant to the Authorization for Use of Military Force (Public Law 107–40; 50 U.S.C. 1541 note) includes the authority for the Armed Forces of the United States to detain covered persons (as defined in subsection (b)) pending disposition under the law of war.

(b) COVERED PERSONS.—A covered person under this section is any person as follows:

(1) A person who planned, authorized, committed, or aided the terrorist attacks that occurred on September 11, 2001, or harbored those responsible for those attacks.

(2) A person who was a part of or substantially supported al-Qaeda, the Taliban, or associated forces that are engaged in hostilities against the United States or its coalition partners, including any person who has committed a belligerent act or has directly supported such hostilities in aid of such enemy forces.

(c) DISPOSITION UNDER LAW OF WAR.—The disposition of a person under the law of war as described in subsection (a) may include the following:

(1) Detention under the law of war without trial until the end of the hostilities authorized by the Authorization for Use of Military Force.

(2) Trial under chapter 47A of title 10, United States Code (as amended by the Military Commissions Act of 2009 (title XVIII of Public Law 111–84)).

(3) Transfer for trial by an alternative court or competent tribunal having lawful jurisdiction.

(4) Transfer to the custody or control of the person's country of origin, any other foreign country, or any other foreign entity.

(d) CONSTRUCTION.—Nothing in this section is intended to limit or expand the authority of the President or the scope of the Authorization for Use of Military Force.

(e) AUTHORITIES.—Nothing in this section shall be construed to affect existing law or authorities relating to the detention of United States citizens, lawful resident aliens of the United States, or any other persons who are captured or arrested in the United States.

(f) REQUIREMENT FOR BRIEFINGS OF CONGRESS.—The Secretary of Defense shall regularly brief Congress regarding the application of the authority described in this section, including the organizations, entities, and individuals considered to be "covered persons" for purposes of subsection (b)(2). H. R. 1540—266

SEC. 1022. MILITARY CUSTODY FOR FOREIGN AL-QAEDA TERRORISTS.

(a) CUSTODY PENDING DISPOSITION UNDER LAW OF WAR.—

(1) IN GENERAL.—Except as provided in paragraph (4), the Armed Forces of the United States shall hold a person described in paragraph (2) who is captured in the course of hostilities authorized by the Authorization for Use of Military Force (Public Law 107–40) in military custody pending disposition under the law of war.

(2) COVERED PERSONS.—The requirement in paragraph (1) shall apply to any person whose detention is authorized under section 1021 who is determined

(A) to be a member of, or part of, al-Qaeda or an associated force that acts in coordination with or pursuant to the direction of al-Qaeda; and

(B) to have participated in the course of planning or carrying out an attack or attempted attack against the United States or its coalition partners.

(3) DISPOSITION UNDER LAW OF WAR.—For purposes of this subsection, the disposition of a person under the law of war has the meaning given in section 1021(c), except that no transfer otherwise described in paragraph (4) of that section shall be made unless consistent with the requirements of section 1028.

(4) WAIVER FOR NATIONAL SECURITY.—The President may waive the requirement of paragraph (1) if the President submits to Congress a certification in writing that such a waiver is in the national security interests of the United States.

(b) APPLICABILITY TO UNITED STATES CITIZENS AND LAWFUL RESIDENT ALIENS

(1) UNITED STATES CITIZENS.—The requirement to detain a person in military custody under this section does not extend to citizens of the United States.

(2) LAWFUL RESIDENT ALIENS.—The requirement to detain a person in military custody under this section does not extend to a lawful resident alien of the United States on the basis of conduct taking place within the United States, except to the extent permitted by the Constitution of the United States.

(c) IMPLEMENTATION PROCEDURES.

(1) IN GENERAL.—Not later than 60 days after the date of the enactment of this Act, the President shall issue, and submit to Congress, procedures for implementing this section.

(2) ELEMENTS.—The procedures for implementing this section shall include, but not be limited to, procedures as follows:

(A) Procedures designating the persons authorized to make determinations under subsection (a)(2) and the process by which such determinations are to be made.

(B) Procedures providing that the requirement for military custody under subsection (a)(1) does not require the interruption of ongoing surveillance or intelligence gathering with regard to persons not already in the custody or control of the United States.

(C) Procedures providing that a determination under subsection (a)(2) is not required to be implemented until after the conclusion of an interrogation which is ongoing at the time the determination is made and does not require the interruption of any such ongoing interrogation.

CHAPTER 1

I remember there was a knock at the front door about 9:30 pm on March 3rd, 2176. The year 2176 seems like such a long time ago. It was a typical night in the Van household. I was watching television and texting my boyfriend Blake while Mom and my three younger sisters were asleep. Dad was in the office doing his usual posting on Craigslist Politics USA forum. Not sure what all he posted, but I do know he despised the so-called conservatives and liberals who posted there. He did enjoy a discussion, though, and enjoyed provoking the other people who posted. My father was all about freedom and liberty. He would tell anyone who would listen—and, a lot of times, those who weren't listening—what he thought. Mom, my three sisters, and I didn't really care about politics nor my dad's discussions. We had boys and school to think about.

I heard my father mumbling about who would be coming to our house this late at night as he passed by me on his way to the door. He was wearing his usual shorts and tee shirt evening wear and was almost to the door when whomever it was knocked again with a lot more force. I looked down at my phone because I had received a text from my boyfriend, but it wasn't from him. It was from an unknown number and said, "Just do what they tell you to do. Friend!" I just deleted it because I didn't recognize the number. Dad raised his voice and said, "Please stop knocking because people are sleeping here."

I heard Dad open the door but didn't really listen to what was being said. I was watching the television again and was quite irritated when I heard my father tell me in a very harsh tone to get Mom up. I yelled "why" because I didn't want to miss any of my show.

He said very loudly and rudely, "Get her up now and don't ask any questions."

I knew that tone, so I got up and went into the bedroom to wake up Mom. She woke from a deep sleep and was quite groggy while putting on her robe and stumbling out to the front door. I followed her to see what was going on.

When we reached the door, three men and my father were looking at each other quite angrily. Mom asked what was going on, and the shortest man told my father not to say anything but to come along with them. My father refused to follow and then turned his back on the men and started to explain to Mom that he was being accused of being a terrorist and they were going to take him down to Homeland Security headquarters. As soon as the words left Dad's mouth, the two taller guys tackled Dad and started beating him with their clubs, saying they had warned him not to talk. Mom became quite hysterical at this point and jumped on top of the one of the guys. The short guy pulled her off, pushed her to the ground, and put handcuffs on her. I was too shocked to do anything but stand and stare.

It seemed like it was only seconds before they were dragging my parents out the door. Dad was yelling at them, saying there were four children in the house who needed to be taken care of. The short man just said, "We will take care of them. Don't you worry." I watched in shock as they led Mom and Dad, in cuffs, toward a car and saw a woman coming up the sidewalk to the door. The woman told me her name was Rita and that I needed to wake up my sisters and pack suitcases with enough clothes to last a few days. She also told me not to say anything to my sisters about what had just happened or I would go to jail, too.

I was very frightened and started walking up the stairs to my sister's rooms, and she followed right behind me. When I got to the top of the stairs, I looked back at the front door, and a man and another woman were standing there. I went into Miranda's room first. She always liked bright colors and had her room painted pink and orange. I spoke her name, and she ignored me as usual. I said, "Miranda, you need to get up." She was still ignoring me when I said, "Someone's here, and you need to get up."

She opened her eyes and saw Rita standing behind me and asked, "What's going on?"

Rita told her not to ask any questions but to get up, get dressed, and pack a suitcase for a few days. Miranda got up and started dressing while Rita and I went to Macie's room. Macie is normally even harder to wake up than Miranda, and this time was no exception. She kept fussing every time I asked her to get up and was still wrapped up with her blanket over her head when Rita spoke up and said, "Macie, get up or you will be in trouble." Macie immediately got up and asked what was wrong. Rita told her the same as she'd told Miranda, and Macie got dressed and started to pack. The last room we went to was the baby's room. Morgan was a sound sleeper and hadn't even woken up during all the commotion. I picked her up from her crib and held her to my shoulder. She was still sleeping when Rita tried to take her from me.

I turned away from Rita so she couldn't take her, but she grabbed my arm and spun me around. She then proceeded to slap me on the cheek and took Morgan from me. I watched as Rita handed her to a different lady who took her and started walking away. I started to move toward Morgan, but Rita gave me an ice cold stare, so I let her go. Morgan woke and started to cry as soon as the woman left the room. I wanted to get my little sister, but Rita stepped in front of me to ensure I didn't follow and told me to go pack. I didn't know what else to do, so I went to my room and began to pack.

As I was packing, I heard Macie ask Rita multiple times where Mom and Dad were, and Rita told her each time not to ask questions or she would get in big trouble. Macie was never one to listen very well, and she was extremely stubborn. I could tell that Rita was getting frustrated with her. I had no idea what to pack, so I threw in a couple pair of jeans and tee shirts along with a nice-looking outfit, too, since I didn't know where we were going or how long we would be gone.

Macie was starting to cry because of how Rita was treating her, and I was getting more and more pissed off the more I thought of what had happened and how Rita was treating Macie. I was almost finished packing and went in to help Macie. Rita was getting very frustrated with her and turned to face me when I entered Macie's room. She said, "Get the hell out of here and finish what I told you to do." I was a bit shocked at her attitude and told her I was going to help Macie.

Macie said, "Thank you, Madison." I started walking over to comfort my sister when Rita spun me around and slapped me on the cheek again, hard enough to knock me down. I sat there and started to cry.

Just then Miranda came out of her room with her suitcase and asked what was going on. Rita told her to take her stuff downstairs and to do what the people down there told her to. Miranda looked at her and then came over to comfort me. She told Rita that she would wait for Macie and me. But Rita didn't like this at all and called out for William and Pat to come up to help. She then told Miranda to go downstairs and wait with William and Pat. Miranda refused and said again that she would wait for us.

Just when Rita was about to explode in frustration, William and Pat arrived at the room. Rita told Pat to escort Miranda downstairs. Pat started to move toward Miranda, saying it would be her pleasure. Miranda started to back up, but Pat grabbed her arm and began to drag Miranda toward the stairs. Miranda tried to resist, but Pat was too strong. She was dragged to the stairs and almost fell while going down.

When the confrontation with Miranda started, William came over and grabbed my arm and started pulling me toward the stairs. I resisted and said I wasn't finished packing. He didn't care and kept dragging me down the stairs and out the front door to a waiting car. Miranda was already in the backseat, rubbing her arm where Pat had grabbed her. William shoved me in beside her. I had barely sat down when Macie was pushed into the car almost on top of me. Rita slammed the door shut after Macie was in. We watched as they threw our suitcases in the trunk, and then William got in the driver seat and started the car. Rita got in the front seat and Pat seated herself next to me. The backseat was very crowded with all four of us in it. We all stared out the car window as we drove away, looking at our house but not realizing it was the last time we would ever see it.

    I did notice that there was a man standing on the sidewalk, staring at us as we drove away. It was too dark to see who it was, probably just one of the neighbors out for a walk. The last sound as we drove away was Pat mentioning to William that some couple would be very fortunate to be getting a new baby. Pat looked over at us when she said that, and all three of us just burst out crying. Pat continued to smile, telling us to shut up and keep quiet.

CHAPTER 2

Let me back up a bit. My name is Madison, and I was sixteen when my parents and little sister were taken away. I miss them very much, and it's incredibly painful to think about them. I can only wonder what kind of a person I would have become if they had still been around and we were still a family. I have three sisters—Miranda, Macie, and Morgan. Miranda is three years younger than me, Macie is four and a half years younger, and Morgan was nine months old. We all have very different personalities. I am, of course, the leader, being the oldest and all. Miranda seems like she follows, but she really just goes along with the things she's not interested in—and then does her own thing when it *is* something she's interested in. Macie is quite headstrong and will do anything or talk to anyone. She is not the least bit shy. Morgan was the sweetest baby I had ever been around. Taking care of her caused problems between Miranda, Macie, and myself. We continually fought over who would get her attention. Usually, Mom would have to settle our arguments and keep track of whose turn it was to take care of her.

Our family was pretty normal as far as I could tell. My father made pretty good money running his Action Park. He would get mad if you called it an amusement park because all the rides were action-oriented. We went to it quite often and had a fairly comfortable life. We were able to take vacations and had a nice house and running cars. I had lots of friends at both school and church at the time my parents were taken, but I didn't really care to be around my annoying sisters. Like most families I knew, we had some money problems, but we all trusted in God. My faith was going to be tested, but He had always come through when I needed him most.

I do miss the rest of my extended family of grandparents, aunts, uncles, and cousins. My father came from a big family, and my mother had only one sister, but there were lots of cousins that we saw quite often. The cousins around my age were all in different cities, so we didn't see them very often. Family doesn't seem that important until it's taken away, and then it hurts to think about them. I also had a boyfriend named Blake who I still think about a lot. I smile every time I think about him and the fun we had together.

Blake and I had met in school. He reminded me of a celebrity singer I thought was cute, so it was just natural that I would fall for him. I was so happy when he asked me to go out with him. We went to a movie with some friends, and we sat next to each other. I don't even remember what movie we saw, but I do remember how happy I was when he reached over and held my hand about halfway through the film. It was one of the happiest memories I had of him.

I often wondered what our lives would have been like if my parents and baby sister hadn't been taken away. Would we have just grown up as other girls did? Would we have gotten married and had kids, and eventually grandkids? Dreaming about those things only makes me more depressed. Suicide was never an option for me, but the continual fight to survive has been a struggle that no one, let alone three young girls, should have to go through.

CHAPTER 3

We had no way of knowing where they were taking us, and none of them would answer any questions. Pat was sitting next to me, so I tried to talk to her, but she kept telling me to be quiet. Miranda didn't say anything the whole car ride, but Macie wanted to know what was happening and would not be quiet. She kept asking me where we were going. I kept telling her to be quiet because I didn't know. That wasn't good enough for Macie, so then she started asking Pat.

"What happened to our parents?"

Pat said, "Be quiet."

Macie said, "I want to know, please tell me." Pat again told her to be quiet. Macie then said in a loud voice, "I want to know, and you are going to tell me." Pat had been calm up to that point, and she reached over and slapped Macie across the face.

I was about to do something when Miranda dove over me and shoved Pat against the door really hard. She held her there, yelling, "Don't ever touch my sister again!" Pat was dazed from hitting her head against the window, so she didn't react much to Miranda's actions.

When Pat slapped Macie, William stopped the car. He was just getting out the door when Miranda tackled Pat. It didn't take him long to circle the car and open Pat's door. Both she and Miranda rolled out onto the ground. William hauled up Miranda and backhanded her across the face, sending Miranda rolling across the gravel to the side of the road. He then picked up Pat and told Rita to get in the driver's seat. He helped Pat into the front passenger seat, glaring at Miranda the entire time. She was glaring right back with the same ferocity. When he had settled Pat in the seat, he walked over to Miranda and grabbed her arm to pull her up. Miranda yanked her arm away, stood on her own, and started walking back to the car. William followed her back and then got in the backseat with us. Nobody said a word the rest of the drive.

TRIO: Getting There

We drove for about an hour. Finally, we stopped in the back of what looked like what could have been a shopping center, but there were only a couple of cars around. It was dark, so I didn't get a very good look. William got out and told us to follow Rita.

As Macie was getting out, she asked William, "When do I get to see my parents?"

William grabbed her hand and started squeezing. He kept squeezing until she was crying and then pulled her face close to his and said in a quiet voice, "No talking." Out of the corner of his eye, he saw Miranda start to move toward him, and he jerked his head to face her and said, "You and your sisters will regret it if you take another step toward me."

Miranda stopped and stared at him with hatred in her eyes. I said to Miranda, "Don't do it. He's too strong."

William squeezed Macie's hand a bit more while saying to Madison, "Didn't I say no talking?" Macie cried out one more time, and then he let go. Rita started walking toward a door in the building. Macie was next, then Miranda, and then me with William behind me. Pat had taken off somewhere with the car.

Rita held the door open as we passed by, and we were met by a man in a gray three-piece suit. As Miranda, Macie, and I stood next to each other, the guy in the suit pulled his jacket back to flash his gun and said, "We aren't going to have any trouble, are we?" We all shook our heads no, and then he started to walk down the hallway. The place reminded me of a hospital because everything was white—tile, walls, and ceiling. We proceeded down the hall and around a corner to an open door. The man in the suit pointed to Macie and told her to go in. The room was illuminated by a plain bulb in the center of the ceiling, and it had a cot with a small mattress on it, but I couldn't see anything else.

Macie grabbed onto me, and both Miranda and I held on to her, as I pleaded with him to let us all stay together. The man in the suit ripped Macie from us and started dragging her into the room. Miranda and I tried to help her, but we were both grabbed by our necks from behind. William forced us to walk further down the hallway. We heard the door behind us slam and Macie's muffled screaming behind it. We came to the next open door, and William shoved me into the empty room. I turned around just in time to see Miranda stomp on William's foot and him hit her in the back of the head right before the door to my room shut. I heard William's muffled cursing, and it brought a bit of a smile, but I was afraid Miranda was going to be seriously hurt by him.

After the sound of William's yelling had died off, I looked around the room. It was a drab square room with no windows. It seemed to be slightly bigger than the living room of our house. In my boredom, I walked it and paced it out. It was thirty-three steps (heel to toe) wide and thirty-four steps long. The walls and ceiling were white, as was the tile on the floor. There were no pictures or decorations of any kind. A bed with a mattress that didn't have a blanket or sheets was tucked in the corner of the room. At the foot of the bed were a fold up table and a chair. That was all there was in the room. I hoped they would let us out soon so we could go home and be with our parents again.

I went over to the bed and sat down. All of the events of the night came back to me, and I just rolled over on the bed, curled up into a ball, and started crying. The more I thought about what had happened, the harder I cried. I must have cried myself to sleep because I woke up, and it was dark. I prayed it had all been a bad dream and called out, "Is anyone there?" No answer. I called out louder. Still no answer, so I yelled, "Can anyone hear me?" Nothing. I was starting to panic, so I scrambled off the bed, and I fell, coming down hard on my knee because I wasn't ready for the height of the bed. I crawled back onto the bed and sat there a minute to try and calm myself down. It took me a few moments until I was able to remember where the bed was in the layout of the room. I didn't remember a light switch but thought there must be one. I got up and almost fell again because my knee hurt so badly. I wasn't going to give up on a light switch. I was already doing everything I could not to panic in the dark.

I made my way to the foot of the bed and touched the wall. I then started to feel my way toward where I thought the door was, toward where I thought a light switch would normally be. After moving a few feet very slowly, I picked up my pace because the dark was getting to me. After a few more steps, my hip banged into something, and I doubled over and hit my head. The table. As I stood still, my head resting on the table top and my hip hurting almost as much as my knee, I started to cry. I seriously considered continuing to rest right where I was, but I craved light too much, so I felt my way around the table and chair and continued to walk along the wall until I reached the door. I felt all around on the left side of it but didn't feel any bumps to indicate a switch. I made it over to the right side of the door and just about collapsed in relief when I was able to flick a switch up—and there was light.

I looked around the room and saw my suitcase, sheets, and a blanket lying on the floor a few feet away from me along with an empty bucket. I then turned back around and grabbed the door handle and twisted. It didn't twist at all, so I pulled. It didn't budge. I was starting to panic and banged on the door, yelling for someone to let me out. I kept it up for a few minutes until I saw the door knob begin to turn, so I backed up a few steps and watched the door open. My heart sank when I saw it was Pat who opened the door and stood in the doorway.

The first words out of her mouth were, "We will have none of that banging or yelling or there will be consequences." I asked her what I was supposed to do if I needed something. She told me to look up to the corner of the room where the camera was mounted. I did, and then she told me to look at the button next to the light switch. She explained it was an intercom to the front desk, but I was only to use it if absolutely necessary. Any use for trivial matters would result in consequences. I was afraid to ask what those consequences were. She also told me that the bucket was for me to urinate in, and if I had to defecate, I should use the intercom. She warned me to push the button only once or it would be ignored permanently.

I asked her what defecate meant and she laughed at me and explained. She said it in a way made me feel stupid. She said that was all and started to turn around. My stomach growled just then, and I asked for some food. She laughed, told me I would get food twice a day, and closed the door. I immediately ran to the door and started banging and yelling again, screaming that I wanted my parents and sisters, and I wanted out.

It took only a second for the door to open and slam into me knocking me down. I sat there looking up at William. He was very angry and told me to shut up or I would suffer the same consequences as my sister. He also said, "Don't ask questions you won't like the answers to." Now about the consequences for not following the directions Pat gave you, he stepped forward and gave me an open handed slap across the face that sent me rolling across the floor. As he closed the door behind him, I heard him say "I hope she learns faster than her sister."

My face was really stinging from the hit, so I sat there a few minutes. Almost without thinking, I picked up my suitcase and the sheets and blanket that were left and walked over to the bed. I laid the suitcase down beside the bed and made up the bed with the sheets and blanket. Even though I had already slept, I was so exhausted from the whole ordeal that I lay down and went to sleep again. I was too afraid to be in the dark, so I left the light on.

CHAPTER 4

Next time I woke up, there was a McDonald's Happy Meal on the table with a small cup of what looked like Coke. It had probably been four or five years since I'd had a Happy Meal. I didn't like Coke very much, but I was so hungry and thirsty that I opened the bag and finished the cheeseburger and fries and downed the drink in what seemed like seconds. I was still hungry and thirsty, so I went over and pushed the intercom button. I remembered to push it only once. I waited and waited, and just as I was about to push it again, a male voice came on and asked, "What do you want?" I held the button down and told him I was still hungry and very thirsty and would like some more. He just laughed. I held the button down again and begged for something more to drink. He told me to leave him alone. I held the button down again, still pleading. I waited for a response and was going to try again when the door suddenly burst open and almost hit me.

It was William. He rushed over to me, put a hand on my neck, and slammed me into the wall, his face a couple of inches from mine. My feet were almost off the floor. Almost drooling in his anger, he said in a low voice, "This is a friendly warning. When I say no, I mean no, and that's the end of it. Any further whining on your part will just bring bigger punishments to you—and to your sisters." I was having trouble breathing because he was pushing quite hard on my neck with his hand, but I knew better than to say anything. He finally let me go and stormed out of the room, slamming the door behind him. I sat down on the bed to try and catch my breath.

I had nothing to do, so I lay down. I thought about all that had happened and had no idea what we'd done to deserve this. I really missed my sisters and would have given anything to be with them. I thought it had only been one day, but I couldn't tell because the room had no windows. I started thinking about what I could do to get out, but I really didn't have any ideas.

I must have eventually fallen asleep because I woke up with a start when I heard the door knob turning and the door opening. A lady I hadn't met before walked in. She didn't say anything to me but smiled and handed me a McDonald's bag. As soon as I took hold of it, she turned around and left. I looked in the bag and was pleasantly surprised to find a chicken sandwich and fries instead of a Happy Meal. At least I wasn't going to be as hungry this time.

No sooner had I finished the meal than I heard a scuffle outside the door and the sound of the door rattling as someone was slammed into it. It burst open, and there were Macie and Miranda. Macie was running in as fast as she could, and William had his hand on Miranda's neck. He gave her a hard shove into the room. She fell but immediately turned around, facing William with a look of pure hatred.

I was so happy to see them that I got up and ran to them, hugging them as hard as I could. Macie hugged back but, as usual, Miranda just lightly hugged back. I asked them what had happened, and they told me there was space needed for others, so they'd been put in my room. I didn't want to stop hugging them, but finally I did and stepped back to take a look at them. The two of them still wore the same clothes as the night we'd been brought to this place. Macie looked unhurt, but Miranda was suffering from a black eye and bruises on her neck. I asked her about them, and she told me they were courtesy of William. She said when they tried to put her in the room, she'd refused. He'd slapped her on the face. She slapped him back, and he had punched her in the eye. The neck bruises were from when he'd tried to force her to leave her room a little while ago. I asked her why she'd refused, and Miranda told me, "Just because I don't like him. I should have taken off running instead of just hitting him. Not that I could have gotten away, but it would have been fun to make him run with that belly." All three of us chuckled about that. It had been the first time I'd laughed in I don't know how many days.

I was so happy to have my sisters with me that I almost cried every time I looked at them. Being with Miranda and Macie made me think about Morgan and how much I missed her. None of us had any idea where she was. We began to compare our experiences from the last couple of days. I related my story, and then Macie told us that she just lay on the bed crying most of the time, wanting to be with her sisters and her mom and dad. Macie said it had been a mistake for them to show her how to use the intercom because she bugged them with every little thing she could think of. It frustrated William to no end, apparently, but he never did hit her for it.

Miranda told us that she'd cried on the bed for a while and then her tears had turned to anger. "I just got madder and madder the more I thought about what was going on. After brooding on the bed for a while, I starting throwing a fit. First, I banged on the door, but no one came, and then I got the chair and started slamming it into the door. It took only a few slams and the door flew open and William ran in and tackled me to the ground. He pinned me on my back and put his hand on my throat like he was choking me. Then he leaned his ugly face right next to mine and said, 'I can do anything to you that I want and no one will care. You and your sisters don't exist in this world anymore so I would advise you to behave.' Then he got up and left."

I asked Miranda what he meant by what he said, but she had no idea. We talked for a long while and then turned off the light and went to bed. Since there was only one bed, we slept sideways on it so all of us would fit, and we took turns with the pillow. I was very happy as I fell to sleep that I had at least two of my sisters with me. I woke up a few times during the night and had to touch Miranda and Macie to make sure they were still with me.

When we woke up, the same lady who had smiled at me the previous day brought in McDonald's breakfasts for us along with orange juice. I asked her when we would be able to get out and go home, and she said, "I'm not allowed to talk to you, so please don't ask me any more questions."

I watched her turn to leave, and right before she shut the door, I said loudly, "Thank you for breakfast!" hoping that she would at least continue to be nice to us in the future.

This was the start of a daily routine that went on for a very long time. I wasn't sure for how long because we couldn't tell night from day except for the fact that one of the McDonald's meals we got was breakfast and the other was a burger or chicken. We were able to go to the restroom a few times a day and very seldom had to use the bucket. They did not provide a shower, so we improvised and washed using paper towels and the soap in the restroom sink. We tried to use that soap in our hair, but it didn't seem to work very well and gave us very itchy scalps for a couple of days. We begged the smiling lady for some shampoo, but she just put her finger to her lips to shush us. The next day, we found sample shampoo and conditioner bottles in our breakfast bags. I wanted to know her name so I could thank her, but she wouldn't give it to us. They also gave us the suitcases we had packed, so we at least had a change of clothes.

It didn't take long for us to get cranky with each other. There's not much to talk about when you're cut off from everything and everyone you know. I don't even remember what the arguments we had were about, but I do remember Macie taking the blanket off the bed and sleeping on the floor on the other side of the room a few times. Miranda and I only let her because we were mad at her and just as happy to have her away from us as she was to be away, even if it was just on the other side of the room. But we learned to get over our disagreements quickly. Otherwise, the days became even more miserable than they already were.

The nice lady would leave things besides the food in our breakfast bags, but only when she was the one to deliver it. She wouldn't converse with us but seemed to listen to what we asked for. We got pencils, pens, paper, and even some books. We even got a couple extra blankets put in our room. They were just left inside the door one morning. I think she thought us to be younger than we were because the books were young children's books, but we were just extremely grateful to have something to do to occupy our time. Even Macie eventually started reading to alleviate the boredom. It took her a few days, but she finally broke down. Before that, she would look at the pictures in some of the books, but I guess she got tired of that. I don't think up until this time she had ever read a book cover to cover. Her attention span just wasn't up to it. She had always struggled in school and didn't like it. Mom thought it was because of her inability to pay attention for very long.

We would put the books that we had finished into an empty McDonald's bag and give it to the nice lady as trash when she brought our meals. It was a secret game we were playing, and we didn't want to get her in trouble.

After seven or so breakfasts, I said, "Even though we only get two meals a day, I'm getting fat eating all this fast food. All we do is sit around napping or reading. We need to start exercising."

Macie said, "I hate exercising."

Miranda said, "I do, too. I would love to be playing soccer, though."

I called them slackers and started to run around the room. Miranda was sitting in the chair, and Macie was on the bed watching. Since the desk and bed were against the wall, I was just running around in a little circle. I did a couple laps, got bored, and stopped.

"Why did you stop? Are you that out of shape?" Miranda asked.

Laughing, I said, "No, it's just too small an area to run in. Would you help me pull the desk and bed away from the wall?" All three of us moved the desk and bed away from the wall.

It wasn't great, but it was much better than before. I ran for a while but wasn't sure how long since none of us had a watch. I was out of breath and thirsty but didn't have anything to drink. The only drinks we got were with the meal and at the water fountain outside of the bathroom. I had to go pee, so I went and pressed the intercom and said we needed to use the restroom. No response. Not that I was expecting one because whoever was on the other end either just did what we asked or ignored us. I knew better than to press it again or badger them. I hoped they'd heard because I had to go quite badly, and I was very thirsty after my run. It was about ten minutes later when the door opened and a man I had never seen before said, "Hurry it up—I'm missing the football game on TV." We hurried to the restroom and then got a drink. I was taking a couple extra sips of water when the man cleared his throat, meaning I'd better hurry. I took one last swallow and hurried back to the room.

CHAPTER 5

I didn't want to be that thirsty again, so I told Miranda and Macie to start saving the cups that came with the McDonald's meals. We would keep them stacked together, and on our bathroom trips, we would fill them up with water and bring them back to our room for when we were thirsty later. I started running multiple times a day to chase the boredom away. Macie started joining me a couple times a day, and finally after a couple more days, Miranda joined in. Sometimes we ran together just to see who could run the longest. I could always outrun them in distance. Miranda was the quickest but would usually tire out first. The extra water we brought back was always gone before the next bathroom break we were allowed. Sometimes we couldn't hold it that long and would have to pee in the bucket.

I really enjoyed the running and wanted to do other exercises, but I really didn't know any other than the basic pushups and sit-ups. I asked the nice lady if she would get us some fitness books to read. She gave a slight nod and then left as usual. The next day I was disappointed to find that there wasn't a book with our breakfast meal, but the following day we were all smiles because each of us had a different exercise book in our breakfast bag. Macie's book was titled *Exercises for Teens*, Miranda's was *Yoga: The Basics*, and mine was *How to Get Fit*. We only glanced at the yoga book because it looked too boring.

Macie said, "Let's start with my book." Miranda and I were thrilled to see Macie willing to exercise. Her book described the best exercises for each part of the body. I was surprised how many we could do in the room, although we had to get creative for some of them.

Miranda and I had already been doing pushups and sit-ups but didn't know about the eight types of crunches or the forty different squat variations. The book said there were four types of exercise: endurance, strength, balance, and flexibility. I tended to do the best when it came to endurance. I could keep running long after Miranda and Macie had quit. Miranda was definitely into strength. Both Macie and I could get on her back while she did pushups and squats without slowing her down. Macie latched onto the flexibility exercises. Miranda and I thought she only did that because she thought it would require less effort. The *Exercises for Teens* book outlined some basic yoga moves that Macie mastered immediately. From then on, she would do yoga while Miranda and I focused on the other exercises. Amazingly, Macie was able to stay perfectly still for minutes at a time. It became a game for Miranda and me to see if we could get her to move or laugh without touching her—sort of like I remembered seeing videos of people doing to the guards at Buckingham Palace in England.

One time Macie was sitting in the yoga pose and had been completely still for about five straight minutes. Miranda and I thought it was our duty to test her concentration. We sang and yelled while dancing around her. That didn't distract her, so we tried jumping over her like a hurdle. That didn't work, either, so we tried assuming the exact same pose. Miranda had trouble sitting in that position and wasn't even flexible enough to cross her legs properly, but all three of us were sitting perfectly still when the nice lady walked in with our lunch.

She looked over at us and smiled and said, "Don't wait too long or your food will get cold."

Miranda and I broke our concentration to thank her and got up to eat. Macie continued sitting perfectly still while Miranda and I began to eat our hamburgers. After she'd taken a couple bites, Miranda got up and threw a blanket over Macie, saying, "I don't like it when people stare at me when I eat." She then went back to her burger. The blanket was still for a few seconds, and then it start to shake. It shook harder and harder until we saw Macie's head slump over and heard her laughing. Miranda and I were cracking up. I was laughing so hard the Coke nearly came out of my nose.

Miranda really enjoyed the strength exercises more than anything else but had to improvise since we didn't have any weights. She mostly used live weights—Macie and me—to build her strength. Aside from having one or both of us on her back while she did pushups or squats, there wasn't much else she could do. She came up with a few ideas like lying under the desk and lifting it like a bench press. But that was too light for her, so she asked Macie and me to sit on top of it. She lifted it easily, but because Macie and I were different weights, the desk started leaning my way. Before Miranda could set it back down, Macie slid to my side, and the desk fell, breaking one of the legs. Luckily, Miranda was able to scramble out before it righted itself. Needless to say, we didn't try that again.

I enjoyed the endurance exercises. I would stretch really well and then move into doing lunges, squats, pushups, and sit-ups. Then I'd start running around the room. I enjoyed running more than any of the exercises because my thoughts could just drift off to happier times. Miranda would start running with me a few minutes after I started but would normally quit before I did. We had to bribe Macie to run with us by agreeing to do yoga with her three times a week. Sometimes Miranda or I would run with Macie on one or the other of our backs. Macie was very adept at getting out of exercising.

Each night—or what we thought was night because we were tired and were going to bed—we would say our prayers, asking God to watch over Morgan and our mom and dad, and then I would tell a family story I remembered. Macie never failed to say, "Please tell one about me!" The story she liked best was about her and the gloves when she was two or three years old. She had a basket with four or five pairs of kids' gloves and matching hats. Our bedtime routine was for Mom and Dad to lie with each of us for a few minutes before we would go to sleep. There were many times Mom went to check on Macie or wake her up in the morning and laughed because Macie would be lying on her back, sleeping with pink gloves and a hat on.

Miranda always wanted to hear about how she beat up on Macie. It wasn't literally beating up on her little sister—it was more like having fun at Macie's expense. Dad would say, "I'm impressed that Macie ever learned to walk. Whenever Miranda saw Macie trying to walk, she would go up to her and give her a little belly bump to get her to fall down. Fortunately, Macie was persistent and able to overcome the obstacles Miranda set in her way." I don't think Miranda ever felt bad about having done it, and Macie took it all in stride as a part of growing up.

The story I most remember my dad telling is about the day Miranda was born. I was three years old, and Dad and I had to leave the hospital so Mom could rest overnight. Dad said I cried all the way home, saying how much I loved her and couldn't wait to see her again because she was my best friend ever. Dad said I did the same thing when Macie was born. Miranda, on the other hand, seemed to see Macie as a new toy. Miranda was only 18 months old at the time, but I guess it was an omen of things to come.

Dancing became our next obsession. After going through more exercise books, the nice lady gave us a *Dancing for Beginners* book. I had always thought you just went out on the dance floor and jumped around—like I did in middle school. But it was actually more like exercising—with a warm-up, stretching, and flexibility involved. Miranda didn't have much in the flexibility department, so she usually led while Macie and I followed. Macie was so bad at leading that neither Miranda nor I would dance with her as a partner.

Macie wanted to jump right into swing dancing because she remembered dancing like that with our father. We weren't very good, but we always had a lot of fun twirling and being tossed around. Macie and Miranda tried to dance like we had with Dad, but Macie hurt her hip when Miranda flung her into the desk. After that, we decided to actually follow the steps in the book. As was typical of most things, we all leaned toward a different type of dance. Miranda liked jazz and hip hop because they were different and had room for more freedom of expression. Macie favored country dancing because our mother always listened to country music—Macie was definitely the sentimental type. I liked the Latin dances because of the love and romance expressed through the movements. As we learned the dances better, we mixed them in with our normal daily exercise routine.

We had stopped talking about getting out and being able to see our parents again. It was just too painful. None of the few people that we saw would talk to us or give us any information, so we quit trying to guess why we had been put where we were and when—or if—we would ever get out. The nice lady must have noticed that our interest in dancing was waning, so she started mixing in some survival books.

Miranda and I read them to pass the time, but Macie really devoured them. Any time a new survival book was in anyone's meal bag, Macie would pounce and whisk it away to read. Miranda and I made a game of it. When we saw one, we would play keep away from Macie until she was on the verge of tears— and then we would end up giving it to her. Oh, the joys of sisters! Macie wanted to hoard all of the survival books, but if we didn't send them back, then we didn't get new ones. So Macie started writing the techniques she liked down on a notepad.

Macie would practice what she could with the limited items in the room. She was able to build shelters and practiced with our blankets and sheets. One time when she was reading, she said, "Madison and Miranda, come here." We turned around from what we were doing. She was rubbing two pencils together and said, Watch this!"

We watched for a minute, and nothing happened. Miranda said sarcastically, "Really impressive, Macie. I wish I knew how to rub two pencils together."

Macie got mad and said, "I'm going to make a fire." Miranda and I laughed and went back to our own books.

Macie didn't speak to us the rest of the day and was really secretive about what she was doing. That wasn't hard for her since we didn't care and were used to ignoring each other when we wanted to. Early on, after a few fights, we had figured out that it was better to ignore each other when we were mad so that no one ended up with hurt feelings.

The next day, we heard Macie snickering, and then we smelled smoke. We looked over Macie's shoulder and saw a pile of shredded paper smoking, and then it suddenly burst into flames. All three of us were mesmerized watching it burn. After about thirty seconds, the fire alarm went off and the sprinklers came on, dousing everything in the room. About fifteen seconds after that, the door flew open and William ran into the room to see what was going on.

The fire was already out, but William flipped the desk over anyway, spilling all of Macie's stuff on the floor. He glared at us for a few seconds and then stomped out of the room, slamming the door. I was relieved he didn't do more to us. We went about cleaning up, complimenting Macie on a job well done. Not only had she been able to make a fire, but William was mad—we were all pleased. We didn't get any food for dinner that night, nor breakfast the next morning, but it was well worth it knowing we had gotten under William's skin.

Macie got much better and quicker at making fires, but we learned to put them out immediately so the alarm wouldn't go off again. She must have gotten that firebug gene from our dad. He loved to build a fire in the fireplace. Even though we had a gas burner, he would always use paper and cardboard just for the fun of it. Miranda and I tried to make a fire but weren't very successful.

Macie also studied the books on plants and herbs. We would quiz her by showing her a picture or saying the name, and she would describe it and tell whether it was edible or not. It was amazing what she was able to learn and memorize. She liked learning much better than just reading for pure entertainment.

CHAPTER 6

We were three teenage girls in a bad situation, and you can't begin to imagine how bored and miserable we were in that room. Our father had owned a recreational park that catered to active people, young and old. Our mother was into working out every day to stay fit and trim. We had grown up always doing something active when not in school, whether it was working out with Mom or helping Dad build or fix something for the park. His park was situated on a big hill and had a ski slope, an alpine slide, a tubing hill, a rope course, a zip line, and a lot of other smaller activities that were fun for the whole family. We were used to keeping busy, and we enjoyed the feeling of accomplishment we got when helping our dad. Being cooped up in a single room as we were now was sheer torture.

I'm not sure how long we were in the room, but it was at least several months if not close to a year. We kept track of the days for a while but got more depressed as the days stretched into weeks, so we stopped. The nice lady would sometimes give us fiction books, but we asked her not to bother with those because none of us were very interested. We wanted to keep learning new things. We should have been in school—learning math, English, science, and social studies—but the people keeping us locked up wouldn't let us go, and we certainly weren't going to ask for school textbooks.

Our differing interests were very apparent. Macie liked the books on how to do things—hands-on kind of stuff. Miranda liked books that taught physical things like karate and wrestling. I tended to gravitate a bit towards learning about weapons. *The Hunger Games* was my favorite book and movie, so one of the first things I chose to read about was the bow and arrow. We didn't have anything to make weapons from, but I still copied down the instructions and studied how to make them. I was really disappointed that I didn't have the materials to make a bow and some arrows, but I planned to try it if we ever got out of here.

We were able to unscrew the legs from a desk they had brought in and use them for sword fighting practice. Miranda's go-to technique for sword fighting was overpowering her opponent. I, however, studied the different techniques for defending and could usually get the better of her—although I sometimes ended up on my back with her on top. As time went on, she got better at defending herself and could break through my defenses, but it wasn't due to her reading and understanding how things worked, it was from trial and error—and a lot of frustration in between. Macie, for her part, just wasn't as interested in weaponry as Miranda and I.

One day, we were all in the middle of using crayons on each other to create a wood camouflage when William opened the door and told us to pack all our things to leave. During our stay, we did our best to keep Miranda away from William, although not always very successfully. Whenever he brought our food—or even when we were taking a trip to the bathroom—Miranda would do or say something to make him mad. Sometimes we would be able to catch her and hold her back, and sometimes we wouldn't get to her in time, and he would hit her. A couple of these confrontations had resulted in Miranda getting a black eye or a bruise somewhere on her body. She was lucky he'd never broken her nose.

I asked William where we were going while Miranda glared at him. He just said, "None of your business. Have your stuff packed, and be ready to leave in thirty minutes." It took about three minutes to pack and two hours before he came back to the room with Pat. It was the first time we'd seen her since the night they'd put us in here. I noticed that Pat didn't get too close to Miranda and kept her mouth shut to avoid a confrontation.

As we were walking out, we saw the nice lady, and she smiled at us. Before William and Pat could stop us, we all went up and gave her a hug. William immediately pulled us away and told us to get moving. We stopped anyway and asked the lady her name.

She said, "My name is Cindy, and I'm praying that you will be safe."

William warned, "Get moving or you'll be sorry."

We went through two sets of doors and were suddenly outside. It was so bright, not a cloud in the sky. It must have been the middle of the day because the sun was straight overhead. It was the first time in months that we had seen the sun, and it felt so good to be outside. Our eyes started watering, partly from the sun but mostly out of happiness to be out of that room. William snickered to himself and said, "What a bunch of crybabies, acting like they've never seen the sun." But surprisingly, he let us stand there for a couple of minutes to enjoy the outdoors before hustling us into a van with no windows. All I had a chance to see before I got in was the building we had just exited and the parking lot.

CHAPTER 7

Pat was standing by the van as we got in. Miranda climbed into the seat at the far back, and Macie and I sat together in the backseat closer to the front. William got behind the wheel, and Pat sat in the front passenger seat. We could see out the front windshield, but the sides and back of the van were all metal with no windows. We all watched in silent wonder as we drove because it had been so long since we had been outside. We were starving to see anything different from the four walls of our room.

We were out in the country a ways, and I could see we were heading toward Dallas. Miranda leaned forward and whispered. "The door is locked. All we have to do is pull up the lock and leave."

Macie and I turned closer to facing each other in the seat, and Macie said, "I'm afraid of what they will do to us if we try."

I whispered, "Where would we go?"

Miranda said, "Anywhere…let's just open the door and run."

"We're going too fast—we'll be killed if we do that," said Macie.

I thought about it and then said, "We're going into Dallas. There will be stop lights."

Miranda asked, "Should we go the first time we stop?"

"No," I said, "let's wait for a lot of people to be around and then go."

Macie said she was afraid, but we reassured her and told her that we needed to get away to find Mom, Dad, and Morgan. She agreed.

Miranda then said, "When we get out of the van, go back the way we came because it will be harder for them to follow us." We all agreed that was a good plan.

William and Pat were talking and not paying attention to us. William would look at us in the rearview mirror every once in a while, but he didn't speak to us. As I had hoped, we were driving downtown, toward the tall buildings. There were a lot of people walking around so this would be as good a place to escape as any. I turned and whispered, "Next light we stop at, let's go."

As I turned to face forward, I saw William looking at me. "What are you girls talking about?"

I said, "Just about how nice it is to be out of that room."

He looked straight ahead but started glancing in the mirror more often as if he suspected something.

We were coming up to an intersection. The light turned yellow, and William said, "I hate them damn lights. I'm so glad I don't live in the city and have to deal with them very often." He pushed hard on the brake and slowed. We stopped behind a yellow VW bug. I was waiting for the cross traffic to slow before I made a move, hoping that William would have to keep driving when the light turned green. Finally, the traffic started to slow and come to a stop. I timed it as close as I could so Miranda would have time to get out before William started driving. I reached over and unlocked the door, pulling as hard as I could. The door flew open, and I grabbed Macie's hand, pulling her out with me. We turned toward the back of the van and started running. I glanced back just in time to see Miranda jump out as the van started to move—and then the brake lights came on.

We had no time to check what was happening back at the van. We just took off running. I heard William and Pat yelling for us to stop, but their voices were drowned out by all the cars honking their horns at William to move the van. I didn't need to worry about Miranda being behind us because she flew past Macie and I and kept going. At the next intersection, the light was green, so we kept running. There were people slowly walking in the crosswalk, so we had to shove our way through to keep going. A few seconds later, we heard William yelling at them to get out of his way. The chase was on!

We ran about half a block and then cut through a parking lot, crossed over some train tracks, and kept running. We heard

William yelling for us to stop, and it sounded further behind us than the last time, so we pushed ourselves to run even harder and faster. We ran on the sidewalk next to the tracks because there were lots of people standing around, waiting for the train. Miranda was getting too far ahead of us, so I yelled for her to slow down. She looked back as she slowed down, but she didn't look too happy at having to wait for us.

As we were running, I looked over to the left. There was a park, and on the other side of it was TXU. I recognized it because my father used to work there. I remembered our mother bringing us down to eat lunch with him, and I remembered playing in Thanksgiving Square. Our favorite part had been walking in the little cement stream. I wished I was back with my parents, just having lunch and playing. Instead, we were running from someone for reasons I didn't know or understand. When we got past Thanksgiving Square, I glanced over my right shoulder and didn't see William. Either he was slow, or we had lost him. I didn't want to stay and find out, so I told Miranda to take a right at the next corner.

We turned right and kept running. At the next intersection, the light was red, but there was very little traffic, so we crossed anyway and kept running. We were getting tired, and I told Miranda to go through the doors on the right. We all hurried inside and went to the back of the store. We ended up in the ladies' formal department of Neiman Marcus. We looked back and saw that no one was following us, and we ducked behind some of the racks near the dressing room. There were a couple chairs there, so Macie and Miranda sat down. I wanted to but chose to keep an eye toward the door where we had entered.

We stayed there about fifteen or twenty minutes, catching our breath and giving each other high fives for our successful escape. It was then that we realized what a mess we were in. We knew they were out there looking for us, and we had no money and no idea of what to do. We slowly made our way over to one of the windows facing the street. No sooner had we looked out the window than we saw William and Pat drive by in the van. Fortunately, they didn't see us. We were really scared, so we went back to the dressing room where we had been previously. A saleswoman came by and asked if she could help us. I said, "No thanks, we're just looking."

"We better keep moving or we'll look suspicious. Store security might ask us what we're doing," Miranda said. We got up and started to walk around the store.

Neiman Marcus is a very upscale store. We loved looking at all the beautiful clothes but were shocked when we looked at the prices. We discussed what we should do as we walked around and tried to look inconspicuous. Calling the police was definitely out of the question because it was the police who had taken us in the first place. Mom and Dad wouldn't be home for us to call, so we decided to call our grandmother or our aunt. The problem was that none of us could remember either of their phone numbers. We'd all had the numbers programmed into our cell phones, and Pat had taken those. We decided to stay in the store as long as we could, but we knew that we'd have to leave at some point. It was well after dark and the store was getting ready to close when we decided it was time to leave. But we had no idea where to go.

Downtown Dallas was very scary at night. We were getting very hungry as we walked back toward Thanksgiving Square. Macie decided she was going to ask someone for money to eat. We told her not to because we would get in trouble. But Macie never was one to listen very well. She approached the next respectable man who walked by. "Could you please spare some money? We're very hungry." He looked at us very strangely. We could tell he didn't want to get involved, so he reached into his wallet and gave Macie a five dollar bill. We all thanked him, and he walked off. Macie asked a few more well-dressed men who appeared to be in a hurry, and in the end, we ended up with about $35. We were so grateful that we each thanked God out loud right there on the street. We thought we might have enough to eat something other than McDonald's for a change.

There were only a couple of times while we were stuck in the room that they hadn't given us something from McDonald's. We got a pizza once, and Arby's roast beef sandwiches another time. I think we had tried everything on the McDonald's menu at some time or another. I enjoyed the McRib while it lasted. That, I remembered. Miranda only wanted a chicken sandwich or McNuggets. Macie wanted something different every day.

We wandered around downtown, looking for a place to eat. The fast food shops had all closed, but there was a Mexican restaurant that was still open. We went inside and sat down to look at the menu. Miranda ordered a taco salad, Macie ordered chicken strips, and I ordered enchiladas. We didn't do much talking as we ate, but we truly enjoyed our first meal away from the room and away from McDonald's food. There were very few customers in the restaurant by the time we had finished and paid. We were full but still had no idea what to do or where to go. The restaurant was about to close, so we had to leave.

We began to wander around, doing our best to avoid the people on the streets. Most of the people stared at us, and some said some things we didn't understand. A couple of guys we saw across the street from us called out and said we should go over to them. As soon as we saw them looking to cross the street, we started running away as fast as we could. Miranda opened the door to one of the office buildings, and I felt fortunate that it wasn't locked. We all went in, hoping that we would be safer inside rather than wandering the streets. We ended up in a hallway. We didn't want to go back out on the street, so we decided to see where it went. We followed it around a couple left and right turns and ended up at some locked doors. There was no choice but to turn around and go back the way we'd come.

We walked around inside the office building for what seemed like a long time, hitting several dead ends, locked doors, and exits to the outside. We didn't want to go outside and were getting very tired when we came upon a hallway that made a sharp left and ended in locked doors. We hoped we would be safe there until the morning so we could get some rest. We lay down on the carpet next to the door and immediately went to sleep. As usual, Miranda and I made sure we were well away from Macie and her normal thrashing around while she slept.

It seemed that I had barely closed my eyes when I woke up to two cops yelling at us. As soon as we started to get up, the policemen started talking on his radio, saying, "We found them— what do you want us to do?"

The reply on the radio was "hold them until I get there." It was William's voice. All three of us became instantly alert and took off running. Macie was the last to get going, and one of the officers grabbed her. I was in the lead and turned when I heard Macie cry out. Just as I turned, I saw Miranda ram her shoulder into the side of the officer who had Macie. She hit him just under his arm on his left side. It seemed to knock the wind out of him, and he let go of Macie.

The other officer went assist the officer Miranda had hit instead of grabbing Miranda or Macie, so we took off out of there as fast as we could. By the time we made it near the entrance to get outside, there were five officers waiting. The officers we had dealt with earlier must have called for backup. We stopped running when we saw that our exit was blocked and were about to go back when the other two showed up. They had us surrounded and were able to seize us as we tried to dash between them. Two of them had hold of my arms so I couldn't go anywhere. I looked over to where Miranda was going wild with quite a few hits and kicks landing on the cops. It took a couple more cops to subdue her completely. Just about the time they had Miranda quiet, William comes walking up with a big grin on his face. "So you thought you could get away, did you?" he said. Miranda started struggling to get to William, but the police had a firm grip on her. William continued. "Your time in the room will seem like Hawaii compared to where you are going!"

Macie asked, "And where is that?" William laughed and ignored her question.

He told the policemen to put us in handcuffs because we were very likely to run if given a chance. The officers did as William asked, and we were led outside. William took personal charge of Miranda, and I could see him half dragging her instead of letting her walk normally like Macie and me. The same van we had escaped from the day before was waiting for us. Pat was in the driver's seat this time. Miranda and I were put in the very back while Macie and William sat directly behind the driver's seat. Before William closed the door, I saw a man standing on the sidewalk who looked very familiar. He was looking straight at me, and I could have sworn that he winked just before William closed the door. I tried to think of where I might know him from but couldn't remember.

We drove through downtown once again, stopping in front of a building that was one of tallest in Dallas. The sun hung just above the buildings as we filed out of the van and into the building. Once inside, we boarded an elevator and rode to the 46th floor. We walked along a hallway and into a small room with four chairs and a table. William said he would take off the handcuffs if we promised not to run again. Macie and I nodded our heads, but Miranda just glared at him.

William removed the cuffs from Macie and me but left them on Miranda. We rubbed our wrists where the cuffs had been but didn't say a word. On William's way out, he hit each of us on the back of the head and said, "Pretty good escape attempt. I was surprised you didn't call your grandmother or another relative — we had all their phones bugged, so it would've helped us find you sooner. And we would have taken them into custody like your parents. Actually, it was lucky for them that you didn't call!" William left the room, and we heard the door lock behind him. We still didn't know what he was talking about or why we were in trouble, let alone why they were keeping us in custody. After we'd been sitting in very uncomfortable chairs for about an hour, William and two other men came in and got us. William said, "I'm more than happy to put the cuffs back on you. Are you going to be a problem?"

I shook my head and asked him if he would take the cuffs off of Miranda. He looked over at her and laughed. Then he told us to follow him. He led the way, followed by Miranda, Macie, and me, and then the two other men.

We all got in the elevator, and William pressed the button for the top floor. We got out on the 60th floor. William opened the door to the stairwell. We climbed the stairs up to the roof and walked out to where a helicopter was waiting. None of us had ever been in a helicopter before. *Where were they were taking us?* I wondered. We all climbed into the aircraft, and as soon as the door closed, we took off. Macie got scared and grabbed on to me. Miranda finally quit glaring at William and stared out the window. Dallas was a beautiful city from above and had quite an incredible skyline. Little did I realize that it was the last time we would ever see it.

CHAPTER 8

It turned out to be just a short flight to the airport. As soon as we landed, we were marched to a waiting airplane. It was a small one that only had about ten seats. As we were walking, we saw our suitcases unloaded from the helicopter and put on the airplane. We boarded the plane and were told to sit in the back. There was one seat on each side of the aisle, so Macie and I sat in the back row and Miranda in front of us. William sat across the aisle from Miranda. There were also five other people I had never seen before on the plane. Two women and three men—all dressed in suits. William finally took the cuffs off of Miranda after she sat down. As he was doing this, it looked like he was whispering something to her. She had a shocked look on her face as William sat down across the aisle from her. I never did find out what he said to her, but he did glance over at her quite often during the flight. I guess he still didn't trust her, even with the threats. Better safe than sorry.

I remembered the last flight I was on was when my grandparents took me to SeaWorld in San Antonio for my fifth birthday. We flew from Dallas to San Antonio and stayed at a hotel by the park. When we arrived at SeaWorld the next day, I wanted to go to the gift shop first. They bought me a bunch of toys but got irritated with me because all I wanted to do was go back to the hotel and play with my toys. I bugged them so much about the toys that we only stayed at the park a bit more than half the day. I had a great time on the trip and remembered more about playing with my toys in the hotel than I did about Sea World. My grandparents had learned their lesson with me, so when they took Miranda and Macie on their fifth birthdays, they didn't do the shopping until they were on the way out of the park.

I barely remember that flight home because it was such a long time ago. This flight was certainly not a pleasure trip, though. The plane started moving, taxied to the runway, and lifted up into the sky. All three of us watched out the window as we took off and said goodbye to Dallas. We were all exhausted and soon fell asleep in our seats. When I woke up, Macie and Miranda were still sleeping. I looked out the window but couldn't tell much about where we were. I was going to ask William, but he was also asleep.

The stewardess came by and asked if I would like a drink. I asked if she had Power-aid. She didn't, but she had Gatorade. I told her that would be great. I asked, "Do you have anything to eat? They haven't fed us all day. Where are we going?"

She said, "I'm sorry, but all we have are peanuts and pretzels. As far as our destination, it's Albuquerque." I thanked her, and she walked off.

After a little while, Miranda and Macie woke up. I waved at the stewardess, and she came over to ask Macie and Miranda what they wanted to drink. While they were answering, she set a couple bags each of peanuts and pretzels in front of them. Macie wanted a Coke and Miranda a Dr. Pepper. The stewardess moved back to her seat in the front of the plane. William still slept, and Macie said, "I wonder where we're going!" I told her what the stewardess had said.

"Why would we be going there?" Miranda asked. I told her I didn't know but sure hoped we weren't going to be left in a room again. Both Miranda and Macie shook their heads in agreement.

A short time after, the stewardess brought us our drinks. While we stared out the window, one of the women on board came back and squatted in between Macie and me. She introduced herself as Judith and told us she would be happy if we called her Jude. While she shook my hand, she said, "Hi, Madison" and then she did the same with Macie and Miranda. William was snoring away, completely oblivious to everything going on around him. Jude told us we would be landing in Albuquerque soon and asked if we would like to go shopping. We all shook our heads yes, and Macie said, "We would love to go shopping, but we haven't eaten all day. Can we do that first?"

Jude snickered and said, "Sure, but there's just one thing all of you have to agree to before we leave the plane. You must all agree that you won't try to leave the group and won't talk to anyone who isn't in our group." We all nodded our agreement, and I thought to myself, with all these people around us how could we escape anyway!

Jude told us that our suitcases were with us, but each of us needed a new wardrobe. We all wondered why but kept quiet. She went on with more explanation and told us we would be buying outfits for both the cold and the warm weather. She recommended that we purchase at least a heavy coat, gloves, and some warm clothes along with boots for cold weather. Also, we should get a sundress, shorts, tops, sandals, and tennis shoes for warm weather. She reminded us not to forget undergarments and makeup. Each group had a checklist of the items to ensure we got all we needed. Jude also explained that there was only enough time to shop for a few hours, and if we finished early, we would get a surprise purchase. I thought this might be fun and keep us from thinking about all of our other problems. It seemed like the rest of the flight took forever. All the three of us could do was talk and think about food. Shopping was going to be fun, but food was on all of our minds—as well as our stomachs. William didn't bother Miranda during the flight, mostly because he slept a good part of the trip. By the time we landed, we were so famished and excited that we practically ran off the plane into the waiting van.

It was one of those long vans that could accommodate all of us. The two women, Jude, and Amber along with William and two other men all climbed in. William made sure he sat next to the door, just in case we tried anything. After getting caught after our last escape, we didn't see much point in trying, especially with five people watching us. We drove for about thirty minutes and then pulled into the Coronado Mall. I was quite familiar with malls, and this one had all the fun stores I loved in Dallas. The first thing we did was head to the food court. All three of us went straight to the Panda Express line. After all those McDonald's meals, we definitely had a taste for something different. Normally each of us would get the Panda bowl, but we were so hungry we each got the two-entree plate. Macie just wanted the double order of orange chicken. Miranda got the noodles and a double order of orange chicken and an egg roll. I got the steamed rice and a double order of orange chicken and an egg roll. The guy serving us looked at us strangely when we asked for six containers of sweet and sour sauce but filled them up and gave them to us. We got our drinks and went to a table to eat while Jude paid.

It was such a good meal. I wanted to savor every bite but was so hungry I couldn't slow down. Macie and Miranda were shoveling in the food as fast as they could chew and swallow. I wasn't far behind. It took only about ten minutes for us to finish eating and to be ready for some shopping! We headed to Macy's first and then Banana Republic, Wet Seal, and a few I can't remember. All I know is that after two and a half hours of going store to store, we'd found everything that Jude had told us to buy along with some extra clothes that we thought we couldn't live without. Miranda was the choosiest shopper, so we visited the same stores multiple times because she had so much trouble making up her mind. Macie and I were used to her shopping habits, but Jude and the others got frustrated with her. Miranda ended up with more tomboyish and athletic clothes than Macie and I but still grumbled at some of the girly stuff she was forced to buy. While we were shopping for our clothes, one of the men went to purchase the essentials like deodorant, toothbrushes, feminine products, and that kind of thing. I saw Jude give him the list, and I saw the angst on his face, but he seemed to know better than to object.

We had finally finished and were about to head out when Jude asked, "Don't you want your surprise purchase?" We were tired but would never say no to more shopping. Well, Miranda might, but certainly not Macie or me. We followed her to Macy's department store and into the formal department. The dresses were stunning. Jude told us that the mall closed in one hour, so we needed to get busy picking one out—and all the accessories to go with it. I think the store knew we were coming because there was a saleslady assisting each one of us.

I went with a woman who introduced herself as Candice. We browsed through the dresses first. I picked out a medium-length blue Ralph Lauren to try on, but Candice told me the dress had to be a full-length evening gown. That really narrowed my choices. I don't remember ever wearing a full-length dress—not since I was forced to wear one for a choir concert in middle school. I picked out a strapless light blue—almost turquoise—gown and went to the dressing room to try it on. Candice had asked me what size shoe I wore and disappeared for a couple of minutes. When she came back, she was carrying a box. She opened the box and showed me the most beautiful blue high heels. They sparkled everywhere but the sole.

I took the shoes and dress into the dressing room and tried them on. I couldn't see the full length of the dress, so I stepped out of the dressing room and up onto a block in front of three mirrors. I could see myself from head to toe. Candice told me I looked beautiful, but something was missing. She presented me with light blue pear-shaped earrings and a matching necklace. After I had put them on, I stepped up on the block again and looked at myself. I was stunned. I hardly recognized myself. A truly beautiful person was staring back at me from the mirrors. The combination of the dress, necklace, earrings, and shoes was dazzling. I just wish I had my hair done and makeup on to complete the look. My parents would be so proud. I felt like Cinderella, but I knew there was going to be a midnight bell ringing, and all of this happiness would go away. Then I thought more about my parents and became saddened that they were not here to see me like this. I would have loved to see their eyes light up when they saw me in the dress. I became tired and dejected and wasn't in the mood to shop anymore.

Candice could see the change in me and asked if something was wrong. I just told her I was tired and went to change back into my old clothes. As soon as I shut the door in the dressing room, I sat down, put my head in my hands, and started crying. Candice knocked lightly on the door and asked me again if something was wrong. I asked her to please go away, and I cried for a few more minutes before changing out of the beautiful dress and exiting the dressing room. Candice was waiting and asked if I wanted to look at anything else. I said, "No thank you, I'll take this one." I was about to tell her our situation when Jude came up. I lost my chance.

"Miranda and Macie picked out beautiful dresses, and I see you have as well," Jude said. "The mall is about to close, so we need to leave." I looked up at her, and she could tell I had been crying. "I'm sorry, Madison, it's time to go."

"Good-bye, Candice," I said. "Thank you for helping me!" Candice waved as Jude and I left her and walked to the front of the store. Miranda and Macie were waiting with our escorts. Macie was so excited to show me what she got. She yanked the dress out of the bag and held it up to her body. She had chosen a dark blue dress with one strap over the left shoulder. It was beautiful and really brought out the blue in her eyes. I tried my best to be happy for her but just was not in the mood. Miranda just said, "I got a green one" and wouldn't even take it out of the bag to show me. Typical.

We left the mall and walked toward the van. Good thing we had all the escorts with us to carry the stuff we bought. Miranda made sure to give William as much of her stuff as he could carry. Jude was very much in charge here, so William hardly spoke the whole time we were shopping and did what she told him to do. Once we got everything and everyone loaded in the van, I glanced back at the mall as we drove away. I saw a man standing and staring at us. His hand was above his eyes, shading them from the sun, but I was sure that he was the same man I had seen in Dallas. I didn't say anything, but I wondered who he could be.

We didn't drive very far before we pulled into an Embassy Suites hotel. Jude went inside for a few minutes and came out with a key card in her hand. She climbed into the passenger seat up front and told William to pull around back so we could head to the room without parading through the busy lobby.

William did as Jude asked and reminded us before we got out that we were not to speak to anyone about anything or there would be a lot of trouble for us. Macie and I said, "Yes ma'am" to irritate him, but Miranda didn't say anything at all. We all got out and followed Jude to the back door and watched her open it with the key card. She held the door for us and instructed us to go up the stairs to the fourth floor. We started climbing the stairs, and Macie said, "I'm too tired to climb. Can't we take the elevator?"

Jude just laughed a little and said, "Sorry—it's only four floors." Macie sighed and kept climbing.

We finally made it to the fourth floor and dragged our tired feet out into the hallway, waiting for Jude to lead the way. She went two doors down to room 456, opened the door, and went in. We followed her in and looked around. There two rooms—a sort of living room with a couch and television and another room that had two queen sized beds—with swinging double doors separating them. Jude told us the couch folded out into a bed and Amber would be sleeping there, so the three of us would have the room with the beds. There was a nice bathroom with a separate shower and bathtub. Just about the time we had finished looking around, the three men and Amber came in carrying all our purchases and luggage.

When the men had put all the stuff on the beds, they left our room, but Amber and Jude stayed behind. Jude told us to sit down so she could lay out the rules and what we should expect the next day. "Number one, no leaving the room. The phone has been taken out so we won't have a problem there. You three will have the privacy of this room tonight as long as you do not abuse the privilege. Amber will be in the next room, so keep the noise level down. Also, I was informed that the three of you have not had a bath or shower in quite a while, so I would suggest you enjoy it tonight and tomorrow morning because it might be a while before you're in this nice of a place again."

Macie asked, "When can we see our Mom and Dad again?"

"I do not know and am not in charge of that," Jude answered, "I am here to ensure you get to your next destination without any problems."

I asked, "Where is that destination?"

"I am not at liberty to say tonight but will tell you tomorrow once we leave here. At that time, I will also be able to tell you your final destination. Please get a good night's sleep because tomorrow might be a very long day. I almost forgot—see those empty duffel bags in the corner? Pack all your belongings in those for your trip. Whatever you cannot fit stays here and gets thrown away. Good night!" She left, and Amber went into the other room and shut the doors.

Miranda started to cry. "Madison, what are we going to do? I miss Mom and Dad so much I want to die." Both Macie and I went over to her and hugged her. As soon as we touched, we started crying, too. The longer we cried, the more we hung on to each other and the more we cried. We all stood there hugging and crying for a while, and then slowly we got our emotions under control.

We sat down to talk, but there really wasn't much to say. We didn't know why we were here or where we were going—and they wouldn't tell us. There wasn't any chance of escape and nowhere to go even if we did manage to get away. Why escape when we couldn't contact Mom and Dad? Since we did not have anything else to do, we started packing so there would be room on the beds for us to sleep. The first thing we did was separate everything into three piles, one for each of us. We then divided all the makeup and miscellaneous stuff into three piles. We decided to take a break before stuffing it all into the duffel bags. Miranda went to take a shower while Macie and I watched television. I wanted to watch the news to see what was going on in the world, but Macie wanted to watch Nick Jr. We agreed that when Miranda got out of the shower, I would take one next and then she could watch whatever she wanted. The news was on, and they were talking about some local crime in Albuquerque. Then came the weather and sports. The forecast of sunny and hot as was usual for daytime in New Mexico, and it would be cold at night. Just before the news ended, Miranda came out with such a relaxed look on her face. She said, "It's been so long since I took a long hot shower. I didn't want to get out. It felt so good—I was actually falling asleep standing under the water. I wish I could have stayed in there forever." She came over and sat down next to me. I was about to get up for my turn in the shower when the last story on the news came on.

The news anchor stated, "Everything is looking good for the AARDE IV space shuttle and its trip to Europa in five days. This will be the twenty-first trip to Europa for this shuttle. I sure wouldn't want to go—the reports coming back are that it is like the Wild West all over again." The anchorwoman also talked about the Spaceport America space shuttles. There would be four of them taking off tomorrow evening from Spaceport America in Las Cruces, New Mexico. Thousands had applied, but only two hundred would get to be part of the brave new world, and one hundred of those were government workers. After she had finished the story, a commercial came on. I got up as Macie switched the channel to Nick Jr. As I closed the bathroom door, I heard Miranda say she wanted to choose the channel. I shut the door so I wouldn't have to be a part of their decision.

I started the shower but forgot to bring clean clothes in with me, so I stepped out into the bedroom to see both Miranda and Macie struggling over control of the remote. I wanted to keep the peace, so I ordered them to stop. They both stopped and looked at me and then went back to fighting about it. Miranda had just yanked it out of Macie's hands when I said, "Stop! Miranda, give it back to her while I take a shower, and then it will be your turn."

Miranda turned to me and said, "Who made *you* boss?"

"Please, Miranda, haven't we been through enough with them not to fight amongst ourselves?" That sort of took the wind out of her, and she gave Macie the remote.

I grabbed my clean pajamas and went back into the bathroom. After closing the door, I undressed and climbed into the shower. I just stood there under the cascading hot water for at least ten minutes. It was the first shower I'd had since we'd been taken from our home. I was starting to fall asleep like Miranda said had happened to her and ended up banging my head on the wall. I decided I had better get clean before I hurt myself, so I took the washrag and soap and scrubbed my body and then shampooed and conditioned my hair. By the time I finished, I was exhausted. I almost collapsed because I was so tired. I shut off the water, slowly climbed out, and dried off. It was very tempting not to get dressed because of the effort. When I opened the door, I saw that the television was still going, but the piles of clothes we had separated on the bed were now on the floor, and both Macie and Miranda were asleep. Miranda was in one bed, and Macie was in the other one. I was so exhausted that I barely had enough energy to turn off the television and lights and climb into bed with Miranda. Macie had always moved around too much when she slept, so Miranda was the logical choice for a bedmate. As tired as I was, though, I don't think it would have mattered. I'm sure that I was asleep before my head hit the pillow.

CHAPTER 9

At about 7:30 am the next morning, Jude was standing over us telling us to get up because we had a big day ahead. All three of us just looked at her and then Miranda asked if she could have five more minutes to sleep. As long as I could remember, Miranda said this every morning when she was woken up.

Jude said, "Tell you what, I will give you fifteen minutes, and then it will be time to go down to breakfast. Have all of you had a shower?"

I said, "Miranda and I have, but Macie hasn't." Macie wasn't moving and still had her head under the covers, sleeping. I said, "Macie, get up. You need to take a shower." All we heard from her was a grunt.

Jude then said, "Macie, since you haven't taken a shower, you need to get up now." Macie did not move nor make a sound.

"Come on, Macie," I said. "Get up and take a shower so we can go eat breakfast."

Macie yelled at me. "Don't tell me what to do!"

Jude had had enough and as she pulled the covers off of Macie, she said, "She might not be able to, but I can! Now get out of bed and get cleaned up so you can go to breakfast." Macie was quiet and lay still a few seconds then got up and stomped into the bathroom. Jude told Amber to get us down to breakfast as soon as she could.

When Macie finished her shower and came out of the bathroom, I went in to get myself ready. I didn't see the need to put on any makeup, so I just brushed my hair, put it in a ponytail, and went out to get dressed. I thought it was going to be hot, so I put on one of my new shirts with shorts and tennis shoes. I encouraged Miranda and Macie to do the same. Miranda chose the same as me, but Macie insisted on wearing a skirt and tennis shoes. The skirt was white as were the tennis shoes, so it matched well enough. We opened the door to Amber's area and saw her sitting on the couch reading a newspaper. I told her we were ready to go down and that we were really hungry. She got up and led us to the elevator. Once inside, she reminded us not to talk to anyone. On the way down, I considered trying to escape because Amber was the only one with us but knew that it would require more planning than just running away. Not surprisingly, William and the two men were waiting for us when the elevator doors opened, so all escape ideas left my mind as quickly as they had come. William led the way to the breakfast buffet.

Macie, Miranda, and I piled huge helpings of eggs and bacon on our plates. Miranda also got some French toast. We brought our plates and were directed to sit down with Jude. The rest of our escorts were at the next table, looking bored. They must have already eaten. I guess escorting three teenage girls wasn't too exciting for them. Maybe we needed to try another escape to entertain them. I doubted that opportunity would present itself, but it was fun to contemplate. I looked around the restaurant and saw that there were a few other people eating. There was a guy by himself who looked up and directly at me when I looked his way. We made eye contact for a few seconds, and then he looked away. It was the same man I had seen before. Jude started to tell us what we were going to do that day. The first thing we needed to do after breakfast was to pack the duffel bags with all our stuff, and then once we were on the road, she would tell us about our future.

When we'd finished eating and were getting up, I glanced over at the guy eating by himself. He was about to leave also. He looked over at me and bowed his head a little and then left. He looked to be not much older than I was—and kind of cute. I hadn't had any romantic thoughts in a long time. The memories of my previous boyfriend seemed like such a long time ago. All of us left the restaurant and went upstairs to start packing.

Macie, Miranda, and I talked about the reasons why we had duffel bags. It was because we had way too much stuff for a small suitcase. It probably would have taken two or three suitcases each to fit all this stuff. None of us wanted to leave anything behind, but it turned out we were worrying for nothing because all of our stuff fit in the duffel bags with room to spare. The bags were too heavy for any of us to carry, so William and the boys had to carry them down to the van for us. Seeing William have to do anything for us was always a source of amusement. When Miranda saw him carrying the bag, she told me that she wished she would have packed the iron and anything else that would have made the bag heavier. If only Pat had been there to help carry our stuff, we would be even happier. We all went down the stairs and through the door and climbed into the van. Miranda got in the very back, and Macie and I sat in the next row up. Jude sat next to Miranda and the rest of the escorts in the front seats.

When we stopped for gas, Jude told William to get us all drinks. I could tell that he didn't want to, but he knew better than to question Jude's orders. Miranda got her usual Dr. Pepper, Macie a Big Blue, Jude got a coffee, and I got a PowerAde. And then we were back on the road again, and it seemed we were heading south, but I wasn't quite sure. I had never paid attention to directions before but was now very curious as to where we were going. After a few minutes, Jude asked us to be very quiet and to listen without interruption to what she was going to tell us. After she was finished, we could ask questions all the way to our destination if we wanted.

"First off," Jude said, "our destination is Spaceport America."

Macie said, "I read about that in the books we had in the room they kept us in."

"You had books in there?" Jude asked. "I didn't think they were supposed to do that, but I guess it doesn't really matter."

Macie said, "We had all kinds. There was a nice lady there who snuck the books in to us with our meals."

"Macie!" I scolded. "Don't talk about that! It will get her in trouble."

Jude assured us she wouldn't tell anyone about it. She reiterated that our destination was Spaceport America and Macie said, "That will be fun! Can we tour the whole place?"

Jude smiled at Macie's question. "There won't be much time for you to tour it because you will be getting ready to leave on the next rocket shuttle."

All of us spoke at the same time. "What?"

I was starting to get emotional. "Will our parents and little sister be going with us? Has all this just been a test for us? What's really going on?"

"I miss my family so much," Miranda said. "Please say they'll be at this Spaceport place."

Macie started to cry and said, "Please, oh please! I want to see my mommy and daddy so much."

Miranda, Macie, and I looked at Jude expectantly, but Jude said, "No, your parents and little sister will not be there."

Macie asked, "But when will we be able to see them?"

"You're not letting me finish what I need to tell you. Please be quiet for a few minutes while I explain," Jude reprimanded. Jude began her explanation again, the three of us getting more and more angry as she continued. "All three of you are getting on the rocket shuttle tomorrow."

"Will mom and dad meet us on the space station?" Macie asked.

Jude bowed her head for a few seconds and then looked straight at Macie. "No, your parents will not meet you there. Nor will you see them for a very long time."

Miranda said, "It's already been a long time." She just stared at Jude, waiting for her to say something.

Jude was quiet for a short while and then continued in a very soft voice. "I'm sorry. I do not know where your parents and little sister are, and I do not know what happened to them. I was given orders to make sure you three got on the rocket shuttle. That's all I know. Again, I'm sorry I am not able to answer your questions. Considering where you are going and what is going happen to you, I suggest you do your best to forget about your parents and little sister."

"I will never forget them, and there's nothing you can do about it," Macie said defiantly through tears. I choked up, too, and was too stunned by this news to say or do anything.

Jude then said, "Now I will tell you the bare bones truth as I know it. You will take the rocket shuttle from Spaceport America to the space station in orbit. You will stay there for a few days and will then board the AARDE IV space shuttle. It will take you to Europa."

"We saw that story on the news last night," I said. Jude then told us it was a one month trip from Earth to Europa. I asked again, "Why are they sending us there?"

"Because the government doesn't want you here," Jude said very bluntly.

"But why?" asked Miranda.

"I think for two reasons," Jude said, "and I will deny telling you this if anyone ever asks. One, they don't want you here to make trouble about what happened to your parents and little sister. Two, they need women on Europa because there are very few there."

I was shocked. "We're just young girls. We're not old enough to get married. You can't be serious!" I protested.

Jude looked down. "I'm very serious. You three are young now but will be of age in just a few years. You don't have to marry, but I highly encourage it so you'll be taken care of properly."

Miranda and Macie didn't get the meaning behind what Jude was telling us. We were going to be given to the men on Europa—whether we liked it or not. All three of us went completely silent for the rest of Jude's explanation. I could tell she was having a hard time telling us and could see the emotion playing on her face, but her voice was steady as she continued. "Let me tell you as much as I know. We have about a four-hour drive until we get to Spaceport America in Las Cruces. Once there, Jacob Verndari, the man in the passenger's seat up front, will travel with you all the way to Europa to ensure your safety. Jacob, say hi to the girls."

The man in the front seat turned around at her request and said, "Hi girls. I'm looking forward to the trip and helping you with your transition to AARDE." Jacob was a nice-looking man and appeared to be in his late twenties or early thirties. I hadn't really paid too much attention to him before.

"What is AARDE?" I asked.

"It's Dutch for Earth, and it's what the people who live on Europa call their planet," he explained. "Did you notice the name of the space shuttle ship is AARDE IV? There are four spaceships traveling to and from Europa. There will be more eventually, but that is all that have been built and are working so far."

Jude interrupted and said, "Jacob, you'll have plenty of time to tell them all about Europa, but I have a very short time to fill them in on what will happen to them from here on, so please hold your explanations!" Jacob turned around, and she started again. "Actually there isn't really a lot more to tell. When we arrive, all of you and Jacob will be taken to the contamination area. It's much like a hotel but is very clean and bacteria-free. The Spaceport personnel will put you and your belongings through a thorough decontamination process. It involves a lot of washing and scrubbing of your skin along with multiple showers in super-cleansed water. I'm told that the scrubbing can be a bit painful, but you will definitely feel clean when they're done with you. Your belongings go through a similar process and then are given back to you on the space station. Once you and your belongings have been decontaminated, they will not let you come out nor be around anyone who has not been decontaminated. Also, they will do a complete physical on each of you to ensure you are not carrying any diseases that could infect people. They normally do not let people as young as Macie go, but we got a special exemption so the three of you could stay together."

She took a breath and continued. "Once all who are going are decontaminated, they will load you into the rocket shuttle. I'm not sure of the name of the shuttle—there are so many shuttles going from Earth to the space stations every day. Once everyone is on board the shuttle, they'll take off and deliver you to the Europa space station. You will be on the space station a couple of days before the AARDE IV will take you to Europa. There are only a limited number of launch windows to Europa, so if they don't go at the proper time, it could take two or three times as long to get there and the ship might not have enough fuel."

Miranda asked, "What do we do while we're waiting on the space station?"

"Just wait—and enjoy the view of Earth. I haven't been there, but it's said that pictures don't really do justice to what the Earth looks like from space. The pictures of Earth are beautiful, and I can only imagine what it must look like in person."

"I can't wait to see it," said Macie.

All I could think about was how lonely and depressing it would be without our parents and Morgan. We asked a few more questions but were mostly quiet with our own thoughts while we drove to the station.

When we arrived in Truth or Consequences, New Mexico I told Jude that I needed to use the bathroom. She asked the driver to pull into the next gas station. We took the Route 25 bypass that went through the town and pulled into a Chevron gas station. As we pulled in, I asked Miranda and Macie if they had to go. Miranda said, "Sure, I can go," but Macie said she didn't have to. I looked sternly at her and then she said, "Okay, okay. I'll go."

Jude was talking to Jacob about the Spaceport and didn't really pay attention when we got out of the van. William escorted us inside and told us he'd be waiting outside. Inside the ladies bathroom were three stalls. Macie and Miranda went into the first two, but the third one was occupied. I heard a flush from the third stall, and a middle-aged lady who looked to be in her 40s, dressed in jeans and a tee shirt, stepped out. As she was approaching the sink to wash her hands, I stopped her and asked if I could have a moment of her time. She looked at me with a look of irritation at first, but it softened because I think she could tell I had been crying. "Yes," she said. "What can I do for you?"

I said, "I don't have much time because the man outside the bathroom door is waiting for us. I know this is going to be very hard for you to believe, but it's the truth. The three of us have been kidnapped by the government and held for the past year. They will not tell us why. We were taken from our home, kept prisoner in a room, and now they're going to send us to Europa. If there is anything you can do for us, I would be eternally grateful." Miranda and Macie started getting emotional and begging for help. I said, "There's a man outside the bathroom to guard us and a van parked outside that they're going to take us away in." We all grabbed her hands and looked pleadingly at her. She pulled her hands away and left the bathroom very quickly. She must have thought we were completely crazy.

I really didn't have to use the restroom, so after the three of us had calmed down a little, I opened the door and started walking toward the exit. Macie asked William if we could get a snack. He said, "Yes, but make it quick." Miranda got her usual Takis, I got sour cream and onion chips, and Macie couldn't make up her mind, as usual. She finally picked out some shelled sunflower seeds. We went up to the cashier and William paid, then we all headed toward the door. A man held it open for us, and we walked through.

Macie was in the lead followed by Miranda, me, and then William. The man holding the door looked familiar, but I didn't immediately recognize him. I turned around to take a second look at him, and he was looking directly at me. He had shut the door in William's face and was holding it closed with his foot. William immediately went into a rage and started yelling at the man and pushing on the door. As I was watching William and the man argue, I felt a tug on my sleeve. I turned around and was pulled toward the open door of a car in front of the store. The woman in the driver's seat was the same woman we had pleaded with in the bathroom. She was waving frantically at us to get in. It took a few seconds to understand, and then the three of us ran and jumped into her car. I think it was a Lexus but wasn't really sure because I've never been very good at recognizing cars.

CHAPTER 10

As soon as all of us were in the car, she took off. The door closed behind us from the force of the acceleration as she screeched the tires. We all looked back and saw William give the man a big push and start running after us, yelling at the people in the van for help. Jude and the others were very slow to react, and we were out of sight before William made it back to them. The lady sped away through town and ended up on some small road. She stayed on it a mile or so and then turned left onto another street. Once she did that, she slowed down to a normal speed and introduced herself as Sharon but didn't give her last name.

I was about to introduce myself, and she said, "It would be best if I didn't know. I really have no idea what I'm doing. Sorry I didn't believe you when you first told me. I thought you were crazy until I walked out and saw the guy standing there like you said. He looked very impatient for you to come out of the bathroom and was dressed like the FBI. When I walked out of the store, I saw the van and all the people in it, and all of them were dressed similarly to that man. I sat in my car thinking about what to do when I saw you three walking out. I started up the car and drove up in front and opened the door. I thought if you were really in trouble you would get in, and you did."

I asked her where we were going. "I really have no idea," she said. "This kind of thing is new to me. I'm heading back to the highway. I went down that two-lane road so they wouldn't know which way we're going."

"Thank you for doing this for us. I don't know how we can ever repay you."

"Don't thank me yet. We have a long way to go until you're safe."

We arrived at the highway and turned south. We drove for only about five minutes and then saw traffic ahead stopping for the police blocking the road. That was quick! I was thinking as quickly as I could and said, "Please slow down enough for us to get out. We're going to make a run for it. Thank you so much for what you did for us. We will never forget you." While Sharon was slowing down, we all gave her a quick hug. She almost stopped, and we hopped out and ran down into the ditch next to the road as she sped up again so she didn't look suspicious. We followed the ditch to a dry riverbed that ran under the highway. Then we followed the riverbed as it wound eastward. We had no idea where we were going, but we sure didn't want to leave Earth, and this was our best chance of staying.

The riverbed emptied out into a river that was running north to south. If we followed it north, we would be back in Truth or Consequences. If we went south, who knows where we would end up? We decided to go north because it was so flat here we would be spotted easily. We walked down the small hill to the river. I didn't want to drink the water but was getting hot and thirsty, so I just dunked my head in it to get my hair wet. When I stood up, I felt much cooler with the water from my hair dripping down my back. Macie and Miranda did the same before we started walking. We tried to walk next to the embankment so it would be harder for people to see us.

We heard some sirens off in the distance, but fortunately none were close to where we were walking. As we walked, we tried to figure out what to do. It wasn't like we could call anyone. William had said that all of our relatives' phones were tapped—and they were so far away in Dallas. Miranda suggested we could hitchhike back to Albuquerque.

"They probably have checkpoints all over the place," I said. "It would be pretty easy for them to identify three girls traveling together, and splitting up is out of the question. There's no way I'm going to leave either of you."

We walked in silence for a bit before Macie said, "Why don't we go live in the desert?"

Miranda and I laughed, and Miranda stated firmly, "I would rather die on some foreign planet than in the desert. Slow starvation and dehydration seem a nasty way to go."

Macie looked mad and said we could survive. "A lot of the books I read were how to survive in the desert," she said. "I know how to collect water, although if we followed this river we might not need to. I can build fires, and we can cook what we kill." Macie was getting more and more excited as she continued. "There are lots of rabbits in the desert along with other wildlife. I think I can remember the edible plants." Miranda and I were impressed but very skeptical.

Miranda asked her, "Who is going to cook the rabbit—let alone kill it?"

Macie replied, "If you kill it, I will cook it."

I laughed and said, "Macie, the only thing you've ever cooked is a bowl of cereal." Miranda laughed, too, and Macie looked hurt. "Macie, I am sorry. I didn't mean to hurt your feelings. We'd better find a place to hide—there's no telling how long until they get helicopters out looking for us. Remember in Dallas? They had all the police helping. It would be nice if Truth or Consequences were too small to have a helicopter. Let's climb the bank and see where we are."

We climbed the bank and looked over. We could see the backs of a lot of houses. They all backed up to the river, some with chain link fences and some with wooden privacy fences. A few hundred yards up the river was a junkyard. It seemed like it would be a good place to hide and would provide some shade. It was getting pretty hot, so we went back down and walked until we thought we were directly behind the junkyard. We climbed the bank again and fortunately we were right behind the junkyard. There was a barbed wire fence across the back of the property with a six-foot wooden fence up the sides. I guess not too many people broke into junkyards. I held the wires apart so Miranda and Macie could go through, and then Miranda held it for me. Macie was already scoping out a place for us to hide. These must have been really old cars because I didn't know what type most of them were. We spotted an old suburban a few cars up one of the aisles and got in. Lucky for us the windows had a manual crank because it was getting pretty hot outside.

The rear seat was missing from the suburban, so there was just enough room for all three of us to lie down comfortably. The carpet looked old and ragged, but at least no metal was poking through. We lay there talking and enjoying the breeze for about thirty minutes before we heard a helicopter coming toward us. Macie climbed up to look out the window, and Miranda grabbed her leg and pulled her back right before her head went out the window.

"Macie, what were you thinking? Who do you think is in that helicopter?"

Macie said, "I don't know! I just wanted to see it."

Miranda popped Macie on the head and said, "Hmmm, let's see! Who just escaped and are on the run, and what would be the easiest way to catch them? Could it be a helicopter?"

Macie blushed a bit. "I'm sorry—I just wanted to see it."

"It's okay, Macie. We just need to stay out of sight until it's dark." The helicopter had been flying pretty low, and I was thankful that it hadn't flown directly over us. We stayed down until it had passed and then watched it fly away over the desert. As I watched it, I said, "When they don't find us in the desert near here, they'll go house to house searching if they haven't already. We don't have any choice but to stay here until it gets dark and pray they don't find us. We should try to rest if we can because it will be a long night of running."

Macie and Miranda nodded their heads, and we all laid down and tried to rest. It wasn't very comfortable without a pillow but not too bad. The next thing I remembered was Macie shaking me awake, asking, "Do you hear that?"

I couldn't tell if my eyes were open or not because it was so dark. I said to her, "I don't hear anything."

Macie said, "Listen hard." I did and could faintly hear the sounds of dogs barking excitedly. "You don't think they're tracking us, do you?" I shook my head no, but the more I thought about it, the more likely I thought it was.

I started shaking Miranda. "Miranda, get up! They have dogs after us."

Miranda, who normally needs five minutes every time she wakes up, shot bolt upright and said, "We need to get out of here."

We hurriedly climbed out of the suburban and went through the fence toward the river. It was much colder than when I went to sleep. I guess the desert doesn't hold the heat very well at night. The moon was not up yet, but the stars provided enough light for us to see where we were going.

When we got to the river, Macie said, "Hurry and take off your shoes and carry them." Miranda asked why and Macie told her, "The only way we can lose the dogs is to go in the river." It seemed like a good idea, so we did what Macie said.

The water was warmer than the air outside but still quite cool. The sandy bottom was a surprisingly hard surface, so it was easy going. I thought we were going to have to swim across, but the deepest it got was up to my thigh. I didn't even get my shorts wet. Miranda and I were just about across when Macie said, "We need to stay in the river or they'll just pick up our scent on the other side." That made sense, so Miranda and I followed Macie up the river. I remembered the water was fairly clear when I had looked at it earlier in the day. They might be able to track us even if we were in the water. The bottom was fairly hard, however, so I hoped we weren't leaving footprints behind. We stayed nearer the far shore but did cut back and forth a few times hoping to cause some confusion.

We weren't at a full run but were going at a pretty good jogging pace. We were all in pretty good shape from our exercise in the room, and it actually felt good being able to run in the open even if we were being chased. Macie told us a number of times she was getting tired, so we walked for short distances before picking up our pace again. I wasn't winded at all, and I don't think Miranda was either, but Macie hadn't worked out as hard as Miranda and I had when we were in the room. We kept our jog up until we came to a road that crossed the river. It was shallow enough there for a car to cross over. On the other side of the road, though, we found it was about five feet deep. The road must act like a dam.

Miranda was in the lead when we crossed the road. She stepped off and sank in up to her chin. Fortunately, she didn't fall over when she went in and was able to keep her shoes and socks above her head. She handed those to me and then climbed out. All her clothes were wet, and she started to shiver. We couldn't hear the dogs anymore, so we decided to rest a few minutes and figure out what to do next.

"We can't stay in the river because it's too deep, so here is what I suggest," I said. "We put on our shoes and socks and stay on the far side of the river until we either come to more shallow part or a less populated part of town. We could cross over the river then to find some food because I'm getting pretty hungry."

Macie said, "I'm really hungry, too. Can't we find some food now?"

Miranda replied, "Whatever, let's go."

So we put on our shoes and socks and took off. We made much faster progress while not running in the water. We had run for about thirty minutes when Macie spotted a gas station near the other side of the river. We were very thirsty and hungry, so we took off our shoes and socks and waded over to the town side of the river. Fortunately, it wasn't too deep, and I only got my shorts a little wet. As we were putting our shoes back on, we talked about how we were going to get food and water with no money. Our hope was that someone there would take pity on us. Becoming thieves wasn't desirable, but it was definitely more desirable than getting caught by William.

We went around to the front of the store by the gas pumps and tried to decide what to do. There was a man filling his car with gas, but he didn't look too friendly, so we looked over at the store. There were two cars parked in front and three people inside besides the clerk.

"I don't think any of these people look friendly enough to help us, I said. "We're going to have to steal some food. When we go in, let's all split up, get some food and water, and meet back by the door like we're looking at something there. When the clerk isn't looking, we'll make a run for it back to the river. Then we'll keep heading the same way we were going."

Macie looked scared. "What if we get caught?"

Both Miranda and I laughed. Miranda said, "Macie, what do you think will happen? We will be right back with William and on our way to Europa, so we really have nothing to lose. Let's go." We followed Miranda into the store and split up. I went and got a couple of sandwiches out of the deli cooler and then moved to the drink cooler to get a couple bottles of water. Then I walked back to the front door and acted like I was looking at the oil. Miranda stood next to me a minute later, and then Macie showed up.

Miranda had a few candy bars, some gum, and a twenty-ounce Dr. Pepper. Macie had her hands full of stuff. I didn't have time to see what she had except for a bag of Flamin' Hot Cheetos and a Big Blue, her favorite drink. I wished we had planned what we needed instead of just what we wanted, but it was too late. There was a little traveling bag on the shelf, so we all dumped all our stuff in it and looked over at the clerk.

He glanced over at me at the same time I looked at him. He seemed to be nervous about us. He kept glancing over at us like he knew something was up. He wasn't able to say anything to us because he was busy with the people in line checking out. We waited until he turned around to get cigarettes for someone, and then we bolted out the door. Miranda went left and Macie and I went right, hoping to confuse the chase. We met up back up at the river and kept running along it. Macie started to complain after about ten minutes of running, so we decided to rest for a couple minutes. I was actually surprised it had taken her that long to start complaining.

I looked back and could see flashing red and blue lights near where the gas station would be. I said, "We'd better cross the river again to hopefully throw them off if they're following."

Macie said, "Don't take your shoes off yet. Let's go up a ways until we see a road. We'll walk up to the road and then retrace our footsteps and cross the river." Seemed like a good idea, so we ran a few more minutes until the road came near the water. We started walking a bit in the water and then turned directly toward the asphalt road. We walked on the road for forty or fifty feet and then turned around to go back to the river. Macie stopped us, felt around in the bag of stuff I was carrying, and pulled out a small rectangular can. I was surprised to see it was a can of pepper. I asked her what she was doing. "I saw in a movie once that these slaves were on the run from dogs, and they spread pepper to mess with their noses."

Miranda and I watched as Macie opened up the can and started shaking out its contents. Miranda asked what was taking so long. Macie said only a little was coming out as she shook it. Miranda examined the tin closely and laughed. "Macie, you needed to open the tab with the *big* hole." Macie grabbed it from Miranda and opened the other tab on the pepper box.

I suggested, "Why don't you pour it into your hand so you can control where you spread it?"

"Good idea, Madison!" Macie said.

She poured some into her hand and began to sprinkle it around on asphalt near where we stepped off the sand. She got bored very quickly and started shaking the box all over the place. Miranda and I started laughing because she was doing a funky dance while she peppered the sand.

She finally finished, and we walked backward in the sand to the river, doing our best to retrace our footprints. We were only partially successful but made it back to the river without falling. We took off our shoes and socks and waded across the river. It was up to about our waist this time, so it wasn't too bad. When we made it to the other side, we jogged near the edge in the water, hoping they would have a harder time following us. We made it a few hundred yards before it got deep again with a higher bank. We put our shoes and socks back on.

We were just about to take off jogging again when I glanced back the way we had come from. There were white lights flashing, and I could have sworn I heard dogs again. Miranda and Macie saw and heard the same thing, so instead of jogging, we ran as fast as we could. We were getting tired quickly and didn't make it far before we all slowed down. We could still see the lights a long way off but couldn't hear the dogs anymore. As we followed the river, we saw a tall structure in the direction we were headed. As we approached, we figured out it was a dam.

CHAPTER 11

We wound our way up to the top of the dam and saw a big lake glistening in the moonlight. There wasn't a beach on either bank of the lake, but it was surrounded by what looked like sandstone cliffs. We climbed up the cliffs to the flat area at the top, and then we walked quickly while I glanced back every few minutes. I was relieved to no longer see the lights nor hear the dogs. We made good time over the sandstone but were getting tired and cold. Our clothes were still wet, and the temperature was falling. Miranda started to complain about being cold and said she was shivering. I remembered she would wear a sweatshirt to school even when the weather outside was in the 90s.

What we needed was a fire, but those chasing us would be able to see it from a long way off, so we just kept walking. There were deep cracks in the sandstone—we almost fell into a few of them. It gave me an idea, so I went to the edge of the cliff and started climbing down. Macie and Miranda asked what I was doing. I told them I was going to look for a cave. Miranda thought that was a cool idea and started to climb down, too. She was a faster climber and got well ahead of Macie and me. We followed various ledges and had to backtrack some but made decent progress along the cliffs. We found some small caves and a couple of decent size ones that they were too shallow. We kept looking and were about to give up when Miranda called out. "Hey! Over here. This one might do."

Macie and I hurried over to her to see what she'd found. We couldn't see inside because it was very dark. Miranda volunteered to go in first.

Macie was freaking out. She said firmly, "I'm not going in there! There could be a bear in there for all we know!

Miranda and I laughed, and I said "Macie, there aren't bears down here. Snakes, yes, but certainly not bears."

Macie said, "Snakes are even worse."

Miranda laughed. "Okay, then you can wait out here by yourself."

"No, that's definitely the worst. I'm coming," said Macie.

Just as we were about to start feeling our way into the cave, we heard a noise off in the distance. It was a helicopter, and it was coming our way. I stepped away from the side a bit so I could see the dam. Sure enough, there was a helicopter with a big search light hovering over the dam. As I watched, it started moving up the side of the lake. The searchlight was moving back and forth from the edge of the lake up the cliff and over the flat plain. I yelled to Miranda and Macie to get in the cave as I scrambled in behind them. I was worried a little worried about snakes or some other animal being inside, but we didn't have any choice.

We scrambled in, feeling our way along the wall. The cave seemed to zigzag about three or four times before we stopped and stood very still. The helicopter was just about on top of us. I guess they were really being thorough because they were going very slow. As the chopper passed overhead, the spotlight was bright enough to light up a lot of but not the entire cave. From what I could see, there were a couple more zigzags before the roof of the cave opened to the bluff above. We all stood very still just in case, but I was sure they couldn't see us, even with the light shining down from the cavern ceiling. Before the helicopter moved on, I took a good look around the cave.

It was more like a wide zigzagging hallway than a cave. The floor was loose dirt, and the walls were about seven feet tall. We were in the middle of the hall and couldn't see the sky or the lake once the helicopter had moved on. We stood still a couple of minutes before walking around the corner to look up at the hole in the ceiling. The hole was about four feet long and shaped sort of like an egg. We decided to climb up and look out. Once we made it up, I could barely hear the helicopter. It was flying further and further away from us. We then climbed back down and sat down to rest.

Miranda asked, "So what do we do now?" I shook my head and shrugged my shoulders, not having any ideas.

Macie spoke up immediately. "I can build a fire so we can warm up."

"How are you going to do that?" Miranda asked.

"Remember when we were in the room, and I could make a fire with a pencil?"

Miranda laughed. "Oh yeah, I remember. The fire that started the alarm and got us all wet with the sprinklers."

"Good idea, Macie. What do we need to get you?" I asked her.

"Wait, if we start a fire they'll find us immediately," Miranda said.

Macie looked heartbroken. "I hadn't thought of that."

"If we built the fire on the other side of the wall where the roof doesn't have a hole, then the light should be mostly hidden," I said. "We don't want a big fire—just enough to get us warm and dry our clothes."

Macie looked happy again. "We just need some dried grass, a couple of skinny sticks, and wood to burn." We all climbed to the top again, peeking out just in case. We didn't see any lights or hear anyone, so we climbed out to search for the wood.

The stars were out, so there was enough light to search. It didn't take us long to gather up enough tinder and grass. Macie was particular about the kind of sticks she wanted and finally found them. We brought everything down into the cave and piled it against the wall in the center of the hallway section. Macie took her flat stick and laid it down and then started rubbing the skinny one on it. It was pretty dark so I couldn't see much of what Macie was doing, but I did hear her rubbing the sticks together along with her heavy breathing.

After about thirty seconds, I started to smell smoke. "Macie, I can smell the smoke! How much longer?"

"Leave me alone," she said. I shut up and waited.

The rubbing stopped, and Miranda asked, "Did you give up?"

"Shut up," Macie said irritably.

"Are you sure you know what you're doing?" Miranda asked just as a flame lit up the entire room. Macie was putting more of the grass on the fire and gently stacking some of the wood on top.

Miranda and I yelled, "Way to go, Macie!" Our yelling sounded extremely loud in the enclosed space, so we stopped quickly.

Once Macie had the fire going, I climbed out the hole in the roof to see if the light from it was noticeable. If I looked straight down into the hole, I could see a faint glow, but from a few feet back I couldn't see any sign of the fire. I walked over to the ledge and looked down, but I couldn't see anything. I climbed down to the entrance and looked inside and could see just a faint glow but nothing significant. Relieved, I went back inside to warm up. As I looked around the last corner, I yelled, "Freeze!" in the deepest voice I could muster. Both Miranda and Macie jumped up and were starting to run for the hole in the ceiling.

As they started to run, they glanced back. I was doubled over, laughing. They turned around and charged at me. I wasn't ready for the attack when they both tackled and pinned me down on the dirt floor. As she held me down, Miranda said, "Don't ever do that again!" I started laughing, and both of them joined me as they rolled off. By now, Macie had the fire going very well, and the room we were in was starting to warm up. We were cold and tired, so we just sat down by the fire to rest and to let our clothes dry.

After a few minutes of staring mindlessly into the fire, Macie asked, "Where's the bag?"

It took me a few seconds to acknowledge her. "I think it's near the entrance to the cave, but I'm too tired to get it."

Macie looked disgusted with me but got up and walked to the entrance, coming back with the bag. She sat down and started pulling things from it. She gave Miranda one of her candy bars and me a sandwich.

"Are there any more sandwiches?" Miranda asked. "I guess I wasn't thinking too clearly when I picked out my stuff."

"There should be another one," I said as Macie pulled it out.

Both were submarine sandwiches with a bunch of different meats and cheeses. Macie dug out her Flamin' Hot Cheetos and started munching. No wonder she stayed skinny, she hardly ate anything. I certainly wasn't going to judge her now after she'd gotten that fire going for us. We ate mostly in silence, listening to the fire and Macie crunching the Cheetos. After we had finished eating, I looked over at my sisters and saw that Macie and Miranda's eyelids were almost closed. I wasn't far behind them in the tired department.

Macie lay down on her side with her head on the bag. Miranda lay down with her head on Macie's leg and closed her eyes. I was about to lay down but thought I'd better get more wood and build up the fire before going to sleep. I walked over to the part of the cave with the hole in the roof and climbed out. It was harder to find wood because there were clouds covering the stars and the moon, but I found an armful of sticks. Then I had to search around a bit to find the hole to get back to the cave. Once I found it, I dropped the wood into the cave, expecting Miranda and Macie to get scared and yell at me. But I didn't hear anything. They must have been sound asleep.

As I climbed down, I could have sworn I heard dogs again—barking and sneezing. I laughed and hoped they wouldn't find us during the night, but I was honestly too tired to worry about it. I made it back into the cave with the wood, added more to the fire, and then lay down. Miranda and Macie hadn't moved, so I lay my head on Miranda's leg and went to sleep without another thought. It seemed like I had barely closed my eyes when a gunshot woke me, and I sat bolt upright. I listened for a few seconds and then heard the rain—and more thunder. I got up and walked to the entrance to the cave that faced the lake.

With the lightning and thunder booming, it was quite a beautiful sight. It must have been close to sunrise because it was getting lighter outside. I watched for a couple more minutes and then decided to go back to sleep. I went back inside and lay down. Macie was lying on her back, her head still on the bag, and Miranda was using Macie's stomach as a pillow. The fire was almost out, so I put a few pieces of wood on it and lay back down. The thunder had stopped, and all I heard was the rain. There is nothing quite as restful as sleeping as the rain fell.

When I woke up a while later, it was still drizzling but not as hard as earlier. Miranda and Macie were still sleeping, and I couldn't think of any reason to wake them. Miranda would probably sleep the whole day away if given the chance. I went again to the entrance of the cave to look out. It was very dreary, but in a way, it was calming to watch the drops drizzling into the lake. Finally growing tired of watching the rain, I went back in and freaked out when I saw Macie trying to get the fire going again. I yelled as I stomped on the coals and kicked dirt over them. "No! We can't start a fire now. The smoke will let the government people see exactly where we are."

Macie said, "I'm cold—I want a fire."

"Macie, please be reasonable. If William finds us, what do you think will happen?"

Macie pouted for a few seconds then said, "I know, but I'm so cold."

All I could say was, "I'm sorry." I *was* sorry, but it wasn't my fault we were here.

Miranda finally woke up and said, "I'm hungry...and thirsty."

Macie dumped the contents of the bag onto the floor—half of her big blue drink, a full water bottle, a couple of candy bars, half a bag of Flamin' Hot Cheetos, and a multipurpose knife.

I asked, "Where did the knife come from?"

"I saw it when we were in the store and took it," Macie told me. "I thought it might come in handy."

Miranda said, "Good idea Macie. You're quite the survivalist."

We were all totally run down from the excitement of the previous night but not enough to go back to sleep, so we explored more of the cave as we finished off the candy bars and Cheetos.

There wasn't much to see past the hole in the roof, just a bigger room. The other end of the cave overlooked the lake. It had stopped raining, and the sun was peeking out as the clouds broke up. The sun was almost directly overhead. We lay down behind some rocks to let it warm us. It felt quite nice, and I think I dozed off for a while. I was just starting to wake up when I heard a noise up on the bluff. We were fairly well hidden by some big rocks unless they looked right over the edge immediately above us.

I glanced over and saw that Macie and Miranda were fast asleep, so I just kept as quiet as I could and listened. As the sounds came closer, I could tell it was two men and a woman. They were talking. William, Jude, and some other guy. I could hear them talking about trying to find us. William was mumbling over and over again, "I can't wait until I get my hands on them, especially Miranda."

Jude finally said, "William, just shut up. You're just embarrassed that these girls got the best of you—not once but twice." William mumbled something else under his breath as they moved further away from us.

I smiled to myself with relief that they didn't find us but was too scared to move. After a few minutes, I scrambled up and peeked over the edge. I didn't see or hear anyone. I climbed back down to Miranda and Macie to wake them up, deciding to wake up Macie first because it would probably take both of us to keep Miranda quiet when we got her up.

Fortunately, both of them were lying on their backs. I straddled Macie's chest and pressed my hand to her mouth. She immediately awakened, a look of panic in her eyes, but then recognized me and saw that I had my finger in front of my mouth, trying to shush her. She was about to say something when I leaned over next to her ear and whispered that there were people near. She shook her head in acknowledgment as I continued whispering that I needed her help to quietly wake up Miranda. I told her to straddle Miranda like I had done to her and put her hand over Miranda's mouth. I would lie on top of her to keep her still until she calmed down.

Macie got up and knelt down, straddling Miranda, ready to put her hand on her sister's mouth. I nodded for her to do it as I positioned myself over her legs. As soon as Macie's hand touched Miranda's mouth, Miranda's eyes shot open, and her body stiffened. She grabbed Macie and threw her about three feet away. She then sat up incredibly fast, about to kick me off her legs when she saw the panicked look in my eyes and my finger in front of my mouth, urging her to be quiet. I should have known that Miranda would fight first before yelling or making noise. We looked back at Macie and started to laugh. She had been thrown and had nearly hit her head, but the surprised look on her face was priceless.

I whispered to them. "William, Jude, and another person walked by on the ridge looking for us. We were very lucky they didn't look over, or they would have seen us. We need to get back to the cave." We all got up and crept back inside. Once there, Miranda climbed up to look out and didn't see anyone.

We huddled in the cave, trying to keep warm and keeping silent in case someone came back. I could tell Miranda was getting restless and wouldn't stay still the whole day, but we had to try to remain invisible for the time being. After about an hour or so, Macie started to complain about being hungry. We still had some of our drinks left, so we weren't too thirsty. I tried to keep Macie calm, telling her that we'd find something to eat after dark.

Miranda laughed and said sarcastically, "Oh really? And how are we going to do that when we can't even see?" Macie was about to cry when Miranda whispered, "Quiet! I hear something."

The noise was coming from the cave entrance toward the lake and was getting closer. We listened intently as the sound moved closer. Miranda picked up a rock for protection. She raised her arm to throw it just as the sound was about to come around the bend in the cave. We were all super quiet as a squirrel appeared. It looked right at us and was about to turn around and run when Miranda threw her rock, hitting it in the back of the head. Macie and I looked at Miranda, shocked.

"Why did you do that? It was about to leave," I said.

Miranda just laughed at me and said, "I just killed our dinner!" Macie and I were aghast that she would kill an innocent animal like that. "How about this plan? I kill our dinner, Madison skins it, and Macie cooks it."

Surprisingly, Macie said, "I'll cook it, but I'm not cleaning it." Both of them looked expectantly at me.

I just stared blankly at the dead squirrel. Finally I said, "But I don't know how."

"Nice try, Madison," Miranda said, "but all three of us memorized those survival books, and now is your chance to put some of it to good use."

I had purposefully put all those books about killing and skinning out of my mind, but once reminded, I knew exactly what to do. I got some rocks to lay the squirrel on and grabbed the knife Macie had taken from the convenience store. First I cut under the tail and around the squirrel's sides. Once the cuts were made, I stepped on the tail and peeled the skin right off. All three of us were completely grossed out, but fortunately we didn't puke. I then peeled the skin off of the bottom of its body and its legs and then held it up to admire what I had done. I wasn't proud of my participation in killing one of God's creatures, but I was getting very hungry, so the morality of the whole thing was becoming less of an issue.

I put the squirrel in the bag and looked over at Miranda and Macie. Macie was enthralled and said, "I get to clean the next one."

It was still a couple hours until dark, but it had finally warmed up, so we all lay down to take a nap. I was surprised that I was tired enough to go back to sleep. I woke up to a blazing fire and three squirrels cooking over the fire.

"Where did you get the other two?" I asked.

"Shortly after we lay down, I heard some rustling around," said Macie. "I looked over at my empty Cheetos bag and saw two squirrels playing with it, so I bumped Miranda to wake her up. Once saw what they were doing, she slowly picked up a couple of rocks. The squirrels didn't even seem to notice us. Miranda nailed one of the squirrels. The other one took off running, but she got him with a rock before he rounded the corner. I tried to clean them, but I did much better with the second one."

"Wow, three for three, Miranda!" I exclaimed. "How long until they're ready to eat?'"

"They're almost done cooking," said Macie, "but I sure wish we had some seasoning to put on them. Mom's Texjoy steak seasoning would have been nice. I'm so hungry I'm ready to eat them raw." Macie kept turning them over the fire until they were a nice golden brown and then held one in front of Miranda to try. She bit into it, chewed and swallowed, and took a drink from a bottle full of water. I asked where the water came from, and Macie said she'd gotten it from the lake. I got upset.

"Don't you know lake water isn't fit to drink? It has all kinds of microorganisms in it!" I looked at them seriously. "Do you want to get sick?"

They both laughed.

"Relax, Madison, Macie boiled it first."

I looked over at Macie and asked, "How? We don't have a pan to boil it in."

Macie said, "It's a good thing at least one of us remembered what we read in those survival books. All you have to do is fill the plastic bottle up so there isn't any air, and the fire won't melt the plastic. You just leave it in a little while, and it boils out the impurities." I was very impressed. I asked for a drink.

It was a bit warm, but it tasted delicious. I feasted on my share of the squirrels. I was surprised—it was quite tasty. The flavor was good and much better than a lot of chicken I had eaten before. But then again, I was so hungry I probably would have eaten almost anything. All three moaned our pleasure as we ate. I was quite full after finishing the meal, and Miranda and Macie must have been, too, because they just lay back against the wall, rubbing their stomachs and groaning contentedly. Once our food had settled, we started talking about what to do next.

We couldn't just stay in this cave and live off of squirrels forever. We needed a plan. After debating food, shelter, and the future of life in the cave, we decided that we needed to leave. We would have to stay here one more day. When it got dark the next night, we would go back to town, find some warm clothes, and then start heading north. We couldn't hitchhike because all three of us together would be too identifiable. I was sure that people had been advised to be on the lookout for three girls. Splitting up was not an option. We would have to travel at night, parallel to the highway, and hope to find food to cook and eat. If we stole from stores along the way, they would know where we'd been and be able to track us.

It wasn't much of a plan, but it sure beat sitting in a cave waiting for them to find us—and possibly starving to death or freezing. We warmed up by the fire and then made short trips out of the cave to gather wood and look for food. We would go back to the cave when we got cold. We found some yucca plants but nothing else that we considered to be edible. Miranda saw a rabbit and was able to hit it with a rock. That dazed it long enough for me to run up and stab it with the knife. I felt bad about killing something so cute, but we needed food for the next day.

We spent the rest of the night cooking up the rabbit and the yucca. We got the fire blazing to heat up the rocks around us but knew we would have to put it out before the sun came up. As soon as it started getting lighter outside, we put the flames out and planned to sleep as much of the day away as we could. We wanted to be well-rested for the next night. The rabbit was cooked, and we had full bottles of water to drink. With all that, we would be able to have a decent lunch when we woke up.

CHAPTER 12

I was having a lovely dream about being in bed at home and hearing the sounds of my mother coming into my room to wake me up for school. I would act like I was asleep, hoping that it was Saturday so I wouldn't have to get up. For some reason, she started shaking me instead of just talking to me until I woke up. As I woke up from the dream, I realized that I someone *was* shaking me, and it wasn't Miranda or Macie, it was Jude.

I sat up with a start and looked around. Jude backed away from me, and I saw that we were surrounded by people in our cave. Pat was still shaking Macie, trying to wake her up, and William was kicking Miranda's feet to wake her up. I think he was afraid of her attacking him when she came out of her sound sleep. He was lucky this time because Miranda sat up quickly and just told William never to touch her again. I almost laughed at how quickly William stopped and moved back away from her. Macie kept telling them to leave her alone, but she finally sat up and started back talking nearly every comment they made.

Jude was nice enough to offer me her jacket when she saw me shivering. She then told Pat to give Macie her coat and William to give her his jacket. As soon as he gave it to her, she passed it to Miranda. Jude didn't want a direct conflict this soon. William didn't say anything, but I could tell he wasn't happy about it at all. There were too many of them to try an escape, so we just started to march obediently out of the cave. It was very bright when we exited and climbed up to the plain. The sun was shining fiercely. As we walked, I overheard William telling Pat that he was impressed with our survival skills. I looked back and saw him eating our rabbit. He smiled at Miranda as he ate it, hoping she would turn around. Fortunately for all of us, she kept her eyes straight ahead.

I started talking to Jude while we were walking and asked her how they'd found us. "We were at a local bar talking about searching for you three all day and not having any luck," she said.

"A man at the bar asked if we had looked in all the caves. William told him that we looked in all that we had found. The man told us we'd probably missed the one he knew about. He gave us directions and told us it looks shallow from the outside, but it's more like a hallway and even has a chimney at the other end.

"We had no idea what he was talking about but asked him if he would show it to us in the morning. Sure enough, that's where we found you. From what I saw, you three were doing quite well for yourselves." I didn't respond, not wanting to give up our plan, but it was a pretty hopeless situation at this point since they'd caught us again. Jude pressed me more. "Come on, you can talk about it. Your chance of escape now is pretty much zero, and even if you did get away, you wouldn't be in the same circumstances anyway." I thought about it for a couple more minutes. We really had no way of escaping again, and Jude was being very nice to us, so I didn't see any point in not telling her.

"We were going to wait until dark to eat and then go into town to find some warm clothes and more food. The clothes were the most important things we needed. After dark, it got extremely cold, so we had to stay by the fire. Anyway, we were going to work our way north toward Albuquerque. Miranda is quite good at throwing, and Macie can build a fire with just sticks almost as fast as you could with matches. We thought we had a pretty good chance of making it—other than the shelter problem."

Jude was shocked that three young girls could survive as they had in the desert and said, "I'm very impressed with all three of you and wish the circumstances were different."

I turned away from her and agreed. "Me, too!"

We made it to the van and started climbing in. William was standing behind Miranda and gave her a hard push as she got in. She took a couple steps but couldn't stop her momentum and hit her head just above the window and fell on the floor. William and Pat started laughing as Miranda picked herself up. Her head was bleeding, but she had a smile on her face and said, "Enjoy while you can, William. You'll screw up and let us escape again. You managed to do it two times already. Maybe the third time will be the charm—then we'll be free, and you'll be fired." As Miranda finished, she wiped the blood from her head with William's coat and sat down.

William's laughter stopped, and his face went from smiling to angry as he started to climb in after her. Jude grabbed his arm. "Leave them alone, William. It was your fault they escaped, and we don't much longer until you will never see them again." William glared at her but didn't say anything and proceeded to get into the front seat. After we were all in the van, we started driving away from the lake area.

We drove to Highway 51 and headed east. We were on that twisty road for only about twenty minutes when we saw a massive building with some strange-looking planes around it.

Macie asked, "Which one will we get to go on?"

Jude said, "I really have no idea. The rocket ships are a couple miles away. I think they're used for large loads to go to space where the planes will shuttle the people back and forth."

We pulled up in front of the building and stopped. While we were getting out of the van, some baggage handlers came over to help us with the luggage. Jude flashed her badge to them and said, "We got it." They stared at her for a couple seconds, shrugged their shoulders, and walked off. Our escorts unloaded the van and handed us our duffel bags. Macie tried to pick hers up and couldn't even get it off the ground. Miranda slung hers over her shoulder but was all hunched over trying to carry it. I picked mine up and just about fell down when I put it over my shoulder. All of our escorts laughed except for Amber and Jude. William was hysterical. Jude glared at them, and they stopped immediately—except for William, who carried on a bit longer. Jude turned toward us and said, "Girls, leave those here. The men will follow us with them, but do remember how heavy they are here because they will be light as a feather in space."

We dropped our bags, took a few steps forward, and watched as the men picked them up. We then started laughing at them as they had at us, and we followed Jude inside. The building was massive. The ceiling was painted with millions of stars to look like the sky at night. On one side of the ceiling was the Earth, just like you would see it from space. "Wow!" Macie exclaimed. Miranda and I just stared without saying a word. Jude gave us a few seconds to admire and then said, "Come on, we need to get you checked in." When started following Jude again, none other than Pat showed up and started to talk to her.

"All the arrangements have been made," said Pat. "Once we check them in and escort them to those tall doors on the other side of the room, we are through with them. Security will not let them back out without the consent of Jacob who will be considered their guardian from that point on." Jude and the rest of us followed Pat up toward the counter. There were many people already waiting in line, but Pat walked right by them up to the person at the counter. The lady looked irritated that someone would cut in line until Pat flashed her badge and said, "We need to check in these three girls and this man who will be their guardian for their journey."

Jacob approached the counter and put his ID and badge down so the ticket agent could enter the information into the computer. When the agent finished, she had each of us step over to the side and stand in front of a blue screen so our picture could be taken. As usual, Macie jumped in front of everyone to be first. She gave her best smile when the agent asked her to and then stepped away. I was next, giving a halfhearted smile for the camera. Miranda was next and didn't smile at all. She scowled. She must have been thinking of William. The agent said to her, "You're going to be wearing this picture on your badge for the next few months—do you really want to look like that?"

I said to her, "Miranda, just think—we'll be away from William forever!"

Miranda smiled and said, "Okay, please take another picture. I'll try to smile." It was probably one of the prettiest smiles Miranda ever gave.

I was getting nervous but didn't say anything while waiting. A few minutes later, the ticket agent presented each of us with a photo ID that had our picture and a bar-code. It was attached to a lanyard so it could hang around our necks. She asked us to place them around our necks and said that we must wear them at all times. "If you are caught two times without it from here on, then you will be required to have an escort with you at all times except when in your room," she told us. There was way too much to see, so all of us hurriedly put them on. We hadn't noticed that she had given an ID to Jacob as well. He must have already had a photo on file because he didn't have to have his picture taken. While we were doing the picture thing, some men had taken our duffel bags away. I assumed they were just being checked in like at a normal airport.

Jude said, "Since you are all checked in, we will walk you to the security checkpoint and say good-bye."

We all walked down the hallway to the security checkpoint area where the TSA agents were waiting to check us in. There wasn't anyone ahead of us, so Amber asked all of us to come over to her. We did, and she gave each of us a hug, saying, "I'm sorry for all that happened to you, but please make the best of what you have to do—and stay out of trouble. On this type of journey, they are very intolerant of anyone who causes problems. Punishment ranges from room confinement to execution, so please be very careful."

We all promised to stay out of trouble. Jacob was waiting for us. Amber waved good-bye, and we walked up to the security guard. He scanned our pictures, but before we headed through the metal detector, Miranda turned and asked Jude, "Are any of you coming past the checkpoint except Jacob?"

"Nope, none of us has the clearance to go past the checkpoint. Jacob will take care of you from here on out."

"Can I say goodbye to the rest of them?" Miranda asked.

"Sure, but you really need to get going, so make it quick."

"Come with me," Miranda said to Macie and me. Macie and I looked at each other, not really knowing what she meant. But we followed her anyway. She walked up to Amber and gave her a hug. "Thank you for being nice to us." Macie and I did the same and then Miranda walked up to the guys — we never did get their names — and shook their hands.

As she approached Pat and William, she said, "I don't really know why you were so mean to us, but no hard feelings, okay?" This was too much for Macie and me — we weren't going to say good-bye to them. But then we saw Miranda's hand motioning us to go around her. We had just gotten to the other side of her when she said, "And here is the best goodbye I can give either of you."

She walked up to William and then stepped back, took a step, and kicked him in the crotch as hard as she could. I think I even heard a grunt out of her from the effort. He doubled over and went to the ground from the pain. Everyone else just stood there, staring at what had happened but too in shock to move. Miranda then slapped Pat across the face as hard as she could and then ran up to security and went through the metal detector. As soon as Miranda kicked William, Macie and I decided that we wanted to get in on the action but didn't know quite what to do. So when Miranda slapped Pat, Macie and I ran over and gave her a big shove backwards. She took a step going back and tripped over William, who was on his knees, holding his crotch. We watched long enough to see her hit her head the floor and then we ran after Miranda. We were through the metal detector before anyone could react to what we had done.

We looked back after we had made it through the checkpoint to see the others helping Pat and William up. Pat looked a bit woozy, but William was super angry. They had to hold him back to keep him from coming after us. The security people we had just passed by were on high alert, watching William. He glared at us but knew that there was nothing he could do and started walking away quite gingerly. Jude looked at us with a smirk on her face, waved, and walked away. The security people told us to move along, most with smiles after watching what we had done.

CHAPTER 13

We followed Jacob down the hallway away from security until we came to two swinging glass doors. We walked on through and saw about fifty people sitting and standing around. Jacob led us up to the counter and introduced himself to the attendant. She said, "Hello, my name is Debbie. Are you a day tripper or traveling? May I please see your ID?"

Jacob replied, "We are going to Europa."

She said, "They're pretty young for that kind of trip, aren't they? I need their IDs also, please."

"Yes, they're young, but they're very strong and healthy. The trip will not be a problem for them," he said as he flashed his badge. "Please do not ask any more personal questions regarding them."

She looked a bit flustered and said, "Yes, sir. I see that you all have priority and will be the next ones in for the decontamination process. I will call you one by one."

"No, when ready, all three of them will go together. I don't want them separated for any reason, and if they are, I will hold you personally responsible."

"But we don't—"

He cut her off. "If you have a problem with keeping them together, then please get your boss out here right now. Otherwise, they stay together. Do you understand?"

"Yes sir, there is no problem," said Debbie. "Please have a seat, and I will call them shortly."

We all took a seat. I was almost crying. "Thank you, Jacob, for keeping us together. I don't know what I would do if I were to lose another sister."

Jacob said, "Let me get a few things straight with you now that I am solely responsible for you. I will do everything in my power to get you to Europa safely and with as little discomfort to you as possible. Given the circumstances of your situation, it should not be a bad life for you out there. I'll give you additional details when we have more time to talk. But on the flip side, just so we all understand each other, if you do not do what I tell you to do when I tell you to do it, there will be severe consequences.

"I have permission to kill you if I deem it necessary—for the safety of myself and the people around us. Let me ask—to be sure that all is clear. Do you understand that if you do not do what I tell you to do that you will regret it?" We all shook our heads. "No," he said, "I want to hear it."

We all said, "Yes sir, we will do what you tell us to."

"Fine, now that that is out of the way, let's try and make the best of this trip. I am afraid that you won't like the decontamination process much. They are going to strip you naked, soap you up, scrub you with brushes from top to bottom, and repeat the process two additional times. It's very unpleasant, but hopefully being together will make it a bit more tolerable. You will then be given a plain white bra and panties and a loose fitting white outfit. Sort of like what they wear in karate. All of the possessions you take off will be thoroughly cleaned and will not be given back to you until we are on the ship to Europa. They will be waiting in your cabin. Do you have any questions? You should be called very soon now. Also, if it makes you feel any better, I will be going through the same scrubbing that you do."

Macie was the most nervous and jumped when they called Robert Mosby. We saw a man go up to the reception desk where he was directed to go through the doors on the left. Just as he went through the door, they were called over the loudspeaker. "Jacob Verndari and family, please come to reception." Jacob got up and we followed suit.

Miranda said, "I didn't know your last name was Verndari. Where is that from?"

Jacob said, "My great great grandfather came over from Iceland."

"Really?" she asked, amazed.

"Yes, but we need to get going. I want to get this part over with as soon as possible."

We followed him up to the receptionist where another person scanned our badges and told us girls to go through the doors on the right and Jacob to go through those on the left. As we started heading toward the doors, Jacob said, "I'll be truly impressed if they can get you three clean" and laughed.

Macie retorted, "At least we don't smell like you." We were all laughing as we went through the swinging doors.

A lady met us immediately and told us to have a seat on the bench because she had a few things to go over with us before we were put through the decontamination process. She said, "My name is Maria, and welcome to the first step in your journey. Unfortunately, this process is necessary so the space station and Europa are not contaminated with viruses and diseases. Also, we don't want any other types of plants or bugs other than what we planned on introducing to Europa. You will all be given complete physicals along with a most unpleasant scrubbing of your body from head to toe. We need you to be as clean as possible. Do you have any questions before we begin with the physicals? We will take you one at a time through the process."

Macie said, "I'm scared to be by myself."

"Don't worry," I reassured her. "Jacob made sure that we stay together at all times."

The lady said, "I'm sorry, but we only take one at a time."

Macie was getting worked up to start crying, and I said, "Ma'am, we are all going together—or we are not going at all."

The lady was taken aback by that and told me, "We're only allowed to take one at a time."

"I don't really care. Either we go together, or we don't go. You better go talk to the receptionist out there or get Jacob in here to deal with this because we *are* all going in together."

Maria picked up the phone on the wall and dialed a number. She talked a few minutes before hanging it up and said to us, "You may all go in now." We got up and started walking toward the door she was holding open for us. But then I stopped dead in my tracks.

It just hit me that now would be a perfect time to escape. Jacob was being processed, and Jude and the others should have already left, so all I had to do was get my sisters and make a run for it the way we came in. But what was the point of trying? They would capture us quickly—just like the previous times—and we would be no better off than we are now. And where would we run to anyway? We were in the middle of New Mexico. I was pretty sure there were other agents around, too, just in case. Thinking about it, I didn't see that we had any choice but to make the best of it. I went through the door.

What we saw when we walked in was a room that looked like a cross between a gym and a hospital. There was a lot of equipment you would see at a gym—treadmills, stair climbers, multiple weight machines that would work out every part of the body, and free weights and benches. I knew all about this equipment, from the books we read when we were locked in the room and from my mother who had worked out at a twenty-four-hour fitness place. We went to work out with her a lot. My dad hated to work out—he got his exercise playing sports like soccer or softball.

A man in a lab coat came up, shook our hands, and introduced himself as Dr. Jeff Arzt. *What a funny last name*, I thought. He asked, "Are you ready for a good workout? Here's what we are going to do. You will all step into that dressing room over there." He pointed across the room to where it said *Dressing Room* above a door. "You will change into the clothes in the room. Don't worry if they don't fit perfectly—you will only be wearing them while we run you through the tests. When you come out, we're going to draw some blood to screen for any physical problems, and then we'll have you do a circuit of the equipment to see how fit you are. Do you have any questions?" We all shook our heads and he said, "Okay then, let's get this show on the road."

An assistant guided us into the dressing room. Good thing she did or I might have ended up in the area with Macie's size clothes. The assistant reminded us to leave all our clothes in the room and she would take care of them. We didn't really have a choice, so we followed her instructions and changed into the clothes left for us. They sure did like white—white shirt, shorts, bra, panties. No shoes or socks needed, I guess. I bet Miranda didn't care for the no socks part. She always had socks on, even outside by the pool. She would only take them off when she got in the water.

We finished dressing and were met by Dr. Jeff as we walked out of the dressing room. He said, "We're going to test your fitness level. Each of you will have an assistant monitoring all of your activities. All of you are going to warm up on the treadmill for a few minutes, and then you will make a circuit of the machines to test your strength. When your strength tests are over, you will get on the treadmill and see how far and fast you can run. Do you have any questions before we begin?"

As we shook our heads no, three women in white lab coats came up to us and introduced themselves. A blond-haired woman shook hands with Macie and introduced herself as Anita. A short, black-haired woman shook hands with Miranda and said, "My name is Magdaline, but everyone calls me Lynn." The third lady came up and shook my hand and said, "Hi, my name is Elizabeth, but I go by Beth." We followed them over to the treadmills where they motioned for us to get on.

The assistants turned them on to a medium walk. As soon as each of us got on, they started the stopwatches. At first it was easy, but then the speed went up to a jog. We did this for five minutes and then they took each of us to a different machine. Beth started me out on the leg press. She said, "You will do two sets of ten, and then we will see the max you can press. I did the two sets, and then she piled the weight on. I impressed myself—and I think

Beth was a bit impressed—with 310 pounds. We then went to the bench press, and I was able to bench seventy-five pounds.

We went through the other machines in the circuit—leg pulls, arm pull-downs, pulling and pushing just about every muscle I had. All the while, Beth was watching and writing down what I had completed. Every once in a while, I would look over at Macie and Miranda and laugh at how much they were straining and sweating. I finally finished, and Beth told me to get a drink of water and rest for a little while. Miranda and Macie finished at about the same time as I did, and we all went to the drinking fountain and then sat down.

I was fairly tired but not too bad. We started comparing our accomplishments. Miranda beat Macie and me at everything and did an impressive 385 pounds on the leg press. We talked for a few minutes more and were just getting relaxed when the assistants came over and told us we had one more exercise. There were three treadmills in front of us. They told us that the speed and incline would keep increasing until we could go no more. We were very tired, so running until we dropped wasn't very appealing. As we climbed onto the treadmills, we were surprised when they started attaching all these wires to us. I wasn't sure how we would run with wires attached to our legs, arms, chest, and head.

They started us out with a fairly fast walk and then started increasing it about every thirty seconds. Every minute or so the incline would go up a bit. Each assistant was on our left side, and three more appeared and were on our right sides to help catch us if we fell. We were all in good shape from our running and exercising in the room that we'd previously been kept in. The doctor and his assistants were impressed with our stamina. The doctor asked each of us whether we preferred to run faster or steeper. Macie said "neither," Miranda said "faster," and I said "steeper." The assistants were controlling our treadmills and increased each depending upon our answer.

Macie was the first to give out after about nine or ten minutes. Miranda and I were both going good at fifteen minutes but were losing energy and having trouble keeping up. At this point, Miranda was in a full sprint, barely keeping up with the treadmill, and I was huffing and puffing running uphill. I wasn't running as fast as Miranda, but it felt like I was going straight up a mountain. Both of us were starting to stumble, but neither would give up and lose to the other. I had just given the sign to quit when out of the corner of my eye, I saw Miranda stumble and fall. Because she had distracted me, I stumbled and fell right after she did, and both of us shot off the back of the treadmill before the assistants could catch us. Most of the wires were ripped from our skin, and a few of them were ripped from the machine.

Macie came running over to us to make sure we were all right. Miranda and I looked at each other and started laughing. We then started check what part of our bodies got skinned by the treadmill. The doctor and assistants ran over.

"Are you all right?" asked the doctor. "No women, let alone young girls, have ever made it that steep or run that fast before. I'm sorry we didn't shut it down earlier, but we were sort of mesmerized and interested to see how long the two of you would go. You both set records for women and were not very far off the time for the men." Miranda had skinned her left knee, the back of her left hand, and her left shoulder when she fell. I skinned my right foot, hip, shoulder, and somehow my back. They helped us up, and we walked over and sat down at the table. They gave us Gatorade to drink and a power bar as a snack. The doctor said, "You've completed the hard part. Now we will just draw some more blood and take your vitals. Once that's finished, you will have about an hour to rest before going through the cleansing process."

"What's the cleansing process?" Macie asked in a worried voice.

The doctor explained, "Your body must be completely clean. The only way to do that is to scrub it. Unfortunately, you don't get

TRIO: Getting There

to do it yourself—there will be a team of women who will scrub your body and hair. It is a very unpleasant process, so just try to think of something else. Please go with your assistants. They'll finish your assessment and physical."

We followed them over to their desks and they proceeded to poke, prod, and draw what seemed like a lot of blood to me. They also took care of Miranda's and my scrapes and bruises from our fall. When it was all over, Anita led us to a door by the dressing rooms and told us to wait there until they called us.

We were in the waiting room for about an hour when a lady opened a door on the other side of the room and asked, "Are you the VanBuren girls?" We shook our heads yes, and she said, "Hello, my name is Emily, and I will be with you throughout the cleansing process. It's not very pleasant so we will try to get through it as quickly as possible. Normally we do one at a time but since you three will stay together, we will go oldest to youngest so you can reassure your younger sisters that it isn't so bad. Please follow me into the next room where you will undress and wrap yourself in the towel provided. After each cleansing, you will be given a new towel just to be sure no germs follow you. Do you have any questions?" We shook our heads and followed her into the next room.

All that was in the room were three white towels on hangers and a bag. "Please put all of your clothes in the bag," Emily directed. We started undressing and were down to bras and panties, reaching for the towels, when Emily said, "Unfortunately, *all* clothes need to be put in the bag. You will get new ones when you are done." We reluctantly finished undressing and hurriedly wrapped the towels around ourselves. Miranda seemed the most embarrassed, but we were all very uncomfortable. Emily opened the door and told us to go through. She did not follow us in but closed the door behind us. How many rooms did we have to go through?

This new room was all white, and there was what looked like a large shower with no door on it and a big drain in the middle.

There were three women standing next to the shower. Two had soap in one hand and a scrub brush in the other. The brushes looked like the kind you cleaned a toilet with, not something you would use in the shower. The other lady was standing next to a table that had shampoo, conditioner, and a number of combs on it. All were dressed in white plastic suits from head to toe. They looked very serious, and I was about to find out just how serious they were.

The lady next to the shampoo said, "Madison, you will go first. Please put your towel in the clothes hamper next to the wall and step into the shower to rinse off. Miranda and Macie, please turn around so Madison does not have to experience any embarrassment from you watching." I waited for Miranda and Macie to turn around, and then I slipped off the towel and put it in the hamper. I walked over into the shower under the water that was already flowing and rinsed off and got my hair wet. One of the ladies with a brush motioned me over to her and told me to hold out my arms to the side. It was very uncomfortable to stand naked in front of these strangers, so I kept my arms crossed over my chest. The second one with a brush came over to me and very gently pulled my hands from my chest, saying, "Please do as we say, and we will get this over with as quickly as we can." I nodded my head and held out my arms. As soon as I did that, both of the women with brushes were all over me, soaping and brushing my body from head to toe. The bristles from the brushes hurt very much on my skin, but the women were very efficient and finished quickly. It was very humiliating, though, and my skin was bright red and hurt all over. When they finished scrubbing me, the one with the shampoo said, "Please step in the shower so you can be rinsed off, and then wet your hair really well."

The ones with the brushes followed me into the shower and used slightly softer brushes to go over my body again. I was very relieved when they were through, and I wet my hair and stepped out. The woman with the shampoo put it in my hair and scrubbed very hard with her gloved fingers. It felt like she was pulling my hair out. I kept wincing as she did it, but was proud I didn't cry. After a few more tugs at my hair, she told me to step into the shower. I did, and she followed and roughly rinsed my hair out. We repeated the shampoo and rinse again, and as I stepped out of the shower, there were two new women there with brushes in their hands.

I wondered what I had done to deserve this! Those two did the same scrubbing treatment on me but were much rougher than the first two. I started crying, but they didn't say a word and just did their job. After they had rinsed me off with the other brushes, I was shampooed two more times by a different lady. They repeated the whole process one more time and then conditioner was put in my hair. I actually got to rinse that out myself. As I stepped out of the shower after the third round, I asked sarcastically, "Is that all?"

The shampoo lady handed me a white towel and motioned me to the other side of the table. She said, "You are almost finished. We just have to comb your hair and examine it to be sure we didn't miss anything."

I asked, "How could you possibly have missed anything with that treatment?"

She said, "You would be surprised what can be missed in shampooing." She came up behind me with a comb and said, "We're going to comb your hair now. I will start with a fairly wide-toothed comb and then go through two others and then a lice comb to check that there is nothing left. I checked your hair initially for lice, but we will check using the lice comb just to make sure." She started combing fairly gently with the first comb, but since my hair is very thick and long, we were soon in a hair tug of war with the fine-toothed comb, and I was crying by the time she used the lice comb. I was hopeful that I would grow enough back to replace what was being pulled out. Finally, it was over and she said I could wait over by the exit door. I started to walk over to Miranda and Macie, but she grabbed my arm roughly and said,

"You are clean now, but if you go over there, you will have to do it all over again." I went to stand over by the door as she had originally told me.

The lady went to Miranda and Macie and asked, "Who's next?"

Both shook their heads and said, "We're not going through that."

The lady just sighed. "If you don't do it peaceably, we have been given orders to complete the cleansing even if we have to get ten men in here to hold you down while we do it. Your only choice is whether you will be held or not. The cleansing *will* happen. I have had someone go through it against their will before, and you do not want that to happen to you. Now please, one of you step forward and come with me."

Miranda said to Macie, "I'll go next if you want."

Macie, who was already crying, said, "I'll do it, but thanks, Miranda."

"Come along then, Macie," said the lady. Macie didn't move so the woman went over and grabbed her arm, half dragging her to the shower. After a few steps, Macie started walking on her own, but the lady held tightly to her arm until she was in the shower for the first rinsing.

Macie cried throughout the whole ordeal and even screamed a few times. Nothing the ladies or Miranda and I said to calm her worked. Finally, they finished with her, and she came running over to me. I put my arms around her, and she slowly calmed down.

Miranda was next. One of the women started to grab her arm, but Miranda jerked it away and told her, "Don't touch me or you will regret it." The lady backed up a step and looked like she was about to call for help when Miranda stepped around her and went to the shower. She endured the cleansing process without saying a word. She kept eyeing the lady who had tried to grab her, but she didn't say anything. Miranda was finally finished, and the three of us were told to wait by the exit door. We stood there in our towels, talking and still trying to soothe Macie, and then a lady opened the door and told us to come through and get dressed. It was another white room barely bigger than a walk-in closet. There were white clothes hanging up that looked like the same clothes we had been wearing before—either they had been cleaned or they were new.

The woman said, "Please put these on and then follow me."

"Do we get shoes?" Macie asked. The lady told her there wasn't a need because everything was sanitized and we would not be walking anywhere but to the space plane. She turned away from us, and we got dressed as quickly as we could. We followed her out into what looked like the waiting area of an airport except that everything was white and spotless. It looked much cleaner than any hospital room I had ever seen. We were looking around when we saw someone waving at us. It was Jacob, and he was dressed in white like us. As we took in our surroundings, it turned out everyone was dressed in white. We walked over and he stood and gave us all hugs. We returned them before I realized we had only just met this man today and didn't know anything about him. We were all so traumatized by the cleansing process that we probably would have given anyone a hug.

We sat and he said, "I talked to the supervisor of the cleansing department, and he told me how mature all of you were for the process. I am very proud that you did so well."

Macie spoke up. "I cried the whole time, but I'm better now."

Jacob patted her leg. "I'm especially proud of you." Macie blushed. Jacob went on. "You've made it through the tough part, and now the adventure begins. In about an hour, they will call us to board the space plane and we'll be off to the space station. You must be exhausted after all of that, so why don't you rest and take a nap if you can. You want to be awake for the flight. I've heard it is like nothing you could imagine."

Miranda asked if we could get a drink. She sure loved her Dr. Pepper. "I'd get you something," said Jacob, "but you really don't want to have to go to the bathroom on the space plane flight. It's a few hours long, and the flight crew doesn't like anyone getting out of their seats for the first two hours. In fact, only in emergencies will they let you. I have read that many people have had accidents in their pants on the flight because they weren't allowed to get up."

Miranda just nodded her head and stretched out on two seats to go to sleep. I slumped in mine to try and get comfortable. It looked like Jacob was going to do the same thing, but Macie started peppering him with questions, so I doubt he even got a quick nap. Macie was usually the last to go to sleep on trips—and the first to get up. Not always in a good mood, either. Next thing I remembered was someone gently pushing on my arm saying that it was time to board.

CHAPTER 14

I must have been in a real deep sleep because I woke all disoriented. I think I was dreaming of the night they took Mom and Dad away because as I looked around, nothing seemed familiar and I was in a very depressed mood. Miranda was having a hard time waking up and looked even more disoriented than I felt. She kept going back to sleep and asking for just a few more minutes. I'm not sure if Macie ever went to sleep because she was standing at the window looking at the space plane. I got up and went over to stand next to her and looked at it with her. It was quite massive and very long. There were only windows near the front, and I guessed that the rest of it was the engines but didn't really know or care. Macie started chattering to me about the details of how it was laid out and how many engines it had and a bunch of other technical stuff she had learned from Jacob. I looked over and smiled at him trying to rouse Miranda, thinking better him than me because she gets really grumpy when she doesn't wake up on her own. She was at least sitting up. Jacob looked very tired, probably because Macie hadn't let him get any sleep.

Miranda was just getting to her feet when the intercom announced, "Boarding in five minutes." I looked around and saw what I presumed was the ticket agent setting the microphone down. She glanced my way and smiled at me. I don't know why, but my depressed mood went away at that instant. This was going to be quite an adventure, but I just wished my parents and little sister were here to enjoy it with us. I hoped that someday I would be able to tell them all about it. Jacob and Miranda came over to look out the window. Lucky for us, Miranda got distracted and wasn't too grumpy. A few minutes later, the ticket agent spoke into the microphone. "Boarding will commence now for those with small children, and then we will board the highest number seats first. Rows forty to sixty, please line up."

I asked Jacob where we were sitting. "Row eight. We board in the last group but will get off first, and the view out the windows won't be obstructed by the wings. Who gets the window seats?"

Macie said, "I want one!"

Miranda and I looked at each other, and Miranda said, "Go ahead, Madison. I'm fine with an aisle seat."

"Thanks. If we get a chance, we can swap during the flight."

Just then the agent called out, "Now boarding seats twenty to forty." We were getting very nervous, watching as the people handed their tickets to the agent and disappeared down the walkway tunnel. Finally she said, "Now boarding all seats." We hurried to get in line. Macie started to push her way to the front, but I held her back and told her to be patient.

"I don't want to be patient," she said. "I want to go now." I just kept quiet, knowing Macie and her impatience.

"Please let me in front of you so I can give the agent the tickets," Jacob said to me.

We made it to the front of the line, and Jacob handed the tickets to the agent who scanned them and gave them back to him. Miranda and Macie were very excited and took off running down the tunnel to the plane. I started to say something to them, but Jacob said, "Don't worry, they can't go far." Jacob and I walked down the tunnel and caught up to them just before they went through the door into the space plane.

Macie turned around and asked Jacob, "We're in row eight, right?" Jacob nodded and Macie and Miranda disappeared through the door.

When we caught up with them, they were already sitting down talking excitedly about what was going to happen. Jacob and I sat across the aisle from them. I was next to the window and looked out to see the open desert of New Mexico. It brought again the thought that I might never see Earth again. I leaned my head against the window and started to cry. Jacob tapped me on the shoulder and asked what was wrong. I guess all the pent up emotions came out right then because I just started sobbing and leaned over toward him. He put his arms around me, and I just cried on his chest. It felt so comforting, like I was in my dad's arms.

After a few minutes, I calmed down. Jacob hadn't said anything but just held me. I was so grateful for that that I hugged him back for a couple seconds and then sat up and thanked him. Then the space plane started to move backward. We were really going to Europa! I looked over at Miranda and Macie. Miranda kept telling Macie to move her head so she could see. If that kept up, it was going to be a long flight. I turned to stare out my window. I could see sagebrush for miles. We stopped going backward with a jerk, and then the engines revved up and we started moving forward. The stewardess came on the intercom. "Everyone please fasten your seat belts and harnesses now. If you are having any trouble, please press the button above you and someone will help you shortly." I latched my belt and shoulder harnesses. A stewardess was helping Miranda and Macie and then she left to help others.

The stewardesses came around for one final check. We went around a couple turns relatively slowly and then stopped. The pilot spoke. "This is Captain Flores speaking. We have been cleared for takeoff, and the flight crew has given the green light that everyone is strapped in. Please do not try to unbuckle during the flight because a loud siren and flashing lights will go off. This is a relatively short flight, so you are only able to get out of your seat in an emergency. We are a go, please enjoy your flight."

All of a sudden the engine got incredibly loud, and we started moving. I turned my head to look out the window. The ground was moving by extremely fast. I was pressed harder and harder into my seat as we went down the runway. We lifted off the ground and were climbing at a steep angle when the engine grew louder, and the space plane pointed straight up. I was pushed so hard back in my seat that I could barely turn my head. Jacob turned toward me and smiled. I looked over at Macie and

Miranda. Macie was still looking out the window, and Miranda had her eyes closed. She looked terrified. She can be so tough standing up to people and then a huge chicken on rides. I turned back to look out the window and saw land far in the distance because we were so high.

I kept staring out the window and thought I was able to see water instead of land but wasn't sure. The space plane started to vibrate more and more and then the engine sound quieted and the vibration stopped. I looked out the window, and all went bright white for a while and then it was all dark outside. It took a couple minutes for my eyes to adjust, and when they did, they saw the unimagined beauty of countless stars and the beautiful Earth. It was curving away from me, so I wasn't able to distinguish the continents, but the colors were incredible. Shortly after it went dark, we were no longer being pressed back into our seats and seemed even lighter than normal. It was hard to really tell because we were still strapped in.

"Now that wasn't too bad, was it?" the pilot announced. "We will have smooth sailing from here on out. We have one hour and eighteen minutes until we dock with the space station, so enjoy the view. I will turn the port or left side toward Earth for close to half the time and then the starboard or right side toward Earth until we dock so you all can appreciate the world you are leaving behind." I didn't want to hear that last part and started to tear up but got distracted very quickly by the view. I thought I was going to be disappointed because I was on the right side and got the space view first. I was wrong because the view of space was mesmerizing. It just went on forever and ever, millions and millions of stars.

I glanced over at Jacob, and he was still smiling. Not sure if he was enjoying the view or checking me out. I got a very uncomfortable feeling. I looked over at Miranda and Macie and could hear Miranda asking Macie to lean back so she could see. Macie didn't do what she asked quickly enough, so Miranda put her hand against Macie's head to hold it back. Macie started to squirm and pushed her hand away. Jacob was now looking to see what they were doing. Macie's voice was rising. He told them to stop. They did for a few seconds and then started fighting again.

"Stop it right now. If you do not, then the flight crew will put you in a closet and you won't get to see anything. Try taking turns." They stopped and looked at him, mouths open.

Macie said, "Really?" Jacob nodded his head. Miranda and Macie got along very well for the rest of the time.

When Jacob turned toward me, I whispered to him, "Do they really do that?"

He whispered back, "I don't know, but it was the best punishment I could think of." I just laughed and turned toward my window.

The stars were amazing, but I got bored very quickly looking at them. When I turned from the window, Jacob was staring at me again. I tried to ignore him. I saw Macie point something out to Miranda right before Miranda pushed Macie's head out of the way to see it. Macie pushed Miranda, and then they both started laughing. I wished I was sitting with them instead of Jacob. Miranda saw I was looking over and laughingly said, "Madison, Macie said she saw our house! I looked out, and we were over Africa. So when she looked out the window again, I pushed her head and she banged it against the window. I asked her if she was seeing stars yet." Jacob and I started laughing. I saw then that Macie's window view was turning from Earth and was now viewing stars. I hurriedly turned around to my own window.

At first, I just saw the stars, but then the Earth came into view. It was so blue. We were just far enough away that the top part of my view was both stars and the edge of the Earth. No words could describe how beautiful it was. I could see just a bit of the sun, and I could see either the sunrise or the sunset on Earth as there was a distinct dark line. On the sunny side, everything was just so dark blue in the middle of the ocean and lighter blue closer to land. We were starting to pass over North America. It was dark there, and I could see the lights from the major cities. As I looked at it, I assumed the cluster in the middle of the country was Dallas and thought of my parents and little sister. I looked down from the window and said a silent prayer for them that they were safe. When I looked up in, again, I saw what must have been a hurricane in the Atlantic Ocean. It was amazing how large it was and how defined the eye was. I just stared out at the beautiful Earth until something new came into view.

It was a space station. It must have been one of many because we passed by it and I could see the Earth again, but we didn't stop. Jacob, who had been looking over my shoulder, said, "I think that was one of the space hotels. I would have thought they'd have signs of some sort on them. Maybe they do near the docking station." I was just admiring the Earth again when what looked like a huge ship came into view. It was docked to a long tube. Jacob said, "I think that's the ship we'll be taking to Europa." I didn't say anything but continued to stare out the window at it. It looked like a big cylinder with holes in the ends. I guess in space, aerodynamics didn't really matter. Our ship had slowed a lot, and I was able to see the spaceship. And then it seemed that we weren't moving at all. Space doesn't give you many points of reference for speed, so I wasn't sure. After a few minutes of slowing, we had just the slightest bump and Jacob said, "We are here!"

CHAPTER 15

The pilot announced, "Welcome to Space Station Europa! This will be your home for a couple of days. Just remember—the gravity here is less than ten percent of Earth's, so try not to bang your head on the ceiling as you walk. We will be disembarking in a few minutes, so please be patient." I looked over and Macie was rubbing her head where she had hit it above her seat. She had unbuckled and jumped up, unprepared for the lack of gravity. Miranda was laughing at her as she slowly unbuckled herself. I unbuckled, too, and sat there, a bit afraid to move. Jacob leaned over and reassured me that it was all right but to just take it slow until I was comfortable. People ahead of us were going out the front of the space plane. I saw a couple of people bounce off the ceiling as they walked with too much pep in their step. They probably got lumps on their head. They should have put padding on the ceiling of the space plane knowing that people would invariably bang their heads as they learned to walk in low gravity.

Our row was next. Miranda stood up slowly and grabbed onto the armrest to keep her from going up, and before she stepped forward, she grabbed onto the armrest in the next row. Macie tried to get around Miranda on the way out, but Miranda wouldn't let her past. Macie even tried to jump over her a couple rows up but just ended up smacking her head on the ceiling, which gave Miranda another laugh. Fortunately, Macie was so excited she didn't get mad. Jacob got up and held out his hand to me. I grabbed it as I got up, very unsteadily, and he stepped back so I could go in front of him. Before he released my hand, he gave it a squeeze and smiled at me. As I started to walk in front of him, similar to how Miranda had, he put his hand on my shoulder and said, "I will help keep you down." Before I could thank him, his hand started to move around on my shoulder. I didn't care for it and asked him to take his hand off so I could learn how to walk on my own. He did but squeezed my shoulder just before removing it. Jacob seemed nice, but it seemed like he was hitting on me. I certainly wasn't interested in someone at that old.

I slowly made it to the front of the space plane and out into a long hallway/tube that curved away in both directions. A lady dressed in the same white clothes I was wearing and a blue badge pinned to her breast directed us to the right. We stopped at the first restroom we saw. When I came out, I saw Miranda and Macie jumping, seeing who could touch the ten-foot ceiling first. Miranda let Macie go first, and she made it about eight feet. Then Miranda squatted and jumped straight up. She jumped so hard and with such power that she had to use her hands to stop her from banging her head. Because she pushed off from the ceiling with her hands, she did a half flip on the way down and landed on her hands on the floor. Instead of falling and getting to her feet, she just started walking on her hands. We laughed at her as she continued to show off. Macie tried to jump the same way Miranda had and almost made it to the ceiling.

Jacob was smiling but asked them to please walk normally. Miranda did a little push with her hands and landed on her feet, looked at Jacob, and asked, "Is this better?" Jacob just grinned. I was walking next to him, and he put his hand on my shoulder. I didn't want to deal with him, so I ran to catch up to Macie and Miranda. When I took a couple steps, I tripped over my own feet because I wasn't used to the lack of gravity. I went down on my right side and caught myself with my right hand. I wasn't just falling but tumbling in cartwheel fashion. My left hand hit the floor, and then my left foot, right foot, and I did about three cartwheels and a round-off to stop. I looked around, embarrassed. Macie, Miranda, Jacob, and a few people around us started to clap. I just blushed and started walking between Macie and Miranda. Jacob followed us a few steps back.

About every twenty to thirty yards, we would step through a door similar to those on a submarine. I guess any hallway could be sealed off if necessary. We passed by doors on three sides of us. There were bars on the walls to assist you in going upward. There were doors to our left and right, but most were closed. We walked through a couple more doors, and then I saw Macie run ahead and stop to stare at a picture. Too many things had been happening too quickly for us to think to ask questions about the space station.

The picture was sort of like one of those layouts at a mall that shows a little dot—"You are here"—and the different floors. This one showed the little dot with an arrow pointing at it. We were on the fifth level in the outer ring. Our level was called E. There were levels A through J and three wings in each level with various rooms hung off of the rings. It sort of looked like a bunch of bicycle wheels next to each other, with inner rings and connectors in between the wheels. There was a legend at the bottom of each level's picture. Jacob pushed us on before we could really study what was up here. He had to take Macie by the arm to get her moving again. She ran ahead of him and caught up to Miranda and me.

"This place is amazing! I want to go exploring as soon as I can." We all looked at Jacob, and Macie asked, "Can we go exploring?"

Jacob looked at her with concern, and said, "Only under supervision so you don't get in trouble. But first we need to get settled in our rooms."

"Okay," Macie said dejectedly, "but let's hurry! There's so much to see." Her pace picked up to match her enthusiasm. Miranda and I were tired and had to grab Macie to slow her down.

We walked for another ten minutes or so and were guided into a big room where we had to stand in line to get our room key. There were about ten people ahead of us. We waited patiently— well, I did. Macie and Miranda were having a hopping contest. First, they did a little jump and bumped into the people in front of us. They apologized to the two men. Next, they stepped out of line to the side and said "one, two, three, now." They sprang into the air before Jacob could tell them not to. Miranda was just a split second ahead of Macie and went almost to the twenty-foot ceiling. Macie only made it a bit over ten feet. The funny part was seeing them come down. Macie was flailing her arms to keep her balance but landed on her butt. Miranda had a bit more forward momentum and was starting to come down head first but threw her arms forward and ended up landing on her feet. The people in the room applauded, and Miranda looked embarrassed. Macie and I were just laughing.

I watched Jacob stomp—if you can call it that in low gravity—over to them and say through clenched teeth, "If you ever do any stunts like that again in public, there will be severe punishments. Do you understand me?" Macie and Miranda looked sheepishly at him and nodded their heads.

A few minutes later, we made it to the front of the line and a woman whose nametag said Carla asked, "What are your names?" Jacob showed her his badge, and she put his name into the computer. She told us we would be in rooms six and seven on Level One.

Macie said, "Those rooms are great and should have a spectacular view of Earth."

"Oh really? And how do you know that?" Jacob asked.

"I remember it from the map we saw."

"I think Macie has close to a photographic memory," Miranda said. "She sees something once and can usually remember it later."

Jacob acted very impressed and said, "I have a map to get us there."

Macie spoke up. "I already know the way. Follow me."

Macie led us down the hall and through a door. We climbed up to an inner ring, through some more doors, and then dropped down to an outer ring. We passed through even more doors, climbed up to an inner ring and finally stopped in front of a door that said Level One. I don't think we took the most direct route, but Macie had a lot of fun leading us. I think Jacob figured out that the climbing and dropping were just for fun. We stepped through the door of Level One and went down the hall to rooms six and seven, right across the hall from each other.

Jacob said, "My room is six and yours is seven. Go check it out, and then let's go eat. I'm starving." We had been so excited that we hadn't even thought about food. Now that he mentioned it, our stomachs all growled at once. We hurried to our room and went in.

It was tiny. One side had four bunk beds built into the wall, and the other side was covered with a big curtain. We pulled back the curtain and had to step back. The Earth took up nearly the whole view through the window. It was so beautiful and looked so close you could reach out and touch it. Tears started rolling down my cheeks, and I just collapsed to my knees on the floor and buried my face in my hands. Miranda and Macie came over to me, and we all began crying together and hugging each other. We missed home, our parents, and our little sister so much. I'm not sure how long we sat like that but eventually we looked at the door and saw Jacob standing there with a very sad look on his face.

He came in and put his hands on Macie and Miranda's backs. "I am so sorry for all that has happened to you and wish it could all go away. But what is done is done, and we have to move on."

Miranda smacked his hand away and said, "Get your hand off of me. You are just as much a part of this as any of the others."

Jacob looked embarrassed. He backed out of the room and said, "I'll wait for you all in my room. Please come get me when you want to go eat." And then he was gone, but the flow of emotion had been broken, and we had all stopped crying.

"Miranda," asked Macie, "did you have to be so mean to Jacob?"

Before Miranda could answer, I said, "Macie, Miranda is right. Jacob is a big part of what has happened to us. He is just doing what he has been told to do. He isn't helping us because he's kind—he is doing it because he was told to. Don't be fooled by his kindness, the only ones we can trust are each other. Jacob will make sure we get where we are going, but I wouldn't count on him to stick around once we get there."

"And we don't even know where that might be," Miranda said. "He plays all nice, but he's trying too hard. I just get the feeling it isn't genuine. If he cared more, he wouldn't let us mess around as much as he does. He just seems to be putting up with us until he can get rid of us."

Macie thought about what we'd said. "I think you both are wrong, but there isn't anything we can do about it right now, so let's have fun and see how much we can get away with."

Miranda laughed. "I plan on doing just that."

God help us! I thought

We went to Jacob's room and looked in. His room was similar to ours, but he didn't have the curtain pulled back. He was just sitting at the small desk reading. He turned around and looked at us then got up. "Okay, let's go eat. Macie, can you get us there or do we need to follow the map? It's on this level, somewhere on an inner ring."

Macie said, "I'll get us there. Follow me." We followed her and were there in just a couple minutes. Macie must have been hungry to lead us straight to the restaurant.

The sign outside the door said *Terre*. I knew that meant Earth in French. One whole wall was just a window of Earth. It was dark, and you could see all the lights from the cities. I realized we were currently over Europe. It was a beautiful sight. We went in, Jacob flashed his badge, and we were immediately seated next to the window facing Earth. You couldn't help but stare at the planet. The waitress had to ask a couple of times what we wanted to drink before we would look away from the view. Before we could apologize, she said, "Don't worry, I've been here three months and still can't stop staring at it."

We looked at the menu but didn't see anything of interest. We wanted American food, not this fancy French stuff. The waitress returned in a few minutes and set our drinks in front of us, asking if we were ready to order.

"Do you have chicken strips?" Macie asked.

The waitress said, "We very seldom have children in the restaurant, but I will see what they can scrounge up for you. Would all of you girls like the same thing?" Miranda nodded but I asked if they had hamburgers. The waitress wasn't sure but said she would check to see if they could whip one up. "There are more restaurants on the higher levels as well, so if you don't like what you get here, there are plenty more choices higher up." Jacob ordered something that sounded like it was a steak but had some fancy name. The only way I knew it was a steak was when she asked him how he wanted it cooked and he said "well done." My dad always said you might as well be eating charcoal if you got a steak well done. Of course, that's exactly how my mother liked it.

Just as she was about to leave to put in our order, Miranda spoke up. "Was that a steak he ordered?"

"Yes, it was," said the waitress.

Miranda rubbed her hands together and said, "Please change mine to a steak, medium rare. That's the way my dad liked it, and this meal is in remembrance of him." Macie and I changed our orders, too.

"I'm so sorry. What happened to your father?" the waitress asked.

Immediately, Jacob said, "That is all. Please bring me another glass of wine." And the waitress left. We all looked at Jacob, and he warned, "Don't go there. It is a topic neither you nor I can talk about." We all were quiet and stared out the window until the food came. It was a wondrous view, but all I could think about was where the rest of my family was and if they were all right. Jacob tried to talk to us as we sat there, but we ignored him long enough that he finally gave up trying.

The food came. The three of us talked to each other about our parents and little sister as we ate. Jacob didn't talk but just listened.

"I finally got a little sister," Macie said, "and just when she was becoming fun, she was taken away from me." She was becoming angry as she looked over at Jacob and asked, "Why us? Why did you take away our little sister? What did she ever do to you?"

Jacob looked down and then slowly raised his head. "I don't know the details of what happened to you, but I have seen families that were torn apart, including the children. Very seldom have they let the children stay together. I'm not saying that you are lucky, but you are an exception, and it's fortunate they kept you three together."

Miranda looked at him disgustedly. "Who is this 'they' you're talking about? From the people who took us from our house, to Jude taking us across the country, to you taking us to a different planet, it's always someone invisible who is responsible. Well, I say that's a bunch of crap. You are just as responsible for the kidnapping and breakup of my family as that mythical 'they' you keep referring to. No matter how many times you try to blame others, it is your fault just as much as theirs, so just quit trying to blame other people and take some responsibility for what you are doing."

Jacob looked directly at her. "You are correct. I chose to work for them and am responsible to get you to Europa safely. I don't always like my work, but I do it and make the best of it. I recommend that you do the same. You are going, and there isn't anything you can do about it no matter how much you dislike me and what I have to do. After we finish eating, I will tell you what is going to happen for the next few days until we leave. It can be quite pleasant if you let it be."

Miranda grumbled a bit and went back to eating just as the waitress came by to check on us. She asked us how our Steak Au Poivre was. Macie's mouth was full of steak, but that didn't keep her from commenting. "It is the second best steak. Kobe steak in Dallas is my favorite." Miranda nodded, and I agree that my steak was very good. Jacob nodded, and the waitress walked away.

Jacob finished first. "Now I will tell you about the next few days. Tomorrow morning after breakfast, we will go see a presentation of our trip and Europa. I heard it was a very good introduction. It will last until about lunchtime. I will let you go free to explore and to eat lunch wherever you like. All you have to do is show them your badge, and it will be taken care of. That reminds me—you always need to have your badge where it can be seen, or they will take you to the holding area and you will lose your privilege to explore. You will just need to be back by 6:30 for dinner. There are clocks everywhere so I will expect you to be on time. After dinner, there's a show we will go to and then off to bed. The two days after that will be very similar. There are also lots of additional activities listed below any of the maps. Do you have any questions?"

"Does that mean that we can go anywhere in the space station?" asked Macie.

"Yes, but let me warn you. If you get into trouble or don't do what any of the adults ask you to do, you will end up in your room for the duration of our stay. There are some cool things to do here, but I will let you find them on your own. I can tell where you are located by your badge. To find me, all you need to do is ask at any of the information booths."

The waitress asked if we were finished, and we all nodded yes. She scanned Jacob's badge and we got up to leave. We walked back to our rooms without saying much because we were all very tired. Jacob said good-night to us at our door, and we nodded and went in. We gazed one last time at Earth before closing the curtain and climbing into our beds. Strangely enough, we slept in the order of our ages, as we did most things. I was on the bottom, Miranda was in the middle, and Macie insisted she get the top. We said our goodnights to each other, and I think I was asleep in two minutes.

CHAPTER 16

The next thing I remember was a knocking at our door. Since I was on the bottom, I got up to answer it. It was Jacob telling us it was time for breakfast. I said we'd be ready in twenty minutes. I turned around. "Macie and Miranda, time to get up." Macie practically flew out of bed and got dressed immediately.

"Just five more minutes?" asked Miranda.

"Come on, let's get going," I said. She just rolled over and ignored me.

Macie said, "Come on, Miranda, we need to get going."

"Let's let her sleep for the five minutes—maybe she won't be so grumpy."

About five minutes later, I roused Miranda again, and she slowly sat up and hopped off the bed onto the floor. I knew better than to push her to get ready, so I just sat waiting and watching Earth. We were going over the Atlantic Ocean. There was the unmistakable swirl of a hurricane, and it looked like it was approaching the Gulf of Mexico. Miranda was finally awake enough to go eat, so we opened our door and knocked on Jacob's door. He answered immediately, and we left for breakfast, stopping by the bathroom on our way.

The restaurant had a breakfast buffet with about everything you could imagine. Macie and I had the scrambled eggs, and Miranda grabbed her usual French toast. Jacob seemed to eat a bit of everything—eggs, bacon, sausage, French toast, and a couple of pancakes.

"After breakfast," Jacob explained, "you will only have an hour or so before the presentation starts. Make sure you are there before nine am. Also, you will have a new set of clothes set out when you get back to your room. I would recommend taking a shower and keeping yourself very clean while here. I've heard that some people who didn't have good hygiene while here were put through a good scrubbing similar to what we went through back on Earth. I sure wouldn't want to go through that again. As you probably saw, there are shower stalls in the bathrooms. Shampoo and conditioner are provided along with the towels."

We hurried, and we finished our meals before Jacob was half finished with his and asked if we could go. He nodded his head, and we were out of there before he finished another bite. Just like he said, there were clothes laid out for us. Of course, they were all white. I was getting sick of white very quickly. We grabbed the clothes and headed to the bathroom to shower. When we had finished, we saw a sign that said to put dirty clothes in the clothes chute. We shoved all our old stuff in there and took off to go explore. I think Macie had the whole place memorized She wouldn't tell us where we were going, but she told us to follow her, and we kept climbing toward the inner circles. Glancing down the halls of the circles, I could see they curved quite a bit. The closer to the center we got, the lighter we felt. It seemed that Macie was taking us to the center bubble. When we got to the final doorway, we could see inside, and people were floating around in midair. The sign above the door said *Zero Grav-Experience It If You Dare!* We stepped through the doorway and met an attendant named Jordan. "Please read the rules over on the wall before you can participate," he said. We moved to the wall to read them.

1. Space Inc. is not responsible for any accidents.
2. Participate at your own risk.
3. Obey attendant.
4. Obey all rules or you will not participate.
5. Reckless participation will not be tolerated.
6. Stay away from others.
7. Only twenty will be able to participate, and there will be a five-minute limit when others are waiting.
8. Have fun!

Miranda and Macie were already squatting to take off when the attendant yelled "Stop!" He barely said it in time. Miranda and Macie had just done a little hop and seemed to float there instead of coming back to the floor. "Did you read the rules?" Jordan asked. We nodded, and he said, "You're lucky because it's early. Most people don't get here until after the presentations, and then it's quite crowded. Go ahead and go—just stay away from others and don't push off of the walls too hard or you might fly into someone."

Macie and Miranda had floated to the ground again. They squatted and flew off the floor as soon as Jordan gave the go ahead. I was more hesitant and just pushed off gently and slowly floated up to the center. I looked up just in time to see Miranda do a front flip right before she got to the other wall so that her feet landed. Then she pushed off again just as Macie was trying to flip the same way. Macie didn't quite make it around and landed on her butt. She just sat there a second and then hopped to her feet, shooting off in the same direction Miranda was going. They were coming straight at me! Miranda was a natural at this, and Macie was doing everything she could to keep up. They came close enough that I was able to slap hands with Miranda as she floated by.

The hand slap caused both of us to do slow cartwheels. I finally made it to the other side and stood there for a second. I shot off again and started doing twists and flips before making it to the other side. I was going to try some of my dive moves. I had taken diving lessons when I was eight or nine. I started with some easy flips, remembering to point my toes, and worked myself into the more complicated twists and turns. I figured out that if I didn't push off very hard, I could twist and flip ten or twelve times before I got to the other side. I wasn't paying attention to the others and just concentrating on my flips. After one particularly complicated one with ten twists, four tuck flips, and four pike flips, I stuck the landing perfectly and did a salute like a gymnast. I heard applause from all around me. Everyone had been watching from the wall while I did that last maneuver. I blushed and looked down out of embarrassment.

Macie and Miranda flew over to me. We were about ten feet off the main floor, and Miranda shot off just above the people standing across the room. She could have touched their heads if she had reached down. She made it to the other side, landed on her feet, threw her arms forward, and flipped up the wall—hands and feet alternating—and then did a twist on her last flip to land on her feet in a squat. Then she shot right back to me. I just watched with my mouth hanging open. I gave her a big high five when she landed right next to me. Macie gave her one, too, and then shot off the wall. But instead of a smooth dive across the room, she flailed her arms and legs back and forth, going all cockeyed instead of straight. I laughed so hard I was crying when she landed on her butt against the wall on the other side. Miranda had pushed off a bit and was just hanging in midair, hunched over and laughing.

It was already 8:30 according to the clock above the door, so I told them they could do two more jumps, and then we needed to get to the presentation. Both of them looked very disappointed. I pushed off to try some more flips, but Miranda grabbed my leg as I went by, and I pulled her with me. I slowed down a bit, but we made it to the other side just as Macie flew up to us. Miranda suddenly said to Macie, "You want to do something cool?" Macie nodded. "Just push off easy, and I'll come by and grab you." Macie and Miranda would do most anything the other asked, especially if involved something fun.

Macie pushed off the wall gently and was slowly floating out to the middle when Miranda shot off the wall and grabbed one of her feet. As Miranda went by, she let go of Macie's foot, causing Macie to start flipping very fast and very out of control. It was funny until I saw the panicked look in Macie's eyes and saw that she wouldn't be able to stop flipping until she hit the wall. I looked down and saw the attendant dealing with someone and not looking up, so I shot off toward where Macie was going to hit and got there just before she did. I gently pushed off toward her at an angle opposite to how she was spinning and was very happy that I was able to grab her by the wrist. As I did this, it stopped her spinning, and she landed on her feet with me holding her wrist straight out from the wall with my feet in the air. The attendant got to us a couple seconds later and told us it was time to leave. Macie pulled me down next to her. We smiled at the attendant and pushed off toward the floor. Miranda was already there, rolling around on the floor because she was laughing so hard. Macie was mad at her for doing that but couldn't stop smiling at what we had pulled off.

It was time to get to the presentation. Macie was still dizzy from the spinning but got over it quickly as we worked our way to the outer rings. Going this way was a lot more fun because, instead of climbing, we got to drop from ring to ring. There was more gravity toward the outer rings, but nothing compared to Earth. Luckily, Macie knew the way, so we got there at 8:58—just in time to get a drink and go in and sit down. Of course, Jacob had front seats for us. We went in and sat down. Miranda was furthest from Jacob with Macie next to her, and that left me sitting next to him. I hoped he would leave me alone to enjoy the presentation.

CHAPTER 17

Jacob leaned over and said, "Glad you three could make it. I was considering sending out a search party." I just glared back at him and didn't say anything.

The lights dimmed, and an old man in a white lab coat stepped out into the spotlight shining on the podium. He tapped on the microphone a couple times and said, "Thank you all for being here. Let me introduce myself. I am Doctor Manual Addison. I was with the first group of men who went to Europa about fifty years ago. I was the third man to set foot on the fourth-largest moon of Jupiter. I can still remember it as if it were yesterday. But I'm sure you don't want to hear my musings on the past, so I will get right into it. In 2017, a series of asteroids that were on a path to strike Jupiter hit Europa instead."

The big screen above Dr. Addison lit up, and we watched an animation of a flyby of Jupiter and its moons as he continued to talk. "Europa was discovered on 8 January 1610 by Galileo Galilei. The discovery—along with the discovery of three other Jovian moons—was the first time a moon had been discovered orbiting a planet other than Earth. The discovery of the four Galilean satellites eventually led to the understanding that planets in our solar system orbit the sun, instead of our solar system revolving around Earth. Galileo apparently had observed Europa on 7 January 1610 but had been unable to differentiate it from Io until the next night.

"Galileo originally called Jupiter's moons the Medicean planets—after the Medici family—and referred to the individual moons numerically as I, II, III, and IV. Galileo's naming system would be used for a couple of centuries until the mid-1800s when the names of the Galilean moons—Io, Europa, Ganymede, and Callisto—would be officially adopted and after it became apparent that naming moons by number would be very confusing as new additional moons were discovered.

"Europa is named after the daughter of Agenor. Europa was abducted by Zeus—the Greek equivalent of the Roman god Jupiter—who had taken the shape of a spotless white bull. Europa was so delighted by the gentle beast that she decked it with flowers and rode upon its back. Zeus, seizing his opportunity, rode away with her into the ocean to the island of Crete, where he transformed back into his true shape. Europa bore Zeus many children, including Minos."

The screen changed so that we watched asteroids approach and hit Europa and Jupiter. I was getting bored already. I looked over at Miranda, and she seemed as bored as I was, but Macie was glued to the screen and was mouthing words like "cool" and "amazing." It was a cool video, but I had seen it all in school and on television many times. When the video stopped, Dr. Addison continued. "As you can see, it was quite a show that lasted for two days. Europa was struck by four or five, and another five or so missed and hit Jupiter. Jupiter absorbed the asteroids, but the ones that hit Europa caused a great deal of damage. They created a number of huge holes or canyons and also caused the instability of the crust. But the biggest change was that the impact of the asteroids moved the moon closer to Jupiter. This was important for many reasons. The biggest was that the moon started to warm up.

"A couple of years before the asteroids hit Europa, the US had launched the James Webb space telescope. It picked up where the Hubble telescope left off. It was designed to see even further into space. When it was determined that the asteroids were going to hit Jupiter, the Webb telescope was pointed in that direction to watch. It was quite a show, to say the least, and Europa getting hit was just the icing on the cake. As Europa was now closer to Jupiter, the radiation increased, as did the gravitational tidal action. One of the most amazing occurrences was that Europa started to turn on its axis. It would be like our moon starting to turn instead of the same side always facing the Earth."

He paused to let that sink in, like we cared. I just wanted him to finish so we could eat. I was starting to get hungry. The video continued on to show the transformation of Europa from a vast frozen planet to a climate very similar to Earth's. I didn't really understand much but did get the gist that it was warm enough for people to live there. I was looking around and wasn't really paying much attention to what he was saying. It was a bunch of technical stuff about what had made Europa warm up. Macie was transfixed on him. I think she actually understood what he was saying—and actually cared. Miranda was still bored and was biting her nails and spitting them on the floor. I was glad I was between her and Jacob. Dr. Addison continued. "We sent probes to test for life on Europa. No life was found, so thus began the big debate. What to do with a new world. Should we just leave it, or should we colonize it? Fortunately for me, it was decided to colonize it. So now what? Lots and lots of discussion took place on how to start up a brand new world."

At this point, I really went into daydream mode. He talked about microorganisms, worms, krill, fish, rabbits, herbivores, carnivores, the cycle of life, and a whole host of other boring stuff. The video showed examples of what he was talking about. Finally, the video started to show trees and grass and then flew out over the ocean. It was very pretty and reminded me of our trips to Panama City Beach in Florida. The best family vacations we had ever gone on.

Now the screen was showing lots and lots of rabbits. Dr. Addison was still talking about the animals. "The rabbits did much better than we thought. As you can see in the video, there are lots of them. We started introducing predators for the rabbit, mostly endangered animals such as the bald eagle. There are now nearly half the number of bald eagles as there are on Earth. They really thrived in a clean environment with plenty of food. We did need some insects, but Europa will be one place where you will never get a mosquito bite."

He continued to drone on about the plants, animals, and insects. I didn't much pay attention to what he was saying, but I watched the video. It was showing a flyover of different parts of the moon. It started over the ocean, then went over fields and trees, and then went through the mountains. It was beautiful but made me very homesick for Earth. I started to daydream about our skiing trips to Colorado. Telluride was by far my favorite place. It was so pretty there and the best skiing of any place I had been to. I didn't notice any snow in the video. I wondered if Europa had snow! It must with all those mountains.

I don't even remember any more of the presentation and was about to pee my pants when Dr. Addison finally said, "That will wrap it up for today. Tomorrow we will talk about your trip to Europa. Enjoy your day and see you back tomorrow at the same time." I ran out of there and almost didn't make it to the bathroom. When I came back to the presentation room, Jacob asked me why I'd left so quickly. He'd thought something was wrong. "What do you want for lunch?" he asked.

I said, "A chicken sandwich would be nice. There isn't a Raising Cane's here, is there?"

"Yes," Macie said. "It's up on Level Six on one of the inner rings."

"You guys go ahead," Jacob said, "but come back in time for us to go to dinner. Try and make it around six."

We took off. Macie led the way, and we ate at Raising Cane's. It was a great meal. We weren't sure what to do next, so we went exploring. A lot of levels and compartments were off limits. We found a gym that was off the outer ring. It had every contraption for exercising you could think of—and some I had no idea how to use. There was also a running track. It wrapped around part of the gym and continued out through the wall, coming back through the wall on the other side of the gym. The track that went through the wall was a clear tube. The floor and walls were all clear. It felt like you were running out in space with nothing but the stars and Earth to look at.

After the past few days without exercise, we all decided to spend the afternoon working out. I was happiest and most at peace when running outside of the gym. I did the different weights and exercises, too, but running was by far my favorite. Miranda enjoyed running also. Macie worked out but just didn't enjoy it like Miranda and me. The people in charge of the gym monitored how much we exercised and would give us a report of our activities before we left. It turns out that the report was sent to Jacob as well. There were a few other people in the gym, but they stayed to themselves as we did.

After we had all showered and cleaned up, we met Jacob for dinner. He let us choose where to eat. Miranda wanted ravioli, so we ended up at an Italian restaurant. It was very good food. We talked about the gym and what we did while away from Jacob. Of course, Macie dominated the conversation. Jacob was impressed that we liked to work out and said our bodies really showed how fit we were. We all felt a bit awkward when he said that but didn't say anything. He told us that to stay fit in low gravity, you needed to work out three to four times as much compared to just walking on Earth. He had received our workout reports, and he told Macie she needed to do more or she would have trouble in the future.

That evening after we ate dinner with Jacob, Miranda and I decided to work out again because we were bored. Macie said she was going to Zero Grav. She liked the attendant and thought he was cute. When Miranda and I arrived at the gym, she decided to work out first and then run. I enjoyed running long distance so just took off on the running track. After a couple laps, I noticed a boy working out. With each lap I ran, he seemed to be one machine closer to Miranda. She didn't seem to notice until he was right next to her. When I entered the gym again, I actually saw him say something to her. She just looked at him and then looked away. She was always very shy. I remembered my parents saying that when she was about one and a half years old, she would put her arm over her eyes as she would walk by men. After another lap, I saw that the boy was gone and Miranda was jogging to catch up with me.

I asked her what had happened, and Miranda told me it was really weird. The boy had told her he was there to help. And then he got up and walked away. I stumbled but was able to keep running when she said that. "What do you think he meant?" I asked.

"I have no idea," Miranda said. "He was sort of cute, and he winked before he left, but that's it."

"Didn't you ask him any questions?"

"He was gone before I came up with any to ask."

We kept running for a long time, both lost in our own thoughts. I'd lost count of how many laps we had run when we decided to stop. We didn't stop because we were tired—we stopped mainly because we got bored. With such little gravity, I felt like I could run forever without getting tired.

We went back, showered and put on clean clothes. The clean clothes were stacked on shelves as you went into the shower area. All you had to do was find your size and you were good to go. A few minutes after we got back to our room, Macie showed up— along with a security guard. Macie told him thanks and came into our room and shut the door.

Miranda said, "Guess what happened to us?"

"Me first!" Macie said.

Miranda gave in and said, "Go ahead, Macie."

"I was playing in Zero Grav and noticed this guy kept staring at me. At first I didn't pay attention, but after a while I was sure he was watching me. There were other people in there, but every time I looked down, he was looking at me. He didn't do any jumping but just stood there watching me. He watched me for about fifteen minutes and then was gone. I was afraid to go back to our room by myself, so I had one of the security people walk me back."

"Wow," I said, "I'm glad nothing happened to you. I didn't think we would be in any danger here. Miranda and I had an incident also. A boy came up to her and told her he's here to help. Do you think we should tell Jacob?"

Macie said, "Yes, let's go tell him now."

Miranda shook her head. "I don't trust him. There is something about him and the way he acts that just isn't right. And besides, nothing actually happened to us. We should be sure not go anywhere alone, though, just to be safe." Macie and I shook our heads in agreement, and then we all went to bed.

CHAPTER 18

The next day's presentation was a lot more interesting. We arrived just after it started. Jacob didn't look very happy that we were late but didn't say anything. The speaker was in the middle of giving her life history and how she came to be giving the presentation. Something about enjoying travel, meeting people, and always wanting to go to outer space. I tuned out most of what she said, still thinking about our latest escapade in Zero Grav. I perked up a bit when the woman said, "Once again, for those who joined us late, my name is Reese Price, and I will be with you all the way to Europa. Although I will be coming back, and you won't!" She smiled when she said this and seemed to be looking straight at me.

She began to talk about history again. "Those of you who were here yesterday for the presentation are probably already familiar with the history of what will be your new home, so I'll keep it brief. Did you know that the people living there refer to the moon as *AARDE*? AARDE means Earth in Dutch. Pieter Schuyler was one of the first settlers, and he coined the nickname. I will cover some of the high points again and add some things that the presentation yesterday might not have covered. By now you are probably aware that Galileo Galilei discovered it on January 8, 1610, and it was named after Europa, a Phoenician noblewoman in Greek mythology. It is also slightly smaller than Earth's moon.

"I'm not going to go into the past of how it became habitable for humans but rather talk about the present and future of Aarde. Aarde has about as much land as Africa but with a chunk about the size of Australia separated off as an island." She showed a simple map of it on the wall. Ganymede was off by itself, completely surrounded by water, and the main continent went from pole to pole with the upper third called IO, the middle portion Callisto, and the bottom third called Thebe.

MAP

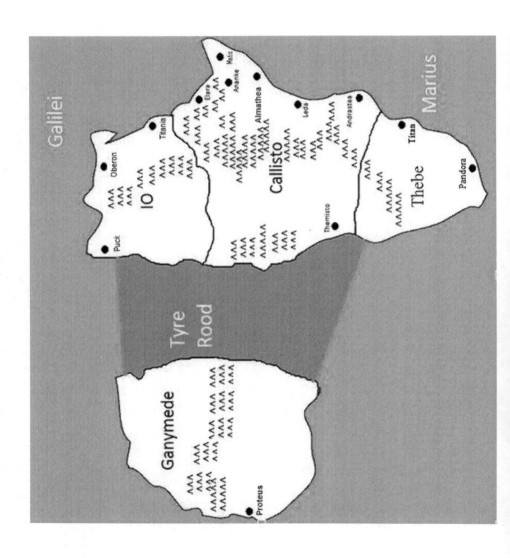

"There are about twenty thousand people so far," Reese continued. "Almost all have come by spaceship. No children have been allowed to immigrate to Aarde because it is such a harsh environment. There have been less than two hundred children born on Aarde so far. Doctors were worried that children born in the low gravity would have a lot of health problems, but it turned out to be just the opposite. The intelligence and physical development has been measured to be faster than on Earth. The reason why is not understood as yet."

I was getting bored and was looking around the room and just happened to glance at a group of women across the room when Reese said, "Only about ten percent of the population on Aarde is women. Women are in such high demand on Aarde that there is actually a market for them. It's primitive but necessary for the new world to thrive. No women means men get cranky and rowdy, like the Old West was in the United States before the settlers. I'm sure they didn't call it the Wild West because of its redeeming qualities. Aarde is such a new and undeveloped world that it's very similar to that era in a lot of ways." At this statement, a number of the women smiled smugly like they were better than all those around them. Looking around the auditorium, I saw there were only about twenty-five women compared to well over two hundred men. I was trying not to be too judgmental, but none of the women were very pretty, and some were downright homely. The women who were smiling seemed to have an air of confidence about them.

Reese continued while I watched the women. "Aarde is just as inaccessible and inhospitable to families now as the West was then. Some other interesting facts are that not all the plants and animals put on Aarde survived. Some have stayed the same, but some have started to evolve to better suit themselves to their environment. As an example, the rabbits that were first shipped to Aarde were able to leap long distances because of the low gravity. As the generations have progressed, they seem to be able to stay away from predators more through intelligence than from being able to jump long distances. Another example of change is the trees. At first, the trees grew hundreds of feet high because of the low gravity, but a lot of them were wiped out during some of the intense storms. The same types of trees that had been growing very tall started to send roots deeper into the soil and not grow so high.

"So back to the lack of women, there were very few single women willing to move to another world. There were even fewer men with wives who were willing to go, especially when there was very little if any chance that they would ever make it back to Earth. The trips to and from Aarde are very expensive, and space is at a premium. We take people and supplies to Aarde from Earth and bring freight, both mined and what can be created in lower gravity, back to Earth. With so much to bring back, there is not room for disgruntled people who do not want to live on Aarde." I looked over at Miranda and Macie and started to tear up. This was another reminder that we were not ever going back to Earth. They were intently watching Reese, so I turned my attention back to her, too.

Reese took a breath and continued, "To be blunt, where there is a demand, there will be a supply. I am only telling you this to emphasize that this is a new and rough world, so prepare yourselves. Fortunately, the demand for—and lack of—women was expected, so shortly after explorers were sent to Aarde, steps were taken to prepare for this. The best and most attractive solution was what became known as "The Proposal" on Aarde. The process involves women on Earth agreeing to marry a man of their choosing when they get to Aarde. Allowing women to remain single was not considered to be feasible because of the rough conditions and lack of protection. Sounds simple, doesn't it?

But it became complicated very quickly. There are not very many women who would just agree to marry someone on a distant world without ever meeting them. The first solution the government tried was advertising for women to go. The advertising showed only the good side of Aarde, so there were a lot of women who applied but ended up backing out when they realized what the real conditions were. The government also tried arranged marriages, but the communication between the two worlds was too slow so it was too cumbersome.

Finally, the government gave in to Capitalism, and "The Proposal" was created. There are "discoverers" who find fairly young, single women who will sign a contract to be married when they get to Aarde. Before they can sign, they must go through a class about Aarde and the life they might choose. If a woman makes the choice to continue, she must pass a physical and then sign a contract that becomes enforceable the moment she steps off the space station onto the spaceship bound for Europa. Once on the ship, she is obligated to fulfill the contract and get married when she arrives on Europa." I thought the entire concept was crazy. Who would agree to do this?

Reese continued. "When the women arrive at Aarde, they are given about a week to relax and get acclimated to their new world. It also gives them a chance to meet the prospective suitors—or "Proposers". It is a week filled with parties and dancing for not just the women and Proposers, but for all of the immigrants to the new world. A new ship brings in not only new people but much-needed supplies.

"On the last night, there is a huge party to wrap up the week. It is a formal ball called "The Proposal Ball." All of the new immigrants are given a tuxedo if they don't have one. The women can wear their own dresses or choose from the elegant ones provided. The ball is open to all Aarde citizens, but they have to supply their own formal wear. Usually the governors of the four states of Callisto, Ganymede, IO, and Europa attend, along with the mayors of the towns near Metis. A few of them are bachelors, and they occasionally bid on the women but very seldom win because government employees of Aarde are not normally paid very well. This is also the last chance for the prospective grooms to impress the ladies with their charm and their assets.

"Near the end of the evening, the real fun starts. All the ladies retire to the dressing rooms for a little rest, refreshment, and last minute prepping of their hair and makeup. The attending dignitaries will confer and then call each of the ladies to the stage to be bid upon. Men being men, they will usually call the most desirable women last. It does usually ensure that the highest and most competitive bidding occurs last. The bidding starts as soon as the first lady takes the stage. The rest of the ladies remain in their dressing rooms until it is their turn.

"The bidding process lasts two minutes. It usually starts with the poorer men bidding first, hoping others will not bid. Quite often, one bid will win because the men with more money will wait for the more attractive women. The top two bidders on each lady are forbidden from bidding again on subsequent ladies. After all of the women have had their two minutes of fame, they have one hour to decide who their husband will be. A document will accompany each bid detailing who the man is and what assets he owns. A woman has a lot of incentive to choose the top bidder. She will get forty percent of the bid to keep as her own and fifty percent of the man's assets if she stays with him for five years. If she chooses one of the other bidders, then she will only get ten percent of the bid to keep as her own and twenty percent of his assets after five years.

After all of the women have been bid on, the music starts up, and everyone goes back to dancing. The women will dance with each of their prospective husbands until making a final decision, and then she will go up on the stage and ring the bell. When the bell is rung, the music stops, and the prospective husbands go up on the stage and get down on one knee with engagement rings held out. She will go up to the one she has chosen, and he will put the ring on her finger. Some women will play coy and walk back and forth in front of the men, acting like they can't decide, before finally choosing. After her choice is made, everyone claps, and the music starts up again until the next bell is rung.

After all of the women have become engaged, the band will play one more song to end the Proposal Ball. The engagement will last until the following day when the marriage ceremonies start. There are only two churches in Metis, so the ceremonies start and finish about every twenty minutes. There is one more reception for the newly married after the weddings are over. Not many show because the people from out of town have already left, and the immigrants who just arrived are ready to start their new life. It is actually a pretty boring party. After the reception, the newlyweds get a free night in the Aardemore and then go on with their new life."

I leaned over to Miranda and whispered, "Wow, I sure wouldn't want to get married that way."

She looked over at me and whispered back, "We're too young. Why even worry about it?"

I thought to myself, *I'm almost old enough to get married, but I sure don't want to do it The Proposal way.*

Reese had stopped talking for a moment and took a drink of water before continuing. "I know there are a lot of details I left out, but all of the ladies have been well informed about the process and their rights. The reason I repeated the information for them is just a reminder that once they step onto the spaceship, they are committed to follow the contract they signed." During her speech, the room was dimly lit, the only light the one on the stage. When Reese pointed to the women in the audience, a spotlight was cast on them, and she said, "Ladies, we are very pleased that you have chosen your new life—although not as pleased as the gentlemen will be when you become their wives." All of the women stood, smiling, and waved. There was a bit of catcalling and whistling while they were standing that seemed to make some of the ladies blush while others licked their lips, apparently enjoying the attention.

They all sat down, and Reese said, "That is all for today. Enjoy your next couple days, and we will see you on the ship."

Before we got up, Jacob said, "I expect you to be here on time from now on. Don't disappoint me."

The rest of our time on the space station was filled with more boring presentations, working out, and playing in Zero Grav. We saw the boy a couple more times, but he left as soon as he saw us and we could never catch him. Macie saw the man who had helped us escape and pointed him out to Miranda and me. As soon as I saw him, I recognized him as the man who'd been at the hotel and had blocked William at the convenience store. I started to wave to him, but he immediately turned around and left. We tried to follow, but we were unable to catch up with him.

CHAPTER 19

Jacob didn't do much with us. The only time we talked with him was when we were eating dinner at one of the restaurants. We tried to question him about the trip to Europa and what we would be doing once we got there. All he would say was, "I'll tell you when we leave the space station." On our last night we ate at a Mexican restaurant called Julio's. Jacob encouraged us to enjoy our last dinner because the food we would have during the trip was not going to taste very good. The next morning we would eat breakfast and then load up into the spaceship and leave. I think all three of us had triple the amount of Mexican food we would normally eat and were so full we skipped working out and just went to play in Zero Grav for the last time.

We were getting used to the low gravity on the space station. We had already been in good shape before we arrived, but something about running and working out in low gravity seemed to enhance our bodies. We could run very long distances without getting tired, and we seemed to be stronger than ever although it was hard to judge very accurately. The other people we saw working out in the gym didn't seem to have near our dedication or strength. Even the men seemed to be struggling at what we would have thought easy on Earth. We really honed our coordination from playing in Zero Grav. There didn't seem to be much we couldn't do, flipping and sailing from wall to wall. When we arrived at Zero Grav, the attendant was not there. There was only one person playing. He was clear up at the top, and he looked down at us. It was the boy who had talked to Miranda. He got a panicked look on his face and seemed to be contemplating how to get away from us. I told Miranda and Macie not to let him get out before we talked to him.

Miranda said, "Madison, you stay down here to block the exits while Macie and I get him. Macie, you go on my left when I tell you. You'll have to jump fast because if you go too slow, he will just jump past you." Macie shook her head. "Look down, and jump when I say now." They looked down, and I heard Miranda whisper, "Now!" Both jumped at the same time.

I wanted to jump with them but knew one of us had to guard the door. If we weren't so serious about asking him some questions, I would have been laughing at what I saw next. After Miranda and Macie jumped straight toward the boy, I saw him panic and immediately shoot toward the floor. The girls couldn't stop their momentum and ended up right where the boy had been before he jumped. They immediately pushed off after him. I saw he was headed toward the floor, so I tried to be where I thought he would end up but didn't get there in time, and I saw him land and push off again just as I reached for him. He went off at a forty-five-degree angle toward one of the walls. Miranda and Macie landed a couple seconds after he jumped and jumped right after him. I stayed on the floor watching but really wanted to be helping.

Miranda and Macie continued to be a few seconds behind him on each jump and weren't really getting any closer to catching him. I saw Miranda tell Macie to stop at the next jump. When they stopped, the boy stopped, too—only on the other side of the room. Miranda and Macie chatted a few seconds and then both took off at different angles, neither one directly at the boy. He just stood still, watching Macie and Miranda bounce around the room, finally taking off when he thought one of them was coming too close. Miranda and Macie didn't really look like they were chasing him, but he seemed to think so and kept moving. Sometimes Miranda and Macie would go sailing right by each other. I noticed that they would say something to each other each time they passed close.

All of this seemed to go on for a long time, but in reality it was just a few minutes. The boy seemed to be really panicking, trying to stay away from their random jumping. On one jump, when the boy jumped and Miranda and Macie were going by each other, I saw Miranda say something to Macie. Macie grabbed Miranda's hand, and that changed Miranda's direction to intersect with the boy. When Miranda and the boy collided in midair, I saw her grab him in a bear hug just before they got to the opposite wall. They both swung around and landed on their feet. The boy was so surprised he didn't struggle for a few seconds, and by the time he started to get away from Miranda, Macie was there grabbing his legs away from the wall. He didn't have any leverage to get away.

So there were Miranda and Macie, holding the boy, their feet on the wall. Both pushed off gently, and they floated to the floor where they landed ever so gently. I took a closer look at the boy. He was very skinny and just a bit taller than Miranda. I couldn't tell for sure how old he was, but he looked like he was about my age. He was taller than Macie but not as tall as Miranda. Miranda still had her hands on him, but Macie had let go.

"What's your name?" I asked.

He just stared at me a few seconds, pondering what to say. Finally he said, "I don't think it would be wise to tell you, for your sake and mine." Miranda tightened her hands on him a bit. He winced but wouldn't say anymore.

"Well then, why did you tell Miranda that you would be there to help?"

He looked around, checking for others, but there wasn't anyone there but us. He said, "We know about your situation and are doing our best to keep you safe."

Macie looked at him with fear on her face, and Miranda said, "What do we need to be kept safe from?"

"You will be safe until you reach Aarde, but you will need to be extremely careful once you arrive."

I was about to ask him some more questions when we heard a noise from outside the door like someone was coming. When we looked toward the door, the boy broke away from Miranda, took off toward the other door, and was out just as the attendant entered. The attendant looked at us strangely and asked what we were doing in there without supervision. I spoke up quickly. "We wanted to experience Zero Grav one more time before we left, and we really appreciate how nice you have been to us while we were here."

He softened. "Thank you, but we need to close up." We begged him for just ten minutes. He looked around as if expecting someone to be watching him and said. "Ten minutes is all I can give or I'll get in trouble."

We thanked him and gave a push straight up to the ceiling. When we landed, I asked Macie, "Where did you come up with that move you used to capture the boy?"

"It was Miranda's idea."

"I thought that if we just confused him by jumping in random directions that eventually we would catch him," Miranda explained. "I didn't think of grabbing Macie to change directions in mid-flight until that last jump. As I was approaching her, I told her to grab me and fling me toward where he was going. I thought it might work but was even more impressed when Macie let go of me at the perfect time."

Macie blushed a bit at the compliment, and I said "Macie, would you do that with me?"

"Sure, but I don't know if I can do it again."

"It doesn't really matter. This is our last time playing here, so let's just have some fun."

I went to one of the side walls and pushed off toward Macie just as she pushed off. Right when I was near her, I put out my hand. She grabbed it and held on until I was at almost a ninety-degree angle, and then she let go. Instead of doing a nice dive to land on the wall, I went spinning and ended up hitting the wall with my butt instead of my feet. Macie made it to the other wall. I watched as Miranda and Macie shot off the walls toward each other and did it perfectly again. I was disappointed that I hadn't been able to do it right the first time, but after a few more tries, I finally got it right.

We continued flinging each other around until we heard the attendant yelling for us to come down. Macie was by far the best at redirecting and Miranda the worst. Miranda used her strength too much and sent us spinning, not knowing in what direction we would end up. Thinking back, I wondered if Miranda was just entertaining herself at our expense. One time, Miranda had tried to redirect Macie and me at the same time. Instead of sending us away from each other, she flung us together and we banged heads. I hadn't seen Miranda laugh that hard in a long time. We did one last jump and then settled down to the floor where the attendant was waiting for us.

When all three of us landed, he said "Wow! That was by far the best flying I've ever seen. I've seen people grab other people mistakenly and send them into the wall, but I've never watched anyone do it on purpose to send them at different angles. I wish you three were staying longer so I could watch your acrobatics some more. I do hope you all have a safe flight to Europa." We thanked him and left. As we were walking out, I wondered what the future held for us. We'd been ripped from our home, taken away from Earth, and tomorrow we'd be leaving for a new world, never to return. I saw no way of escaping, so the best plan was to stay safe and together—no matter what.

As we went back to our room, I said, "I wish we could have got more information from the boy. If only the attendant hadn't come back. What do you think we have waiting for us when we get to Europa?"

"He was kind of cute. I hope we see him again." Miranda and I just looked at her and laughed. She always came up with off-the-wall comments like that. "Why don't we talk to Jacob about Europa?" she asked.

"Don't you remember him saying he wouldn't tell us anything until we were on our way? I don't trust him to tell us the truth anyway."

We made it back to our room a few minutes later and got ready for bed. We were all talking about what the trip to Europa was going to be like when Jacob knocked on our door. I was in the bottom bunk, so I answered it. He came in and sat down in a chair while I climbed back in bed.

"I hope you enjoyed your time here at the space station, but this is only the first part of our adventure."

Miranda cleared her throat and said, "Excuse me, Jacob, this is not an adventure for us. We are being sent away from our home and family against our will, so do not refer to it as an adventure. We do not want to go, and you are forcing us to. Just tell us what's going to happen and what we are supposed to do, okay?"

Jacob hadn't been expecting the pushback because his face showed distress before it morphed into a snarl. He said harshly, "Fine, have it your way. It's your choice to make the best of it or not. We all are going to Europa, and there is nothing you can do about it. I will get you up at about 6 am so we will have time to eat and you can take your last shower before we load into the spaceship and leave—you will only be able to take sponge baths on the spaceship. Also, the duffel bags that contain your belongings will be on the spaceship. You will be given two sets of clothes similar to what you have been wearing here on the space station. There isn't a washer so I would recommend that you wear the same outfit when you work out so all of your clothes don't smell. Any questions?" We did have questions but were too tired to ask them.

None of us could get to sleep. We were lying in our beds, lost in thought, when Macie climbed down and opened the curtain. She stood still a moment and then began to cry. Both Miranda and I got out of bed and hugged her. Through her tears she said, "I miss Mom, Dad, and Morgan so much, and I'll never get to see them again." Miranda and I just hugged her and each other tighter and began to cry ourselves. Earth was so beautiful—I couldn't believe we were never going to see it again. We stood there hugging and crying until we could barely stand from exhaustion and then crawled back into our beds. I just lay there looking at Mother Earth until sleep finally overtook me. I imagine Macie and Miranda did the same.

CHAPTER 20

My whole family was sitting in our living room watching the television show *Full House*. It was a show that all of us liked, even my dad. He would always leave the room when we watched *SpongeBob*. My mother had made popcorn with butter. The show had just started when someone started banging on the door. I jumped up, banging my head on Miranda's bunk, and realized I was dreaming. There was banging on our door again, and I realized that I was back on the space station, and it was Jacob banging on the door yelling for us to get up.

Miranda yelled out, "Go away! We don't want to go."

"We have two hours until we board the ship. You can sleep it away and be hungry until lunch, or you can get up, eat breakfast, and enjoy your last shower for a month," he said. "And don't even think of trying not to go to the ship. I will have security tie your hands and feet together and carry you onto the ship if necessary. Do not test me. I am going to eat in fifteen minutes and expect you to be there."

Jacob left, and I got out of bed to get ready. I told Miranda and Macie to get up, but they just lay there. I started shoving them on their beds.

"Don't push me again. I will get up in five minutes." Miranda glared at me, and I backed off.

Macie just kept pulling the blanket back over her head, crying out, "Leave me alone!" I kept pulling her blanket down, telling her this was the last good meal we were going to get. She finally sat up and climbed down. Miranda got up at about the same time.

When dressed, we walked over to Jacob's room and knocked. He opened the door and we all went to get some breakfast. Jacob had his usual omelet, Macie had eggs and triple order of sausage, Miranda ate French toast, and I had the strawberry pancakes. We were all lost in thought with very little conversation. If Jacob would have blessed the pancakes and orange juice, it would have felt even more like the last supper before we died.

After breakfast, Macie, Miranda, and I went back and took long showers. I could have stood there all day, it felt so good, especially knowing it would be at least a month with just sponge baths. We ended up back at the window in our room, staring at Earth as we waited for Jacob to get us to go to the spaceship. We were depressed.

Miranda didn't talk much, but when she did, it was usually something important. As she stood there, she said, "You know it isn't over, don't you? We'll have about a month to prepare for what awaits us on Europa. We were warned that we will be in more danger on the trip, and in even more danger when we get to Europa. Jacob said he's going to tell us about it once we leave here. He probably thinks we'll cause trouble if he tells us before we leave but will be helpless once we do. I can't imagine what it will be like where we're going, but the three of us need to be strong together and not let them separate us, no matter what. We're just three girls, but we need to be prepared to fight and protect ourselves. We must not let them separate us." Macie and I nodded.

I added, "We're all pretty fast runners, and with this low gravity, I think that's our best way out of trouble. But if one stays to fight, all of us must be willing to help. Fighting should only be our last resort. I imagine they'll have some sort of workout facility on the ship, so we really need to hit it hard to be prepared. I doubt it will be as good as on the space station, but a month is too long to go without exercising."

Macie chimed in. "I wonder if they'll have something like Zero Grav."

"I doubt it," I said, "because a ship won't have enough space. I do wonder if there will be any gravity at all on board."

We sat there a few minutes in silence, and then Macie said, "We can't escape from here and certainly not from a spaceship, but once we get to Aarde we can."

Miranda and I looked at her in surprise and Miranda asked, "How?"

Macie got excited. "Do you remember all those books we read when we were first taken and put in that room? I practically memorized every survival book, and I actually paid attention during the orientation presentations—unlike you two." Miranda and I smiled because Macie was right. "Aarde is just like America was right after we became a country—lots of uninhabited land but rich in natural resources. It is about a quarter of the size of Earth with only twenty percent of the gravity. With what we learned from the books, I'm sure we could survive if we escaped."

I had lots of questions for Macie, but we were interrupted by a knock on our door. I answered it, and Jacob was there. "It's time to go." I said we'd be right out and closed the door.

"Time to go," I told my sisters. "We will have plenty of time to discuss this on the trip. Let's get our stuff and go."

"I can't wait to see the inside of the ship," Macie said.

We got our belongings together, looked out at the Earth one more time, and left the room. Jacob was waiting for us outside. "Ready for the next part of your adventure?" We all looked at him but didn't say anything. His face changed from happy to mad very quickly and he said, "Okay, if that's the way you want it to be. Follow me."

We followed him, not really paying attention to where we were going because we were all depressed. Eventually, we came to a room full of people waiting to board. We trailed Jacob up to the counter where he handed the attendant his badge. Her nametag showed her name was Cassandra. She didn't even look at his badge but put a check by his name on her list. We walked up and gave her our badges. "These three girls are with you?" she asked. "You didn't tell me about them before." The three of us looked at him, and he seemed to blush a little bit. So this must be who Jacob spent all his time with when he wasn't with us.

"Yes, they are. I am their temporary guardian. Their names will not be on the list because they are with me."

"I thought everyone was supposed to be on the list," Cassandra said, "but based on your credentials, I will take your word for it." She then handed our badges back to us and said, "I hope you all have a nice flight," staring at Jacob when she said it. Miranda, Macie, and I turned to go sit down while Jacob stood there talking with Cassandra. I heard her say, "I wish you were staying here longer" as we walked away.

There were a lot of people sitting and milling about. The women I saw at the presentation were there. The men seemed to be fairly young and in good shape. A few of them were older. All of the women were older than I was, but only a couple of them were what I would call attractive. They were walking around and flirting with the men but glancing over at us sometimes with a look that wasn't friendly.

We were there about thirty minutes when a door opened and what looked like an airplane pilot stepped out. He walked over to the counter and spoke with the lady there. Jacob was off to the side of the counter but had been talking to her the whole time we were sitting. The pilot left and went back through the door as the lady said something to Jacob. He looked over at us and motioned us to follow. We got up and walked toward the door the pilot had gone through. Everyone in the room watched us, and I heard a bit of whispering but not well enough to understand what was being said. We went to the front of the line and everyone else lined up behind us. We went through the door and headed down a large tube toward another door which led into the spaceship.

Jacob went through first, followed closely by Macie, who was so anxious to see inside that she pushed Jacob out of the way. He looked a little irritated but seemed amused. Miranda was next and then me. I was expecting it to be like an airplane with rows of seats. It wasn't like anything I could have imagined. I looked around and thought the layout made sense. I can only describe it as entering a restaurant where the tables and chairs were not just on the floor but on the walls and the ceiling, too.

"Isn't it cool? Macie said, awestruck.

"The tables and chairs are clamped down now but won't need to be once we leave the space station because the whole tube spins to give us gravity," explained Jacob. I looked around, and sure enough, there were clamps at the bottoms of all the table and chairs. There were also what looked like storage bins in the center of the cylinder. It was all very strange.

Looking to my left, I saw a number of doors that all said *Crew Only* on them. To my right, I saw three doors labeled *Gym* along with two hallways with signs that said *To Sleeping and Storage*. As I continued to look around, I saw a lady across the room motioning us over to her. She was the lady who had given the presentation. Reese. She said, "Please come over here. It will be crowded in here until we pull away from the space station. The sooner we all get on board, the sooner we will leave and have more room." People continued to stream through the door until a lady in a uniform stepped through and closed it. Reese spoke up again right after the door was closed. "Welcome to the *Europa Four* spaceship or— as it is affectionately known to the captain and crew— *Cigar IV*, so named because of the shape of the ship. Please be patient as the crew goes through the final checks before we depart. We will have a more formal presentation after dinner tonight, but here are a few things to know and keep in mind. Number one—this is a long trip in what seems like a large ship, but after a few days it will feel very small and cramped. Because there are a lot of passengers and few crew members, disturbances will be dealt with very quickly and severely. The captain will make all final decisions. I have had passengers who have spent nearly the whole trip in one room for causing problems. It makes for a very unpleasant thirty days, let me tell you." We looked around uncomfortably.

"Number two—the crew's quarters are off limits for passengers. Please respect our space, and we will respect yours. That is all for the rules, but you are expected to be courteous and respectful to all others on the ship. We are about to disconnect from the space station. As soon as we do, you will feel weightless as we will lose the gravity provided by the space station rotation. A bell will sound right before we disconnect, and I ask that you please grab onto a table or chair at that time so you don't float away. About thirty seconds after the disconnection, the floor will start to rotate, giving us enough gravity to remain grounded. It seems strange at first, but you will get used to it very quickly." I looked over at Macie and Miranda, and they were whispering to each other. I didn't get a chance to find out about what because a bell started ringing.

"Please grab onto something to keep from floating," Reese directed. I grabbed a table, and we felt a little bump as the ship disconnected from the space station. Immediately, I felt like I was back in Zero Grav. I looked around just in time to see Miranda take off toward the ceiling with Macie right behind her. Miranda did a tuck somersault and a straight body somersault before assuming a sitting position right before she landed perfectly in a chair on the ceiling. Macie held her arms out like an airplane and did a couple twists before flipping at the last minute, trying to sit in the chair on the other side of the table from where Miranda sat. She missed the chair and ended up sitting on the floor. Miranda would have fallen out of her chair if there were gravity because she was laughing so hard. I was just about to follow them when Reese appeared right next to me, put her hand on my shoulder, and shook her head no. Reese then jumped, did a flip, and landed on her feet right in front of Miranda and Macie. I couldn't hear what she told them, but she said it with a smile. As she was talking to them, I became a little disoriented because the floor started to rotate.

As I looked out the window, the space station moved out of view. I continued to stare out the window as the space station moved in and out of my sight. The rotation seemed to quicken, and as it did, enough gravity was generated so that I did not fly into the air with each step. I walked around the curved wall until I got to where Reese was talking to Miranda and Macie. Reese stuck out her hand and said, "Very nice to meet you, Madison." I shook it and she said, "I was just telling Miranda and Macie here to be careful about their conduct. I thought their performance was great, but some others on the crew might not. They could end up confined to a room if they aren't careful."

Reese pulled a microphone out of her pocket and began to speak to the passengers again, her voice carried through the room by hidden speakers. "Welcome aboard again. We are now on our way to Europa." There was some applause from some of the passengers as Reese continued, "You are now free to explore the ship. We are in the dining room. The next room is the gym. Next to that are the bathrooms and the storage area. Past the storage area are the bedrooms. Your name will be on the door of your room. There are eight beds per room, so please be courteous to your roommates during the trip. Past the sleeping quarters are more crew quarters. Does anyone have questions before I let you go check out the ship?" No one raised their hand or spoke up. "You are free to go, but please return at noon for lunch and the presentation."

CHAPTER 21

Macie immediately started toward the gym and Miranda and I followed. I looked back to see Jacob watching us but not following. I guess he knew we couldn't escape and figured why bother. We went through the door into the gym. There was a running path that traveled across the floor, up the wall, across the ceiling, and down the other wall. I guess it made sense that you could keep running in a straight line to end up where you started from. There were lots of workout machines but no free weights. I recognized most of the machines, but there were a few that looked unusual. There was also a big closet on one side. We looked around for a few minutes, knowing we would be spending a lot of time there during the trip. We made it to the other side of the gym and saw on the set of double doors that said *Ladies* and another that said *Gentlemen*. We definitely needed a bathroom, so we headed in.

We had to go up a flight of stairs to get to the stalls. I guess the plumbing was below the stalls. I really didn't want to know what they did with the waste. Finished, we went down the stairs on the other side of the stalls and through the door at the bottom. We ended up in the sleeping quarters. The hallway led to both the left and the right with doors all along it to our left. We decided to head right and look for where we were going to sleep. Next to each door was a list of names. We found our names by the fifth door.

There were four other names below ours. We opened the door and went in. There were two sinks with big mirrors above them opposite the door. On the left side were four beds attached to the wall with two or three feet between the beds, not much room above you when you slept. There was a ladder to the left of the beds for access to the top beds. The right side of the room was identical to the left with four more beds. We were still looking around the room when four women entered. One was blonde and very skinny, two were overweight brunettes, and the fourth was very plain with red hair and freckles all over her face.

They were the women we had seen before we boarded. I said "hi," but they just looked at me and didn't say anything for a few seconds. When the blonde finally spoke, she said in a mean voice, "We get the bottom two beds on each side, and I don't care if you don't like those arrangements. I'm Emily." She pointed at the other three women and said "And this is Blaise (the redhead), Huxley, and Portia (the brunettes). We already know your names. You three have been quite the talk around the space station. It is going to be a long trip together, so don't mess with us or you *will* regret it." And then the four of them left the room.

All three of us just stood there for a minute, speechless at their bad treatment of us. Macie asked, "Why were they so mean?"

"I have no idea!" I said in shock.

Miranda said, "I don't know or care why they're mean. They looked like four little pigs, especially the one called Portia."

Macie laughed and said, "What kind of names are Blaise, Huxley, and Portia anyway?" We all laughed at Macie's comment but still didn't understand the women's attitudes. There wasn't anything else to see in our room, so we left to go explore the ship some more.

The one place we hadn't been—besides the crew quarters—was the storage area next to the bathrooms. We left our room, and the hallway led us past the bathrooms to a door marked *Storage*. We opened it and went inside. It was laid out like a locker room. There were three aisles with lockers on each side and a bench down the middle. Each locker had a combination lock. We wandered around a bit and saw our names on three of the lockers. We tried to open them, but they were locked and we didn't have the key. We saw that Jacob's locker was right next to ours. It was getting close to twelve, so we headed back to the dining room to eat.

When we got there, almost everyone was already in their chairs talking among themselves. We saw Jacob sitting at a table by himself, so we went over and joined him.

"Hi, did you find your room?"

"Yes, we did," I said, "but we have to share it with four women who were downright mean to us for no reason."

"You didn't tell them anything, did you?"

"No, but why would it even matter?"

"It matters a lot to me," he said, "and if you tell anyone on this trip anything about your background, you will be in a room by yourself for the rest of the trip and only able to come out to use the bathroom under supervision. Do you understand?"

"Seriously, what does it matter? We're here against our will and don't have any choice about where we are going," Miranda said. "It isn't like anyone we told would be able to do a thing to help us go back."

Jacob just glared at her. "You are correct, but if you don't follow my rules, you will suffer the consequences. Let me ask again, do all three of you understand that rule?" We all nodded, and Jacob relaxed a little bit.

As I looked around the room, I noticed that all the other tables were crowded with eight to ten people while it was just the four of us at ours, and I asked Jacob about it. All he said was "Rank has its privileges!"

"What does that mean?" I asked.

He smiled, looked at me, and informed me, "I will be governor of Callisto when we arrive." I had no idea what he was talking about.

Macie was listening. "Madison," she said, "if you had paid attention in the presentations on the space station, you would know that the land on Europa was divided up into states named for the largest moons of Jupiter. Callisto is the second largest moon and the largest state on Europa. I thought it was funny the way they named one of the states Europa even though the moon is called that. Maybe that's one of the reasons the people of Europa call the moon Aarde."

CHAPTER 22

Jacob looked at her, clearly impressed with what she knew, and said, "Very impressive, Macie."

Miranda spoke up. "So now that we are on our way, Jacob, when are you going to tell us our future?"

Jacob just looked at her with a smug look and said, "All in due time, just be patient. We have a long trip ahead of us."

Miranda was getting upset and said, "I'm tired of all your crap, Jacob. You take us away from our family and home, drag us all over the country, and are sending us to a moon somewhere, and you have the nerve to tell us to be patient? What kind of monster are you to think you can treat people this way? My patience has run out, and I want to know now!" As Miranda spoke, her voice got louder, and people around us were staring at our table.

Jacob was furious, but just as he started to speak, the waitress came up and asked what we wanted to drink. Jacob forced himself to calm down and said, "I'll have a glass of red wine. Girls, what do you want to drink?"

We gave the waitress our orders. "Just remember," she said, "that after today, only water will be served during breakfast and lunch because we have a limited supply. My name is Rachael, and I am your server. Also, I'm here to help you with any questions you might have during the trip to Europa—or Aarde as the natives call it. For lunch, your choices are chicken fingers or a hamburger." Macie wanted a hamburger while Miranda and I settled for the chicken fingers. Jacob looked at Rachael and told her he wanted a steak, cooked rare. "I'm sorry, but that is not available for the passengers."

"I am to be the governor of Callisto," Jacob said, "and you will bring me what I asked for—and quickly—or there will be serious consequences when we arrive. Do you understand?" Rachel looked about ready to cry, responded in the affirmative, and walked away quickly.

"You didn't have to treat her like that," said Miranda. "She was just doing her job. I knew you were a mean and nasty person."

Jacob spoke very calmly. "Miranda, I will treat her in any way that I please, and it would be wise of you to consider that before you are disrespectful to me. I have put up with quite a bit from you three—and especially you, Miranda. I am warning you not be disrespectful to me again or do anything that will embarrass me during this trip. Do you understand?"

Macie and I were quiet, but Miranda started laughing. "And just what are you going to do about it, Mr. Governor?"

Jacob very calmly raised his hand and gestured for a person in a uniform to come over to our table. "Miranda, I asked you not to be disrespectful to me. Now you will get a taste of what will happen if you are." The uniformed man walked over to our table and asked what he could do for us. He was wearing a badge and a patch on his sleeve that said *Security*, and his name tag said Matt. Jacob. "Please have another officer help you to escort this young lady to one of the confinement rooms until after dinner."

Matt gestured to another officer standing in another part of the room. "Right away, sir." Just as the other officer arrived, Matt turned to Miranda. "Please stand and come with us." As Miranda stood up with tears in her eyes, she asked them where they were taking her.

Before Matt could respond, Jacob said, "I warned you about being disrespectful. You will serve as a good example for everyone on the ship of what can happen. Enjoy your alone time, and please consider how the rest of the trip will go for you."

Matt and the other security guard were much too strong and easily had Miranda under control. She glared at Jacob as she was led off. Everyone had stopped talking and was staring at us. Macie and I were getting up to go with them when Jacob said harshly, "Sit down or you will be joining her." Macie and I did as we were told.

"Where are they taking her? When will she be let out?" Macie asked.

Jacob just smiled. "She will only be in the cell until after dinner. Hopefully, she will learn her lesson so harsher punishment will not be necessary. I will allow you to visit her after we eat so you will also understand what can happen if you do not do what you are told. I will have very little patience with you from here on out."

Macie and I sat quietly and didn't even speak during lunch. The chicken strips tasted bland, and they wouldn't give us ranch dressing to dip them in, so we just ate in silence. Reese came by a little while before we were finished eating to give us each a lanyard with a card and a key. "The card is for getting into your room and taking showers. The key is for your locker where all your belongings are. I would highly recommend taking very little back to your room with you because the sleeping quarters are small and very little will fit in there besides the beds. Also, you will become very unpopular with your roommates if you keep unnecessary stuff there. If you have any questions or need help with anything, I'm usually in here or in the gym. Oh, about the gym—please use it anytime you like but be courteous to others or your time will be restricted. Do you have any questions?" She paused. "If not, then I hope you enjoy your trip." She moved on to the next table, and I couldn't help but wonder why we would need a card for showers.

As soon as I finished eating, I asked if we could go see Miranda. Jacob motioned to Matt, the security guard and asked him to take us to see her. Matt walked toward the crew quarters where we went through a door and down a short hallway. We stopped in front of a door with a small metal slide in it—a slide large enough for a tray of food. The guard unlatched it and slid it to the side so we could see Miranda sitting in a chair next to a small mattress on the floor. As soon as she saw us, she ran over and grabbed our hands and wouldn't let go, all the while just crying her eyes out. She apologized over and over to the guard and asked if he would let her go. He said he couldn't or he would be in much more trouble than she was. He stepped back a few steps to give us some privacy while we tried to console our sister.

We mostly held her hands and told her how sorry we were she was in there. We told her that she would get out right after dinner. She said she was really hungry, and we looked over at Matt. He said he was given specific instructions not to feed her so she would learn a lesson. I thought about that for a few seconds and remembered that Jacob didn't give any instruction while we were with him, and he hadn't left the table all during the meal. I asked Matt about it, and he said, "Don't tell Jacob I told you about this, but he came to me before lunch and wanted me to watch for his signal to take Miranda away. He told me then not to feed her."

"Why would he do that?" I asked.

"I think he wanted to teach all of you a lesson and knew Miranda would give him that opportunity."

I looked over at Miranda and her tears had dried up. I could see her eyes burning with anger and hatred. Good thing Jacob wasn't here or Miranda might have done or said something that would have kept her confined for the whole trip.

"Miranda." She just stared at Matt, so I said her name again and she finally looked at me. "Miranda, I understand how angry you are, but you can't take it out on Jacob when you get out or you will spend the whole trip in this room. Do you want that?"

Miranda looked down. "No, I don't want that, but Jacob is going to pay for doing this to me." There was venom in her voice.

Matt interrupted us and said that our time was up and that Macie and I had to leave. We gave Miranda's hands one more squeeze and watched as Matt clicked the slide shut.

We emerged from the crew quarters and looked over at Jacob. He wore a smug smile. I wanted to go over and slap him, but I didn't want to end up where Miranda was, so I didn't say anything until he asked how she was.

"Fine, not that you would care," I said.

He just looked at me a few seconds and then said, "That is what will happen to anyone who disrespects me. Take heed of that." Macie and I didn't say anything and just stood there waiting for him to tell us what to do. "Do you think she has learned her lesson?" We were silent. "Answer me or I will let her stay there the whole trip." We nodded. "I certainly hope so because there are other punishments at my disposal. Matt, please release her so she will be able to watch the presentation." Matt did as he was told and left.

A few minutes later, we saw Miranda come through the door with Matt. Macie and I got up and ran over to her to give her a big hug. She barely hugged back and just glared at Jacob. I grabbed her face and forced it to look at me instead of him. Her neck muscles fought my hands, but I slowly won the battle. When we were eye to eye, I leaned my head to hers and whispered, "Miranda, I am begging you, please don't do anything to make Jacob mad. He has the power here and seems intent on showing us he can use it. He will use any excuse he can to put you away for the whole trip, and he threatened harsher punishments if necessary. Please just take a deep breath and let it all go until this trip is over. Who ever thought your patience with Pat and William would ever create a situation where you and Macie could get them back? Just be patient and the opportunity will present itself. Jacob, it seems, has the power of life and death over us right now, so don't provoke him into using it."

Miranda's eyes started to water and tears rolled down her cheeks. "I just hate him so much. I want to rip his eyes out."

"Miranda, channel that hate into something good—or at least productive. If Jacob sees you reacting to things he says and does, then he gets what he wants. He's on a power trip, so don't react to the things he says and does."

Miranda stopped crying and closed her eyes for a few seconds. When she opened them, I could see that she had changed her attitude and wouldn't give Jacob any more problems.

We leaned away from each other and walked over to where Jacob was sitting. "Hey Miranda, did you enjoy your alone time?" he asked cruelly.

Miranda looked him square in the eyes and said, "I am sorry I was disrespectful to you. It will not happen again."

Jacob was shocked because he had been trying to provoke her. I almost started laughing but thought better of it when Jacob tensed. "I'm glad you learned your lesson. Don't let it happen again."

Miranda smiled "Yes, sir."

I could tell Jacob was surprised by her new attitude but wary of it continuing. "All of you sit down, the presentation will start shortly." A few minutes later, the lights dimmed and a spotlight lit up Reese on the other side of the room.

CHAPTER 23

Reese was standing on a makeshift platform with a microphone in her hand. She put it up to her mouth. "Hello again. I hope everyone is having a pleasant trip so far. Before we get into the movie, I would like to introduce a dignitary we have on this flight. Everyone, please give a warm welcome to Jacob Verndari. He is the new governor of Callisto." Everyone started clapping for him as he stood and waved. The look on his face was certainly not one of a humble person but of someone who had come into power and was going to enjoy using it. I did notice that Miranda's hands kept missing each other when she was trying to clap for Jacob. I snickered a bit and looked over to see Macie doing the same thing. I did more of a golf clap that didn't make any sound.

Jacob finally sat down and Reese continued. "The presentations on the space station went into a lot more detail than I am going to, but I did want to review some of the important points that were covered. Most of you probably already know the history of your new home, Europa. Did you know that the people living there refer to the moon as *AARDE*? AARDE means Earth in Dutch. Pieter Schuyler was one of the first settlers and coined the name. By now you are probably aware that Galileo Galilei discovered it on January 8, 1610, and it was named after Europa, a Phoenician noblewoman in Greek mythology.

"It is slightly smaller than Earth's moon. Hopefully, you paid attention when they talked about how it became habitable for humans. I am going to focus more on the present and future of Aarde. Aarde has about as much land as Africa but with a chunk about the size of Australia separated off as an island." She pointed to a map on the wall. Ganymede was off by itself, completely surrounded by water, and the main continent went from pole to pole with the upper third called IO, the middle portion Callisto, and the bottom third called Thebe. Jacob was going to be governor of one-quarter of Aarde. Reese continued. "There are about twenty thousand people so far. Almost all have come by spaceship. Very few have been born there since the mining began.

"Congratulations, ladies! In another month, you will be married. As soon as you stepped foot on this ship, you committed yourselves to marrying when you get to Aarde." I looked around the room and saw smiles and grins on some of the men's and women's faces. I guess they saw a big paycheck in their future.

I looked over at Jacob and wondered why he was smiling so big. It wasn't like he was going to get anything out of it unless he was one of the discoverers, which I doubted. I leaned over to him and whispered, "Are any of the women here yours?" He looked at me and held up three fingers. I was shocked because I'd had no idea. I hadn't seen him so much as talk to any of the women.

Jacob continued to look at me as I turned back to the presentation. I looked over at the women and wondered which ones were Jacob's when it hit me. He couldn't mean the three were us, could he? I turned to look at him, and he was still staring at me as I leaned over again and whispered, "You don't mean *us*, do you?" A big grin spread across his face, and he turned away from me to look back at Reese. I sat there and stared at him for a few seconds. Then I turned away from him and bowed my head, starting to tear up. Miranda looked over at me and asked what was wrong. I was starting to shake as I thought about what was going to happen to us, so instead of answering her, I got up and walked out of the room. She followed me out. As soon as the door shut, I hugged her and put my head on her shoulder and burst out crying. She held me there for a few seconds and then guided me toward the bathroom.

In the bathroom, I went over to the sink and splashed some water on my face to clean up a bit. Miranda just kept staring at me, waiting for me to tell her what was wrong. After I had dried off my face with a paper towel, I said in a very shaky voice, "Jacob is going to sell us." Miranda stared at me while I continued. I started to cry again. "He is going to sell each of us to the highest bidder. We might never see each other again. A few minutes ago, I asked Jacob jokingly if he was one of the discoverers and had women to be auctioned off. He held up three fingers, so I asked him if the three were us, and he just smiled and turned away from me. We are going to be sold like cows to the highest bidder, married, and forced to move to God only knows where."

"They can't do that—we're not adults," Miranda said.

"What do you think Jacob *cannot* do? He is the governor and our legal guardian. You heard Reese say Aarde is like the Wild West. The women will be like property." I could see the anger rising in her face and her fists clenching. I was going to have to talk her down very quickly or there was no telling what she might do. "Miranda! Miranda! You have to calm down. You can't do anything right now or you will be thrown into the room again—or Jacob will come up with something worse. Please calm down! We need to figure out what to do. There is very little we can do on the trip, but we can come up with a plan before we arrive."

Miranda just burst into tears of frustration. "I am going to hurt him bad for all he has done to us."

I pulled her into a hug, and we both cried. I wasn't sure how long we stood there hugging and crying, but eventually Macie came in and asked why we'd left. I saw Miranda was about to tell her and shook my head, so she just said that we were homesick and were crying it out. Macie looked at both of us and knew there was more than we were saying, but she didn't question us further because some of the other women came in.

As they passed by, they looked at us with disgust. I now knew why they were so mean to us. We were competition. They had chosen this life, but we hadn't. It just wasn't fair. Miranda was about to say something to them when I grabbed her arm and said, "Don't, it won't help us." She looked at me in agreement, and the three of us left the bathroom. We didn't talk as we walked to the locker room. We tried our keys in the lockers below our names and opened them. There we saw our duffel bags. I thought that the bag was going to be heavy when I pulled it out, but it felt about heavy as a grocery bag full of groceries. This low gravity was nice. Looking through my things brought back memories of our shopping trip and all the pretty clothes. I was sure that all of the clothes were a wrinkled mess by then, but it was nice to see something familiar. "Why don't we get our shorts and tennis shoes on and go running?" I suggested.

Macie looked at us and said, "I guess there isn't anything else to do."

I dug around in my bag, finding a white shirt, red shorts, red Nike running shoes, some socks, and a sports bra. I looked over at Miranda, and she was half dressed. Macie had dumped her whole bag on the floor and was searching through the pile. I asked what she was looking for.

"My blue shorts. I know they're in here somewhere. Ah ha! I found them!" After a few minutes, we were changed and ready to go, but we had to help Macie stuff her things back into her bag. When we had all the bags back in our lockers, we locked them and left.

When we arrived at the gym, there were a few guys working out with weights. With the low gravity, I wondered how much they could lift. I would pay attention to that later, but right now I was ready to run. All three of us started running, but I could tell Macie wouldn't last long. She just didn't enjoy it the way Miranda and I did. It was a new experience to run like you were on a roller coaster loop. We all took longer strides with the low gravity and were turning the laps at a pretty good pace. Miranda said she was getting bored running so slow, so she started running faster. I picked up my pace to keep up with her. We went way ahead of Macie, and after we had lapped her a few times, Macie stopped to rest and watch. She knew she was in for a show because of how competitive Miranda and I were. Miranda was going faster each lap. I hadn't seen her focus so hard in a long time. I could run a long distance, but not at the pace Miranda was keeping, so it took only a few more laps before I slowed down and Miranda ran on ahead of me by herself.

She ran like something inside was pushing her, probably her hatred of Jacob. I ran a few cool-down laps and then sat down next to Macie. I was sweating a lot and pretty tired. Miranda was taking longer and longer strides as she ran. She was running a whole lot faster than I had ever imagined she could. The few men who were working out stopped what they were doing to watch her run. Miranda was too focused on her running to even notice the audience she was gathering. On one of her laps, I thought I saw just a little sparkle in her eyes as she passed by. I wasn't sure what it meant until she began to increase her stride to jump instead of just run. It reminded me of the men bouncing on the moon when they walked. Before long, Miranda's steps were thirty to forty feet between. It sent her around the track even faster and was quite a sight to see.

Never to miss an opportunity to show off, Macie got up and began to run again. Her steps weren't as big as Miranda's, but she got the hang of it after a few tries and was making good time. It seemed like Miranda was flying around the track rather than running, and she actually jumped over Macie just as Macie was doing the push for her step. It surprised Macie so much that she got off balance, and her step actually turned into a flip. It was either from being lucky or extremely coordinated that Macie managed to land on her feet and keep running. Miranda saw what Macie had done and wasn't about to be outdone by her little sister, so she started doing a flip every few steps and then started doing double flips and twists, landing after each one and continuing to run. Macie was not as powerful as Miranda, but she started doing the flips and twists, too. All that playing we did in Zero Grav on the space station must have really helped our coordination.

I was too self-conscious to start running again because of the audience. Miranda and Macie enjoyed performing too much to stop—it looked like they were going to collapse from exhaustion. When they did stop, both were huffing and puffing and barely able to speak, but they had huge smiles on their faces. The men watching just started clapping, telling them how impressive they were to watch. Miranda blushed with the compliment, but Macie smiled even bigger and actually took a bow.

Miranda said, "That was so much fun. I think after some more practice, I could jump clear across the ship."

I threw them a towel to dry off with, and we walked back to the locker room to take a shower. There was a sign in the shower stall that said, "You have five minutes to shower twice a day. The water will start as soon as you pass your card over the card reader. The water will stop after exactly five minutes." I had never thought about how much time it took to take a shower. I got everything set up and ready before I swiped my card over the reader. I sure didn't want to have shampoo in my hair when it stopped. It turned out that five minutes was just about right if you didn't dilly-dally around. I was done rinsing my hair and just standing and enjoying the water when it turned off. Jacob was apparently wrong about us only getting to take sponge baths on the trip.

As I was drying off and stepping out of the shower, I heard Macie yell, "Noooo! I am *not* done yet!" I turned around to see her come stomping out of the shower with suds still in her hair, looking quite mad. Miranda was already digging through her duffel bag, looking for something to wear. She always took quick showers by only conditioning her hair.

Macie cried, "What am I going to do now?"

Miranda just laughed and said, "There's always the sink."

Macie frowned but went over and started to rinse her hair out in the sink. But it was a faucet that turned off after ten seconds. She said, "Exactly how am I supposed to rinse it out in ten seconds?"

Miranda, still laughing, went over and kept pushing the faucet every few seconds to allow Macie to rinse her hair. The water in the faucet was on the cold side, so I don't think Macie enjoyed it very much.

CHAPTER 24

We all decided to wear our sundresses to dinner because it was plenty warm on the ship and we were tired of wearing the same old clothes we had been issued on the space station. It had been a long time since we had dressed up at all. Miranda went along with wearing the dress, but she wasn't real happy about it. I hadn't even remembered that she had bought a dress when we went shopping, but it was on the list, so she must have. She was always so self-conscious about dressing up. As I was searching through my duffel bag, I pulled out the formal dress I had bought, wondering at the time when I would ever get a chance to wear it. I dug out all of my makeup, and I started getting ready.

Before we were taken from our home, Macie had been just starting to learn how to put on makeup. Miranda had never had an interest, so she very seldom wore any makeup at all. She didn't want put any on, but Macie and I were able to talk her into wearing some this time since we were going to do the same. She looked pretty without makeup, but just the bit that I put on her really made her hazel eyes look beautiful. Macie had light blue eyes, so the makeup she wore made her eyes' shade of blue change depending on the lighting in the room and made her look a few years older. I got my brown eyes from my grandfather and was complimented quite often on how pretty they were. By the time we finished getting ready, we all looked very pretty and were ready make an appearance outside in the sun. What a waste that we were stuck on the ship with just fluorescent lighting.

As we were stepping out of the locker room, a bunch of the women on the ship were just entering. They all looked at us, and then Portia said, "What do you think this is, the Greek Islands? This is just a dirty old ship—I don't know why you all dressed up." All of them laughed at what she had said and followed her into the locker room. I saw Macie and Miranda's faces go from happy to about to cry. My feelings were hurt the same as theirs. We decided to go to our room for a while to decompress before dinner. Since all the women were in the locker room, we knew we would have it to ourselves for a while.

After sitting in our room for a few minutes, Miranda said, "As soon as those mean women get out of the locker room, I am going to go change."

I said, "Please don't, Miranda. If you change, we'll feel uncomfortable in our dresses, and we will want to change, too. We all look nice, and if it irritates those women, then so much the better."

Miranda looked up at me and smiled, enjoying the thought that she could get them back by looking good, but I could tell she didn't really want to wear the dress anymore.

Macie said, "Please Miranda, it's been so long since we got to wear anything nice." Miranda nodded her head, indicating she wouldn't change clothes.

I didn't want to make Macie's evening worse, but we had to tell her about what Jacob was planning to do with us when we arrived on Aarde. When I told her we were going to be sold, she was very surprised and said, "I'm too young to get married."

I told her, "We're all too young to get married, but that's what Jacob is planning to do with us. I don't think there is anything we can do about it. Did you see how security did exactly what Jacob told them to do? We certainly can't count on them for any help. We'll have to wait until we get there to try and escape. One way or another, we're not going to let them separate us. Miranda and I talked about it earlier and came to the conclusion that we need to be good passengers and not cause any trouble. If we cause trouble, then they'll watch us closer. Miranda, that especially means you!" Miranda just snickered because she knew it would be difficult not to talk back to Jacob. "Jacob said he would tell us about our future, so hopefully we can get enough information from him to plan an escape." Miranda and Macie nodded in agreement.

It was just about time for dinner. We got up and were just about to leave the room when the gaggle of women came out of the locker room, heading toward us. Every one of them was wearing a dress. Miranda burst out laughing and said, "Ladies, why are you wearing dresses if it is just a dirty ship?"

They gave us nasty looks but didn't say a word as they walked away. We didn't want to walk in with them, so we went around to the other side of the locker room to enter the dining area from a different door. Before we entered, we looked through the glass window in the door and saw that everyone was seated and eating their salads. The women in dresses were flirting with the men nearby. The men were dressed nicely in shirts and dress pants, but the only man wearing a suit was Jacob. We were all nervous because we were late and would have to walk across the entire room to sit with Jacob.

Hunger overcame our nervousness, so we opened the door. As soon as we passed through the doorway, everyone—including the women—stopped eating and just stared at us as we walked to Jacob's table. When we were almost there, three young men seated at the table next to us got up and held our chairs for us. I couldn't ever remember anyone holding a chair for me, and I was completely embarrassed. Glancing around, I noticed that all of the men in the room were standing. The man closest to me was holding a chair out, saying, "Please sit." I wasn't sure what to do, so I sat, and he helped me scoot my chair close to the table. The other men did the same for Miranda and Macie. We were all too shocked to say anything other than "thank you" to them. As soon as we were settled in our seats, the men sat and resumed their meals.

Miranda laughed and told me to have a look at Portia and the other women. I saw every one of them staring at us with what would best be described as pure hatred in their eyes, especially Portia. The man next to her said something and put his hand out to calm her down. She just batted it down and glared at him. I would have started laughing but was afraid it would make her hate us even more. This made me realize it was going to be a very long trip. I was slowly coming to the realization that the other women saw us as competition for husbands. We needed to stay away from them as much as possible to avoid getting into trouble.

When I turned around to face the table, I looked at Jacob. He had an amused look on his face. He said, "That was quite the entrance the three of you made." We all looked at him, perplexed, wondering why he would say something like that.

Macie was all smiles. "We didn't do it on purpose," she said.

"I get the feeling those women don't like competition."

I said, "Who's competing?"

He just laughed and said, "All of you! You're competing for husbands!"

All three of us said, "What?" We didn't know what he meant.

Macie followed up with "I'm way too young to get married." Miranda just glared at Jacob instead of speaking. I was glad she held her tongue or she might have been put in solitary again.

"Why would we be looking for husbands?" I asked. "You won't even tell us our future. Are you going to sell us in The Proposal like all these other women? Tell us, Jacob—or should I call you Governor? We're tired of your games, and we want to know what you're going to do with us." My voice was starting to rise in pitch, and I was near tears as I was speaking. I saw Jacob tense up.

"Keep your voice down or you'll be where Miranda was earlier today," he said. I was about to yell at him when he put his hand up and said, "I will tell you this much—I haven't completely decided what I'm going to do with the three of you. You're quite young, but on a world like Europa, that can be of great value." His body relaxed, and he smiled and said, "All in due time, ladies. Please, now let us all eat in peace."

I glanced over, and I saw that Miranda was about to come out of her seat. I put a hand on her arm and said quietly, "Please, Miranda, it won't do any good." She tensed up, looked over at

Jacob, who was watching her, and then relaxed and sat down with a smile of satisfaction on her face. I was at a loss as to how she got control of herself so quickly, but I was thankful that she did and even more surprised that she had managed a smile. We settled down and ate in silence. I thought it was interesting that all of the wait staff referred to Jacob as Governor when addressing him. He sure did enjoy the stroking of his ego.

Jacob had a steak while the rest of us had some sort of stew of meat, potatoes, and vegetables. It tasted good and was very filling. Miranda asked for a second helping, but the waitress said it wasn't possible because they had to conserve food for the whole trip. Macie only ate the meat and gave the rest of her stew to Miranda. No wonder Miranda was hungry—she'd been locked up and hadn't gotten a lunch.

When dinner was finished, Jacob told us, "Please be here promptly for breakfast in the morning or I will tell the staff that you would prefer to skip your meal." We didn't say anything in response but had started to scoot away from the table when those three young men at the next table rushed over and helped us with our chairs and offered their hands to help us get up. We felt uncomfortable grabbing their hands but managed to pull ourselves up without falling, giving them polite thank yous."

The men said, "You're welcome, ladies. We are at your service," as they gave slight bows. We didn't know what to do, so we started walking toward the door.

As we walked by each table on our way out, all the men said, "Good evening, ladies." All three of us blushed each time it happened. We finally made it out of the room.

The first thing Miranda said was, "I am not ever wearing a dress on this trip again." All three of us laughed as we walked back to our room. When we got there, we were relieved that Portia and her gang weren't there.

After hanging out for a while, we decided to get into our pajamas because we were getting sleepy, so we went to the locker room and changed. When we got back to the room, Macie turned on the light. Immediately, Huxley yelled, "Turn it off! Can't you tell we're trying to sleep?" Emily and Huxley were lying in the two bottom bunks on the left side while Portia and Blaise were on the right.

Macie stood there a few seconds, not sure what to do, when Portia spoke up and said, "Are you going to turn it off, or do I need to get out of bed and make you?"

I looked over at Macie and she was about to cry, so I said, "Macie, go ahead and turn it off. We can find our way in the dark."

Before she had a chance to turn it off, Miranda stepped between her and Portia and said to Portia, "I'd like to see you try it!"

Before any of them reacted, I put my hand on Miranda and told her, "They aren't worth it. We don't want to get into any trouble."

Emily spoke up, laughing, and said "Yeah, we heard what happened when you got into trouble earlier. Poor little girl...all by herself! Get in trouble again and you might end up there for the entire trip. The Governor doesn't seem to like you, so you'll probably end up there anyway."

Miranda turned to Emily and took a step toward her and then stopped. I gently pressed on her arm and felt her relax. Miranda didn't say anything more but headed to the right side and started climbing the ladder to the top bunk. As she was climbing past Portia, who was in the second from the bottom bunk, she grabbed Portia's blanket and threw it to the floor.

Portia just stared at Miranda, a shocked look on her face. Miranda snickered to herself and continued her climb to the top bunk and lay down. Portia didn't say anything, but she hopped out of her bed, retrieved her blanket, and climbed back in. I nodded to Macie to turn off the light and asked her which bed she wanted. She told me the top one on the left side, and I nodded okay while she flipped off the light and I followed her to the ladder on the left side. It wasn't completely dark because of some indirect lighting near the ceiling. Macie climbed up first to the top one, and I followed her to the third one.

After everyone was settled and it was quiet for a few minutes, Portia spoke up and said, "You do realize, don't you, that everyone was laughing at you after you left. You all made quite a spectacle of yourselves."

I thought about saying something but realized it would just cause more problems, so I bit my tongue and tried to go to sleep. I saw Macie's bed shaking a little and could hear her crying. I don't think anyone else could tell, so I stood on the edge of my bunk in order to lean over hers and gave her a hug, saying quietly, "Don't think about what they say. They're just jealous of how beautiful you were tonight."

Macie sniffled a bit, wrapped her arms around me, gave me a big hug, and said, "Thank you, Madison. I love you." I teared up a little and lay back down on my bed.

It was quiet for a few minutes, and then I heard a thud on the ground. I looked over and saw a shadow leaning over Portia's bed and heard what sounded like a muffled scream and then complete silence as the shadow climbed up into the top bunk. I asked Miranda about it the next day, but all she would say was that she didn't think Portia would be mean to us anymore.

It took me quite a while to get to sleep that night. There was too much to worry about. I only refer to it as night because it was the time we were supposed to sleep. The sun was always shining in space once we left the shadow of Earth. Miranda seemed to be calmer, but if she talked back to Jacob or didn't do what he said, she could find herself in solitary for the whole trip—or worse. I didn't want to find out what they meant by worse than solitary.

I wasn't really too worried about Macie because she was very sensitive and would normally just go along to get along, but I was worried about all these women hating us because they deemed us competition for The Proposal. I had no idea what were we going to do about that. The whole idea of bidding for women scared the heck out of me. Was Jacob really going to sell us off? He appeared to have a lot of power as the governor, and it seemed he was going to get paid for us being part of The Proposal. We had to escape, but I didn't know how. We certainly couldn't escape on the ship. And Aarde was a world we knew nothing about, so where would we go even if we did manage to escape?

CHAPTER 25

I awoke the next morning to Macie jostling me and saying we needed to get up. "Jacob said we will not get to eat breakfast if we're late."

I slowly rolled over to look at her. "How much time do we have?"

"About fifteen minutes. Miranda, your five minutes is up."

I sat up and looked around the room. Fortunately for us the other women were already gone. I climbed down from my bunk at about the same time as Miranda. We hurried to the locker room and changed into shorts, tee shirts, and running shoes. We made it to the dining room and sat down with Jacob just as Rachael, our waitress, was pouring coffee for him. I ended up sitting next to Jacob with Macie on his other side. Miranda was as far away from him as she could get on the other side of Macie. Jacob smirked and asked, "Can you three ever be anywhere early?" We all glanced over at him as Rachael asked if we would like cereal or oatmeal.

Miranda said, "Can I have French toast with some bacon?"

Rachael shook her head. "Sorry, we will only have eggs and bacon once a week. All the other days are either cereal or oatmeal." Miranda said.

"Okay then, I'll have cereal with no milk." Rachael looked at her strangely and listened as Macie and I said we would have cereal also. Jacob told her he would have an omelet.

Before any of us could question why he was able to have egg, Rachael said, "Very good, Governor." And that title explained his special treatment, so we all kept quiet.

As usual, we didn't say much while we ate, so I did a lot of looking around at the other people. It could have been my imagination, but it seemed like a lot of the men—especially the younger ones—were looking over at our table. Most would turn away when I met their eyes, but some would nod their head slightly and keep on looking. At first, it was a little disconcerting to look up and see the top of other people's heads, but I was slowly getting used to it. I happened to look up and saw a man look away very quickly but not quickly enough for me not to recognize him as the one who had blocked the door against William at the convenience store. And the boy that we'd met at Zero Grav was sitting next to him.

I was so shocked that I didn't move and kept staring until Jacob said, "Who are you staring at, Madison?"

It took a few seconds before I responded, "Those women don't like us, do they?" Lucky for me, there were women seated at the same table as the man and boy I recognized.

Jacob looked up and laughed, "I would imagine they wouldn't. They recognize you as competition."

"So are you putting just me up for The Proposal or will all three of us be sold?"

I could see the amusement on his face as he replied, "I haven't decided when the other two will participate. Miranda and Macie are quite young but would fetch a very good price. I might wait until they're fifteen. There have been girls younger than them who have participated, but they were born on Aarde. The actual wedding would not take place until they are fifteen."

I was speechless. He raised his hand, and three security personnel appeared. One stood behind each of us. I was only slightly aware of them and said, "So you and all the others have been lying to us this whole time about keeping us together. Not only will we not be together, but you're going to sell us. Now you have us on a ship, so we have nowhere to go to even try to escape."

Miranda and Macie were listening to our conversation now, and I turned just in time to see Miranda raise out of her seat and start to come around to where Jacob was seated, saying, "We'll see who gets sold." She had barely gotten out of her chair when the security guard behind her grabbed her shoulder to push her down. Miranda twisted away from him and continued to move around the table. The guard behind me turned toward Miranda to stop her. Miranda put some steam behind her steps and lowered her shoulder right into the guard's stomach. He went down hard on his butt. I had spun out of my chair, standing between her and Jacob. "Stop, Miranda! Stop!" I cried just as she reached me. I held out my hands to stop her. She plowed into me, and we went down with my arms tight around her. She was struggling against me while I spoke into her ear. "Miranda, stop. It won't do any good. All it'll do is get you sitting by yourself for the rest of the trip. If you hurt him, you might even get punished even more or put in jail when we get there."

She still struggled but not as much when I whispered very quickly in her ear, "Please stop, and I promise we will get him back once we get there. I just saw the man who helped us get away from the convenience store and the boy we saw on the space station. They'll help us. Just let this go—we'll get our revenge later."

Miranda stopped struggling. "You better be right," she said.

Both she and I got up, looked at Jacob, who hadn't even moved, and started to walk away. Jacob said, "Wait, I haven't finished with you two yet." We turned around, and he continued, "Sit down and finish your breakfast, and I will let the incident go this time. I know I shocked you with what I said, but you had told me that you wanted to know what the future held for you. Now you know. Apologize to the security guards and there will be no punishment. But make no mistake, if I get even an inkling that it might happen again, I will happily have you confined for the rest of the trip."

I moved and sat down while Miranda stood a few seconds and then apologized to the guards and sat down as well. I glanced around the room, and it was deathly silent while everyone stared at us. I blushed and hurried to finish my meal. It took about three minutes for us to finish eating, and then we got up to leave. As we walked away, Jacob said, "Don't forget to be on time— or you will not eat!" He always had to get in a jab. As we walked out, a lot of people stared at us, but we were beyond caring at that point.

While walking to our room, Macie said, "What was all that about? I didn't really understand what he was talking about."

I could tell Miranda was still fuming when she said, "Macie, did you not even listen? All three of us are going to be sold and married."

Macie stopped dead in her tracks and said, "I'm only thirteen—I'm too young to be married!"

Miranda said, "It's much worse than that...what if some old man buys you for his wife?" We kept walking and went into our room. Luckily for us, the other women were still eating, so we had the room to ourselves. Miranda was the last to enter, and she closed the door. "What are we going to do?" Miranda asked.

"Guess who I saw?" I asked. "The boy we talked to on the space station and the man who helped us escape when we were at the convenience store. Jacob almost caught me staring at them. They were right above our table in the dining room," Miranda chimed in "We need to be very careful not to get them caught; they might be our only hope when we get to Aarde. If they're able to help us, then great, but we can't count on them. Our lives are at stake. We need to find out as much about The Proposal as we can so we can make a plan to escape before we're married and they split us up." Macie and I agreed with Miranda.

Macie said, "I already know quite a bit about it but will ask Reese for more information. She seems to know more than some of these women, and we all know they wouldn't help us anyway."

I said, "We can't ask too many questions of Jacob or he might become suspicious and block us from escaping. We also need to make contact with either the man or the boy to see how—and if— they can help us. What do y'all want to do now? How about we go work out? We need to be in the best condition we can to escape." Macie and Miranda agreed, and we left our room, went to the locker room to change into workout clothes, and then walked to the gym.

When we arrived, there wasn't anyone there, so we hit the weight machines first and then ran. We got into a routine over the next few weeks of eating breakfast, resting a little while, working out, going to lunch, working out, resting before eating dinner, participating in some after dinner activity the ship provided, and then going to bed. I can't say that we were perfect angels, but we tried to keep our noses clean and didn't do anything to cause us to be put in solitary confinement. We tried to avoid our roommates as much as we could, and I think they did the same. The only time we were together was when we all went to bed. Miranda developed quite a reputation among the gym-goers for her strength and speed. I think they were a bit wary of her temper, too, after she'd tried to attack Jacob.

We tried to talk to Reese as much as we could about The Proposal. She told us a lot more about the parties and the week leading up to the bidding. She felt sorry for us, knowing that we were going to be part of it, but there was nothing she could do. She told us Jacob was a very powerful man on the ship and would be even more powerful on Aarde. He would have near complete power once he arrived. He would control the government and security. "You would be best served by making the most of your situation and not fighting it because you are guaranteed to lose. Women have very few rights on Aarde," she told us.

We learned a lot from Reese but wouldn't be able to count on her for any help. During the week, there were several possible opportunities that might have provided escape but without knowing where to go after we escaped, what was the point? I saw the man who had helped us and the boy we'd met every once in a while but wasn't able to talk to them because there were always other people around. I finally got an opportunity to talk about five days before we were supposed to arrive at Aarde.

I wasn't feeling too well at dinner one night and went back to the room to rest, and the man appeared at my room the same time that I did. He ducked in and told me to hurry inside. He then shut the door and said, "We only have a few minutes. I know you have a million questions, but let me talk first." I sat down on the bed on the right side of the room while he continued, "Sorry I haven't spoken to you on this trip, but it would be very dangerous if we were caught together. Jacob has enough power to question whomever he wants, and he has the law behind him. I'm sure I wouldn't talk, but my son might, so we could not take the chance. I'm only here to remind you to be very careful and to just go along with whatever Jacob has planned for you. You do know that all three of you are going to be sold in The Proposal, right?"

I nodded yes.

"Good, at least he let you know that much."

I looked at him questioningly and asked, "Is there more that I need to know?"

He answered, "Aarde is a very new world with very few people to enforce the limited number of laws that exist. Those who have power can do pretty much whatever they want. I have knowledge of some of Jacob's plans but not how he will implement them. I need to leave before someone sees me talking to you. I doubt we will talk again until we arrive on Aarde, so you will just have to trust me."

I was all flustered as he got up to leave. He was about to open the door when I asked, "What is your name?"

He turned around and looked at me. "It is too dangerous to tell you." And then he opened the door and walked out.

I just sat there, looking at the doorway, until I heard someone outside. It turned out it was Emily by herself. I started to get up to leave when she said, "Please wait, Madison." I was startled that she even acknowledged me at all. "I know we haven't been nice to you, but we didn't know you were brought here against your will." I just stared at her has she continued, "We were talking to some of the crew who said they heard Jacob boasting about how much he was going to get for you three. He said that he was just supposed to be your guardian until all of you were eighteen. But after he left Earth, he decided to be a finder instead of a guardian. He wanted to make as much money off of you as he could. He seems to be a very greedy person."

I nodded my head in agreement and said, "Thanks for telling me all this, but please don't let Jacob know that you talked to me about it. He expressly prohibited us from talking to or becoming friends with anyone on the trip." Emily looked puzzled and asked why he would do that. "There is a lot more to our being here than I am able to tell you," I explained. "Maybe after we arrive, it won't matter, but for now, I'm too afraid to cross him. Please don't treat us any different for the rest of the trip because Jacob is keeping a close eye on us and who we talk to."

Emily said, "That shouldn't be a problem for most of the girls, but I'm sorry it had to be this way." Emily gave me a hug and left me standing there, shocked. I almost started to cry because it had been so long since someone other than my sisters had hugged me and acted like they cared.

CHAPTER 26

When we were close enough to see Mars, Reese told us to look out the window. It wasn't very interesting because we so far away. It only looked to be about half the size of Earth's moon. It was also difficult to look out the windows because we were rotating around to give us some gravity. The only places that weren't rotating were the observation areas in the front and back of the ship. They only held about ten people at a time, so we weren't able to look for very long. I had never really cared about the stars and planets, so I had spent very little time visiting the observation area. Macie, on the other hand, was fascinated by all that happened in space and spent quite a bit of her time watching the stars and talking to the crew about them.

About seven or eight days before we arrived, Macie came to find Miranda and me in the gym working out. She was so excited she could hardly talk. She said, "You guys have to come and look—you can see Jupiter!"

I just looked at her and said, "Okay, we'll be there after we finish working out and shower."

When we finally arrived at the observation room in the front of the ship, Macie pointed and said, "That is Jupiter. Europa is on the other side of it right now."

It wasn't any bigger than Mars was when we had passed it, so I said, "Big whoop, Macie. Come get me when it's bigger than a star billions of miles away," and turned to leave. Macie looked so disappointed that I didn't share her enthusiasm, staring at the planet again as I left.

A few more days passed, and all Macie could talk about was how big Jupiter was getting. She told us that one of the crew had pointed out Europa to her, so she was able to identify it after that. She also wanted Miranda and me to come up to see it. Miranda joked about going up with her, but neither one of us wanted to.

After many days of Macie bugging us, we finally gave in and went. What we saw was remarkable.

When we went into the observation room, Macie closed the door so the room was completely dark. I asked Macie what the big deal was, and she said "Jacques, please open the curtain." As he did, I saw that only Macie, Miranda, Jacques, and I were in the room. As the curtain slowly pulled back from the viewing window, I took a step back. I was speechless because the view was indescribable. Jupiter almost filled the entire window. The orange, blue, and white swirling stripes were mesmerizing. I glanced over at Miranda, and she was as enchanted as I was. Macie had a huge grin on her face as she watched our reactions. After a couple minutes of us just staring out the window, she pointed out two of the moons on our side of Jupiter. Macie told us that one was Europa, and the other one was IO. They looked like tiny little balls next to a huge one.

Macie was so excited she was practically jumping up and down. She told us it takes about three and a half days for Europa to orbit Jupiter, so the next time we saw it, we will be less than a day from being there. I enjoyed the view, but all I could think of was that we were that much closer to being sold. Miranda didn't say anything, but I saw the tears rolling down her cheek, so I went to her, put my arm around her, and said, "It'll be all right." She looked at me and said, "It *won't* be all right, and you know it," and shrugged off my arm and left the room.

Macie started to go after her, but I caught her arm. "Let her go," I said. "She just needs some time to calm down. I do hope that she doesn't run into Jacob because there's no telling what she might do when she's in that kind of mood. Macie, thank you for forcing us to come up here—the view is extraordinary."

Macie and I stayed there a little while longer and went back as often as we could. Each time we returned, there was a crowd, so it was difficult to get in to see. We weren't able to talk Miranda into going back. She said it reminded her of all that we would never see and experience again on Earth. I understood her feelings, but the sight of Jupiter kept drawing me back to the viewing room. When we saw Europa again a couple of days later, it was much bigger and took up about one-fourth of the viewing window. The backdrop of Europa was like a beautiful moving picture that was Jupiter. It was quite breathtaking. As we approached, Europa filled up more and more of the viewing window. Its colors were similar to Earth's with lots of blue and brown with swirling white clouds. It was quite beautiful to behold. Europa had only two continents, compared to seven on Earth.

It became even more difficult to get into the observation room because everyone wanted to see their new home. Macie never had a problem because of her friendship with Jacques, so when I was with her, I didn't, either. We ended up parked in orbit next to two huge cables that went from outer space down to the ground. Jacques had told Macie that the cable was how everything transported from the ground to space and vice versa. She said it was made of carbon nanotubes—like I knew what that was. There were two elevators attached to the cable for carrying people and supplies. Jacques had also told her that the cable worked on Europa because of less gravity. The cable wouldn't be strong enough to work back on Earth because of the planet's stronger gravity.

The excitement on the ship had been growing, and everyone was even more anxious once we were parked in orbit. It was excruciating having to wait to take the elevator down. We had been told to be sure everything was packed in our bags—whatever wasn't would be left behind. We were also told to wait in the dining area until it was our turn to leave. As we were waiting, Reese got the microphone and said, "Welcome to Aarde! On behalf of the crew, I would like to thank you for a very pleasant and uneventful trip, and we wish you the best in your new life. A couple things before we disembark. The elevators can only hold about twenty-five people at a time, so please be patient and wait for your group to be called. It takes a little less than two hours to reach the surface, and there are four elevators, so you can do the math and figure out when your group will go."

I heard some grumbling from some of the people I assumed were to be in the last groups as Reese continued. "Really, you have the rest of your lives to experience Europa, surely you can manage waiting a few more hours. I hope you all have everything packed. Otherwise, the crew will either claim it or send it into space! Another reminder is that your belongings will be delivered to your hotel room sometime in the next few days. You will have the room for one week and will then have to vacate because the next ship will be here. As you might have noticed, the tables and chairs are buckled to the floor again. For us to connect to the elevator, the ship cannot be rotating. When we stop rotating, guess what happens? Zero gravity! So please hold on to something while the others disembark."

I was taking one last look around and saw Macie and Miranda whispering to each other, so I went over to see what they were talking about. Fortunately, Jacob was not within earshot of what we were saying. As I got close, I heard Macie whisper, "I don't think I can do that."

Miranda asked, "Does it matter? It's our last time in zero gravity. Madison, do you want to do it with us?"

Knowing Miranda and Macie's imagination, we would either put on quite a show and get in trouble or be embarrassed and get in trouble. I thought, what the heck. "Sure, I'm game."

Miranda said, "Even better! It will be even more fun with three."

The three of us were discussing it when Reese came by and whispered, "What are you three going to do?" We all shook our heads, mumbling it was nothing, but Reese knew better and said, "Come on, spill it! I know you three are planning a big finale. I promise I won't tell if you let me join you."

We were all shocked that she would want to participate, and Miranda said, "Why not?"

Just then Reese's microphone beeped and she flipped the button on it, saying, "Everyone, we have five minutes until the rotation stops and the first group of twenty-five disembarks. Group one, please move toward the door." We were in group one and moved over toward the door but made sure we were in the back of the line. I did notice that Jacob was in the front of the line so he would be first in the elevator.

The rotation of the ship slowed and stopped. It felt strange to be weightless again. About a minute after we stopped, we heard a clang and a whoosh near the door. The elevator was attached to the ship, and the door opened. A man peeked through the open door and waved to everyone. Then Jacob followed him into the elevator using the straps on the wall for balance in the weightless environment. As soon as he disappeared, I looked over at Macie and Miranda and nodded.

We all bent our knees and pushed off at different angles to the other side of the room—Miranda went straight, Macie went left, and I went right. Everyone in the room turned to watch, even the ones that were in the first group slowly making their way into the elevator. As Miranda flew, she acted like a dive-bombing plane, her arms spread wide and her legs straight with toes pointed. Right before she landed, she did a flip to land on her feet. Macie flew like someone doing cartwheels and ended up landing on her hands. She looked a bit dizzy as she put her feet down. I flew with my hands at my side and did a flip to land on my feet. About one-third of the first group was on the elevator by this time.

Before we kicked off again, Reese gave an easy push off from near Miranda and was slowly floating across the room when all three of us kicked off right at her. We all arrived to her at the same time, grabbing her in a bear hug as we continued to the other side. After we had landed, we all gave her a squeeze, and she gave an easy push to float into the center of the room. By then, all but a couple of people from the first group were in the elevator. Macie pushed off at an angle. Miranda pushed off to a different angle at about the same time Macie hit the floor and pushed off toward

Reese, who was still floating in the center. I pushed off just before Miranda landed, and Macie was near Reese.

I saw Macie hold out her hand, and Reese grasped it. Reese held on to Macie as they twisted in the air, letting go just in time to send Macie toward the open door. The last person had gone through just before Macie floated through and landed just inside the elevator. Miranda had kicked off just as Reese let go of Macie. Reese held onto Miranda and sent her toward the door. As Miranda floated toward the door, she turned around so she was facing the room, waving as she went through. I saw Macie catch her just as she landed. I kicked off the floor, and Reese directed me to the door as well. I decided to float upside down, facing the room and waving goodbye to the people in the ship. I was almost to the door when I saw Reese start clapping with tears in her eyes.

The rest of the room started clapping loudly just as the back of my feet hit the top of the door that flipped me to land on my feet next to Miranda and Macie. The last thing we saw as they closed the door was Reese floating in the air waving to us, and everyone in the room standing and clapping. Macie, Miranda, and I had very mixed feelings about leaving the ship. We immediately started our journey away from the ship toward Aarde. I saw the ship start to rotate again and was sad that we would never be in zero gravity again. I was really scared about what was going to happen next.

CHAPTER 27

As we started moving down, I looked over at Jacob. He was just smiling and shaking his head. I was expecting him to be furious, but then again we didn't give him any trouble getting on the elevator. I was very sad that Reese wasn't coming with us because she was so nice and really had become our friend. I know Macie was going to miss Jacques. She was always telling us what she learned from him about space and the ship. Miranda and I let her talk on and on about it but never really paid much attention.

The elevator we were in was about twenty feet by twenty feet and had smooth metal walls with lots of holes it. At just about eye level for me, there were shades that could be lifted up so you could see out the windows. The elevator operator introduced himself as Toby Halliday. He spoke with an accent I had never heard before. It sounded like a strange blend of Scottish and redneck. He was very friendly and talkative and was dressed like a bellman at a hotel in a bright red suit that seemed to fit his personality.

After his introduction, he said, "I would like to be the first to welcome all of you to Aarde, especially you, Governor Verndari. If you care to look out the windows once we are below the clouds, you will see the state of Callisto with water on the right and left of it. The state of IO is further to the north, and the state of Thebe is to the south. The boundaries between the states are major rivers that flow from the mountains to the sea. IO has the highest mountain range and an elevation similar to Alaska on Earth except with a very moderate temperature on the west coast. Callisto is the largest state with a varied climate similar to the United States. The state of Thebe has a climate similar to Hawaii except for a few weeks a year when it heats up like Saudi Arabia.

"The gravitational pull of Jupiter, the surrounding moons, and the sun affect the temperature and conditions on all of Aarde. The state of Ganymede is on the other side of Aarde from where we are. It is completely surrounded by water with a lot of volcanoes along its eastern shore. If Ganymede keeps growing at the same pace and direction, it might connect with IO in couple thousand years, but that is pure speculation because Aarde is so young. There is only one city—if you can call it that—on Ganymede called Proteus. By the way, did you hear that all the cities in Callisto are named after other moons of Jupiter, the cities of Thebe are named after moons of Saturn, cities of IO are named after moons of Uranus, and the cities of Ganymede are named after moons of Neptune? Well, if not, then now you know."

I was happy to be standing next to the window, but all I could see was it going from dark outer space to white clouds. I was very anxious to see land again and was a little surprised that I missed it so much. As I was staring out the window, the clouds started to thin out until our view was completely clear. I wasn't sure if the clouds had burnt off or if we were just below them. The view was astonishing. We could see the ocean on both sides of what I assumed was Callisto. On the eastern side, or the right side as I looked down, was an ocean that looked very much like the oceans of Earth—light blue near land and a darker blue further away. What took my breath away was the water on the left side of Callisto. Instead of shades of blues, its color was shades of red. It was a light red near the shore and a deep almost blood red further away.

Toby went on without skipping a beat. "The reason for the red water color is the heat from the all the volcanic activity on the eastern shore of Ganymede that causes a large algae bloom. The ocean Tyre Rood is named after the Kingdom of Tyre from Greek mythology along with Rood, which is a Dutch translation of red. The water near the coast of Ganymede is so hot that it's almost to the point of being scalding. Not that you can see it, but air circulates west to east, similar to the northern hemisphere of Earth. The wind current causes the red algae to move predominantly toward the west coast of Callisto." He went on to explain a lot more, but I just tuned him out to enjoy the view. We didn't get to see the red for long because we were lowering right toward the furthest point east in Callisto, the city called Metis.

I was half listening when Toby explained, "The elevator cable is anchored right on the edge of the coast so that if it ever did break, it would fall into the ocean and not onto the land where the people are. Twenty-five miles of cable this large would make quite a splash. The city of Metis is the largest city on Aarde with about ten thousand people, but it's growing quite rapidly and has a diverse culture. There are people from many countries on Earth who traveled to Aarde, so a lot of cultures and religions are now mixing. Not always with good results."

I continued to stare out the window at what would be our new home. It was very beautiful. As we got lower, we could see what Toby confirmed were snow-covered mountains inland from the water and long beaches along the shoreline. I overheard him say, "In Themisto, you can surf in eighty-five-degree water in the morning and climb in snow six feet deep the same afternoon. Sorry, no ski resorts yet."

Toby talked the whole trip down, either telling us about Aarde or answering questions. When we were getting close to the ground, he said, "Now even though the gravity on Aarde is only twenty percent of Earth's, it is going to hit you like a ton of bricks when we get to the bottom of the elevator. It will take about thirty minutes to depressurize and decontaminate the elevator before the doors will open to your new home. When the doors open and you try to walk, please use the handrails for support. Compared to the gravity of the spaceship, you will feel like you weigh four hundred pounds. If you're in good shape, your body will recover in a couple of days. Do you have any questions?"

A few people asked questions that I didn't pay attention to because the elevator had just gone through a hole in the roof of a building and stopped with a clunk. As soon as we stopped, my legs buckled, and I got very weak. I looked around and most of the people were either sitting or unsteadily standing. I saw Miranda jump a couple feet and almost fall when she landed.

Macie and I started to laugh at her and tried to jump ourselves. I made it about three feet but fell to my hands and knees when I landed. I heard Miranda laugh and say, "Macie, you only made it a couple of inches." As I got up, I looked around and saw that everyone was smiling but Jacob. It would be nice to be away from him even if I were going to have to be married for that to happen.

I then heard a whooshing sound, and it looked like it was raining through the window. The decontamination process of washing and depressurizing the elevator did take about thirty minutes, just like Toby had told us. My ears popped over and over during the process and were hurting when the door finally opened. We were nearest the door since we were the last ones to get on, so we got to go out first. I glanced over my shoulder and saw that Jacob was irritated that he didn't get to go first. As I walked down the steps to the floor, I looked around and saw a big door slide up and four men in suits come through it.

I could see a crowd outside the door being controlled by security guards. As soon as they saw us start down the steps, they started waving to us, and I heard a band start playing. I politely waved back as one of the security guards ushered us over to the corner of the room where the four men were waiting. I did notice that all of them smiled as soon as Jacob started down the stairs. They almost fell over themselves rushing over to shake his hand. As Jacob walked over to them, he had a clear air of superiority over them. The short man who shook Jacob's hand first cleared his throat and said, "Welcome to Aarde, Governor. I am Dexter Dunbar, mayor of Metis." Dexter turned to his right and motioned to a very tall black man and said, "This is Jack Underwood, Mayor of Ananka." Jack and Jacob shook hands. Then Dexter introduced Bob Crowly, mayor of Almathea, and the man behind him was his deputy mayor, Lee Ngyun.

Dexter turned to all of us and said, "Let me extend a hearty welcome from Aarde, your new home. I am Dexter Dunbar, the mayor of Metis. Don't worry about your weak legs—that will pass in a day or two, and you will feel fine. The recovery time is different for everyone. Please follow Deputy Mayor Lee Ngyun to your quarters." Jacob, Dexter, and the two other mayors went out the door with the rest of us following. As we left the building, there were a couple hundred people crowding around the exit but I didn't see any women. As we walked out, the crowd parted, and Jacob waved at them like he was a king. Miranda, Macie, and I just snickered as we followed.

As we emerged from the dark of the building, we all had to hold up our hands to shade our eyes because it was so bright out. On Aarde, there was light from two sources. It seemed like there were two suns. The sun was brighter than Jupiter, but it was smaller from the Aarde perspective. Lee told us about the different phases of an Aarde day that depended on the rotation and location of Jupiter. It was dark when Aarde was on the far side of Jupiter, away from the sun. It was twilight when facing Jupiter without the sun. And it was sort of a dim daytime when Aarde faced away from Jupiter toward the sun because of the greater distance. It was a bright daytime when you could see both Jupiter and the sun at the same time. All those different phases were quite a bit to comprehend ten minutes after we stepped out into a whole new world. I figured I would get used to it eventually.

Our eyes adjusted pretty quickly, and we were able to admire the beauty of Jupiter. At that moment, we could only see the top part of Jupiter, but its colors seemed brighter. Lee told us that the colors were enhanced because of the atmosphere and that Jupiter would be even more beautiful when the sun went down. He also told us that the complete rotation of Aarde was twenty-six Earth hours long instead of twenty-four and that all the clocks were thirteen hours instead of twelve. Lee told us it seemed confusing at first, but we'd get used to it very quickly.

All of us were following Jacob and the Mayors as we walked toward what looked like the town square. Looking back toward the building we'd left, I saw that it was the largest building around, and it looked very strange as the elevator cables went up into the sky and disappeared. I started getting choked up as I thought about my mother, father, and little sister. The more I thought, the more depressed I became. Miranda and Macie noticed me and put their arms around me as I walked, asking what was wrong. After I told them, they got emotional as well. The people around were staring, but they didn't say anything. After a few minutes of moping along while walking, I stopped and turned to see where Jacob was. He was just about to get into a car and happened to look over at us. I could have sworn that he looked directly at me and smirked before climbing into the car and being driven away.

I told Macie and Miranda, "I hate that man and will get him back if it's the last thing I do."

Miranda and Macie smiled and said, "And we will help you do it."

We had fallen behind the group and jogged to catch up. It felt very strange to jog with more gravity pulling you down. I would go a few steps, and then my legs would give out and I would almost fall. Each time I recovered, though, I felt more coordinated and my legs felt better. Macie was really struggling to keep up, but Miranda ran on ahead of me like she wasn't even affected. Once we caught up with the group, we looked around the town square. It reminded me of downtown Carrollton, and I half expected to see a Babe's Restaurant around the corner. That would have been nice, but there were just a few shops, a couple of hardware stores, a feed store, some real estate offices, and, of course, a couple of bars. There was also a bank.

Just off the square we saw what must be the government offices. The biggest building had a sign on it that said *Metis City Hall*. With the parking lot, it took up a whole block. Across the street were two hotels. One call Hotel Metis and the other one called The Aardemore. *How original!* I thought Hotel Metis looked like a typical Holiday Inn, nice but not fancy. The Aardemore reminded me of the Gaylord Texan in Grapevine, Texas. It looked big and expensive. The first thing Macie said when she saw it was that she hoped we would be staying there. We all smiled wide when we followed Lee into The Aardemore.

It was almost as nice as the Gaylord but had more of a country décor with paintings of mountains, lakes, trees, and flowers. There was one really beautiful painting that showed a white sandy beach with red water and what looked like two suns—one was the sun, and the other was Jupiter. It was so striking that our whole group just stopped and stared at it. Lee saw us stop and said, "Yes, nearly everyone stops and stares at that painting. It is the sunset and Jset over the Tyre Rood Sea. We call Jupiter rising and setting *Jrise* and *Jset*. Aarde is a very new and beautiful world." Lee continued, "Please check in at the registration desk when you are ready. Your luggage from the spaceship will be delivered to your room later tonight. All the passengers will disembark, and then the luggage and supplies will be brought down." After another few minutes staring at the painting, we went up to the counter to check in. Of course, Macie crowded her way almost to the front. We stepped up right after two men finished. They were dressed very nicely but acted rudely to the lady at the registration desk. I didn't hear exactly what they'd said, but they seemed to be complaining about not getting as good a room as they had expected.

The lady—her nametag read Lia—said, "Welcome to The Aardemore, you must be Madison, Miranda, and Macie. We are very happy to have you here. You will be in one of the penthouse suites right next to Governor Jacob Verndari. He is our honored guest, as well as you three. Fortunately for us, his governor's mansion won't be finished for a few weeks."

I thought to myself, *Will we ever be away from him?* She gave each of us a key. I looked at it and asked, "Exactly how do you use this?"

Lia laughed and apologized. "I'm sorry—I didn't realize how young you are. On Earth, everything is electronic, even the keys. While Aarde does have some technology, it's still quite primitive. When you get to your room, just slide the key in the hole below the doorknob and turn. It will unlock the door, and you will be able to turn the knob and open it." I felt very stupid and nodded to Macie and Miranda to follow me. Lia said, "Don't forget—there is an introduction dinner tonight in the first-floor dining room at 7 pm. The dinner dress is casual since you might or might not have your luggage delivered by then."

We all went to the elevator, and of course Macie had to be the one to push the button to call it and then to push the floor number. She pushed four when we got inside, and the doors closed. It sure was a slow elevator, but we finally arrived on the fourth floor. When we got out, we saw a door to our right that had a one on it. There wasn't a hallway past that door. We walked a little ways to the left and saw a door with the number two on it. That was our room. Past our room was a long hallway with doors quite a ways down. Before I could put the key in the hole, Macie had already grabbed the key and unlocked and opened the door. We stepped inside.

CHAPTER 28

What we saw inside was a combination of opulence with a country accent. The couches were covered in velvet, but the style was more country with lots of hardwood. The chairs and desk were hardwood stained dark. The living room was huge, and there was even a kitchen. Macie noticed right off that there wasn't a television. I couldn't even remember how long it had been since I watched a TV show. There was a door next to the kitchen, and a hallway that led off to the left. Behind the door was a bathroom with a sink and a toilet. Down the hall were three bedrooms and a bathroom between two of the bedrooms. One was very large with lavish furnishing including silk sheets and a king-size four poster bed with an attached bathroom. The other two were quite a bit smaller but still furnished very nicely with what looked like double sleigh beds.

Macie immediately called the large bedroom. Miranda was about ready to push Macie out of the way to take the room when I suggested, "Why don't we do rock, paper, scissors to see who gets it?"

Macie cried out, "No! I called it first, so I get it!"

Miranda said, "No, Macie. Either rock, paper, scissors, or Madison and I will ensure you *don't* get it."

Macie pouted for a few seconds and then said, "How about we take turns—and I get it first?"

I said, "That's fine, but let's do rock, paper, scissors for who goes first. We can each do two days. We're only going to be here a week before we're forced to get married." That statement made us all sad, and we were silent a few seconds as we got our hands ready for the game.

We decided that when you lost two times, you were out. We all recited the lines—rock, paper, scissors, shoot. Macie opened her hand, signifying paper, and both Miranda and I kept a fist that signified rock, so Macie won round one. Next round, both

Miranda and I did rock while Macie spread her middle and index finger signifying scissors. All of us were tied at one loss. Round three, Macie and I did rock while Miranda did paper. Miranda was the winner. Now Macie and I had to go to see who got the big bedroom second. "Rock, paper, scissors, shoot!" Macie and I said. I did scissors and Macie did paper. I smiled and said, "Cool, I get it second."

Macie rolled her eyes and immediately said, "I get the room on the right!"

I just smiled and said, "Okay, Macie, you choose."

We were all tired from the day and the increase in gravity, so we decided to just stay in our room and rest until dinner. I wasn't sure how long we had been up because what constituted a day had changed from the spaceship to Aarde. The spaceship didn't have real days and nights, so we must have gotten up this morning in the middle of the Aarde night that had been morning on the spaceship. Aarde was only twenty percent of Earth's gravity, but that was about nineteen times more gravity than we'd had on the spaceship. No matter what the cause, I was wiped out and went into my room. I was too tired to even crawl under the covers. I just lay down on the top of the comforter and was asleep almost immediately. I vaguely remember hearing Macie start the shower before I nodded off.

I wasn't sure how long I slept, but I felt very disoriented when I woke up. It didn't take long for that feeling to pass once I remembered where I was and how I got here even though we still hadn't been told why we were sent. Eventually, I got up and went into the living room, but no one was there. I figured Miranda and Macie must still be asleep.

I went into the kitchen and looked in the refrigerator. It wasn't a large one, but it was fully stocked with drinks and some vegetables. I looked in the cabinet and saw little bags of chips. I didn't recognize the labels, but the flavors were the same as I was used to. I selected a bag of barbecue-flavored chips and went into the living room to sit down. I remembered doing this at my home in Carrollton except here there was no television to watch. I wondered how people filled all their time without television. I guess I was going to find out because it didn't look like this was going to be my home for a long time.

I looked at the clock, and it was six. I would have started getting ready for dinner, but we didn't have any clothes except for what we'd worn down from the spaceship. I decided I should at least take a shower, so I went in the bathroom. It was a mess. Macie left two wet towels and a washrag on the floor. I kicked them over to a corner and started the shower. It was going to be so great to have a nice long shower with no one waiting and no time limit. I was standing there, enjoying the hot water for about twenty minutes when Macie banged on the bathroom door. I yelled, "What is it?" she yelled back that our stuff had been dropped off. I was looking forward to unpacking and organizing it all in drawers and a closet instead of having to put it all back in the bag every time we changed clothes. I quickly finished washing my hair and got out of the shower to go unpack.

I wrapped a towel around me and opened the bathroom door. My duffel bag was sitting right outside my bedroom door. I walked over to Macie's door, opened it, and looked in. Macie had dumped everything on the bed and was going through it, picking out what she was going to wear. What a mess, typical Macie — stuff thrown everywhere. I closed her door and opened Miranda's. She had just put her bag next to her bed and was back asleep. Very typical Miranda. I said, "Miranda, are you going to be ready for dinner in thirty?"

She opened her eyes and looked at me seriously and said, "When have I ever been late?"

I just shook my head and carried my bag into my room. It was about as heavy as a full backpack. I think I could get used to this low gravity. I unpacked and hung up all the stuff in my duffel bag as I searched for an outfit I wanted to wear. I picked the yellow sundress in memory of my father. He loved most anything yellow. One time he showed me a picture when he was about four or five.

He had on a yellow suit. He looked so cute, and he told me his brothers and sisters called him "banana boy" for a long time after wearing that suit.

I chose the white sandals and put my hair in a ponytail. Just as I finished up in the bathroom, Macie came out of her bedroom wearing a very pretty green sundress. I went to check on Miranda since it was almost time to go. She was wearing jeans and a black tank top. Not quite dressed up, but this was what she normally wore when given a choice. Everyone was ready, so we went into the hall and locked the door. I handed the key to Miranda to carry since she was the only one with pockets. She put it in her front pocket, and we walked to the elevator.

As usual, Macie rushed ahead to push the down button and the first-floor button once we got inside the car. The elevator stopped on the third floor, and some women from the spaceship got on. All of them were dressed in tank tops and short shorts that showed way too much of their body. We had avoided them as much as we could on the ship and had hoped we would be able to do the same for this next week, but it looked doubtful.

Portia and Emily immediately looked us up and down, and Portia said, "How do you expect to land a husband in *those* outfits? We didn't say anything, but I could tell Macie's feelings were hurt because she really liked to dress cute. Miranda looked indifferent to her comment, much as I expected she would. Miranda enjoyed revenge much more than immediate reactions.

We made it to the first floor, and the doors opened. As I expected, Portia was the first one to go out the door. Just as she stepped off, Miranda bumped her back leg enough to hit the back of her front leg. As it did, she fell forward and landed on her hands. The other ladies were in such a hurry to get off that three of them tumbled over Portia and fell also. When they all glared up at us, Miranda said, "Oh, excuse me. May I help you up?" and offered her hand to Portia.

Portia glared at Miranda and slapped her hand away as she struggled to get up. Once up, she glared at Miranda and said, "I will get you back for that one!" Miranda didn't say anything but was smiling as the women walked away.

We followed a distance behind them into a huge room filled with tables. As we walked around the room, we observed the paintings on the walls. The paintings were of mountains, rivers, and what looked like oceans that were completely unfamiliar to me. The paintings must have been of different places on Aarde. There was a beautiful one of the sun and Jupiter setting on a red sea. That had to have been the Tyre Rood they had told us about. On each table, there were name tents. We looked and looked but didn't find ours until we got to the table right next to the stage. All of the names on our table were men's names except for ours. I only recognized one name and that was the deputy mayor's—Lee Ngyun. I was very glad I didn't see Jacob's name.

I looked at the table up on the stage and was sure that was where Jacob was going to sit. Along with the table on the stage, there was a podium and microphone. We wandered around a little while and then sat down to wait. Behind each name tent was a piece of paper with the week's agenda on it. It was as follows:

Day 1
- Orientation Dinner

Day 2
- Breakfast in room or dining room
- Meet and Greet Lunch on the deck
- Intro Ball (dinner and dancing, formal attire required)

Day 3
- Champagne Brunch
- Date Night Dinner

Day 4
- Breakfast in room or dining room
- Lunch Date
- Date Night Dinner

Day 5
- Brunch
- Dinner Cruise

Day 6
- Breakfast and lunch in room or dining room
- Proposal Ball

Day 7
- Engagement Breakfast on the deck
- Marriages in church

Just after I had finished reading through it for the second time, I felt a tap on my shoulder and looked up at the same time Miranda and Macie did to see Lee Ngyun. He said, "Very nice to see you ladies again. I hope you enjoy your week." And then he sat down in his assigned seat next to Macie. When I looked around some more, I saw that the table on the stage was now occupied by Jacob and the mayor of Metis, Dexter Dunbar. They sat next to each other. I wasn't sure if Jacob's head could get any bigger or whether he could paste a more arrogant look on his face than what he had at that moment. He just happened to look at me the same time, and I felt my anger and hatred of him shifting deeper and deeper into my soul.

We kept staring at each other until the mayor got up and walked to the podium. He tapped on the microphone a couple times to ensure it was working and then started his speech. I call it a speech because he droned on for about ten minutes about how excited he was to have new immigrants here and then introduced all the dignitaries at his table. Of course, Jacob was the last one to be introduced as the new governor of the largest and most populous state of Callisto. Everyone clapped as Jacob stood, waved, and walked over to the podium to shake Mayor Dexter's hand. The mayor seemed a bit surprised that Jacob had come to the podium and even more surprised as Jacob stepped around him to stand in front of the podium like he was going to address the audience. Since we were so close to the stage, I could hear what they were saying.

The mayor said to Jacob, "What are you doing? This isn't on the agenda for tonight."

Jacob whispered back to the mayor, "Please go sit down. I'll explain later. Remember, you work for *me* now." The mayor looked flustered but did as he was told. Jacob stood straight and started to speak into the microphone. "Thank you all for your warm welcome to Europa, and thanks to Mayor Dunbar."

A few people were snickering, and I heard somebody say, "He's governor and he doesn't even know to call our home Aarde!"

Jacob continued. "I have been looking forward to coming to Europa for a long time and am very proud to be your governor." I glanced over at the table on the stage, and a few of the men there didn't look too comfortable with Jacob speaking. Jacob went on. "I had heard about problems on Europa, and I am here to do everything in my power to address and correct those problems. With that, I will turn things back over to Mayor Dunbar."

Jacob sat down, and the mayor went back to the podium again. He still seemed quite rattled as he started to speak once again. "If you look at your agenda, you will see the week's activities. This is a very special week in Aarde. We celebrate the new world along with all the new families we will have at the end of the week. Remember parties are not all that Metis has to offer. Feel free to go exploring around Metis and Ananke. Metis is very well known on Aarde for its variety of beautiful beaches. On the north side of the Texas point is the whitest and softest sand you have ever laid eyes on. The wind almost always blows from south to north so the north side of the point is very calm. Texas point was named by some early workers from Texas who though it looked like the part of Texas near El Paso.

"The south side of Texas point has better surfing than Hawaii. The steady south wind and northward current from the sea of Marius meets the Sea of Galilee just south of Texas point and provides perfect surfing waves. As you will notice, there are very few cars and trucks here, and even fewer airplanes. The cars are used mostly for special occasions and by dignitaries. The airplanes and helicopters are for the exclusive use of the military, and the trucks are used for mining. That leaves horses and walking for the rest of us. Guides will be provided for you during your exploration so you will be safe and can learn about your new world. If you look at the agenda, you will see that you have most of the days free to rest and recreate as the parties occur during the evenings. With that said, please enjoy your week and make yourself at home, especially since this is now your new home. Dinner will be served shortly."

Mayor Dunbar finally sat down, and a waiter appeared at our table. There was a wide selection of foods to choose from. As always, when presented with a choice, Macie chose steak cooked medium rare and Miranda chose chicken strips. I was very hungry, so I followed Macie's choice of steak. After we and the others at our table had ordered, I looked around and saw that Jacob's table on the stage and ours were the only two that had waiters. The rest of the people were lining up at a buffet. Being associated with Jacob did have its perks, even though I despised him and what he had done to us.

While I was looking around, the man sitting next to me introduced himself as William Hickok, owner of the Silver Dollar mining company. He looked to be at least forty because I saw a bit of gray hair above his ears. He introduced the gentleman to his left as John Steele, part owner of the Metis Thermisto railroad company. John looked quite a bit younger than William, but then again I had never been very good at guessing people's ages.

I introduced myself, Miranda, and Macie to them. Miranda said hi, but Macie was busy asking Lee questions and didn't even acknowledge me. William asked me where I was from and why a beautiful woman like me would want to come to a new and wild world. I was very flattered by his compliment, but remembered well Jacob's warning not to tell anyone why we were there, so I lied and said my sisters and I were just looking for adventure because we didn't have any family left on Earth. He looked at me like he wasn't sure I was telling the truth, so I started peppering him with questions about himself and his company. I wanted to distract him from asking more questions about us. He asked me to call him Bill.

"When I was younger," Bill said, "I was a manager of a steel mill in Pittsburgh, Pennsylvania. Allegheny Steel. The owners wanted to start a mining company on Europa and needed someone to run it. I talked to my nephew about the opportunity. He had recently graduated with a doctorate in metallurgy and was working in the research department. This was a perfect opportunity for him to work with minerals no one had ever worked with before, so he didn't hesitate in saying yes. We named the new company Silver Dollar Mining Co. We have enjoyed every minute we've been here. The only thing I regret was not bringing a wife with along with me." I blushed a bit, suddenly realizing why he was at this dinner. He was here to bid on a wife.

I asked him, "Where's your nephew?"

"Wyatt is up the coast near Titania. Our iron mine struck gold. He's testing to estimate how much gold there is. Iron is more useful here on Aarde, but gold is popular everywhere. Wyatt despises the whole Proposal thing and always leaves Metis during that week. He wants to get married the old-fashioned way. I'm not sure there is an old-fashioned way on Aarde." I laughed politely at his joke but was thinking that I would prefer the old-fashioned way to being bid on like a cow. Wyatt did sound like a nice guy. I thought I might like to meet him sometime. Our food came as I was finishing that thought.

My steak was cooked perfectly with just a tinge of red in the middle. Bill noticed my steak and said to me, "Do you taste that extra flavor in your steak?"

I took another bite and after swallowing, I said, "Yes, it's very subtle, and I don't think I would have noticed it if you hadn't pointed it out." I looked over at Macie to tell her, but she had already finished her meal and was talking with Lee again. Bill laughed at Macie having eaten so fast, and I said, "She'll only eat the meat and no vegetables. Our parents always had to force her to eat her vegetables. Watch this. Macie, eat your vegetables."

Macie looked at me and said. "You're not my boss!" All of us at the table laughed.

"That extra flavor in the meat is the hay that the cows eat," Bill explained. "Before they brought cows to Aarde, they seeded miles of open range with the best grass seed from Earth. The cows thrived on miles and miles of perfect grass."

Miranda had listened to my conversation with Bill and to Macie's with Lee but had hardly spoken at all. That was not unusual at all for Miranda. She would just stay quiet until someone asked her opinion, and then her response would usually be surprising because it would become obvious she'd been paying attention the whole time. Bill asked her how she liked Aarde so far. Miranda got right to the point "I don't want to be here, and I haven't seen anything outside of this hotel. So what's there to like?" Bill looked surprised but didn't question her and seemed to know better than to push the conversation. Since all of us were finished eating, I suggested we go up to our room. As we stood, all the men at the table stood up, too. We were walking toward the exit when I glanced up to the stage and saw Jacob motioning us over to his table. I just feigned confusion about his gestures and waved as we left. He probably wanted to show off for us some more.

CHAPTER 29

We went up to the room, put our pajamas on, and were sitting in the living room chatting when we heard a knock on the door. Macie got up and opened it. Jacob burst in, red-faced and in a rage, and started yelling at us. "Don't you ever turn your back and walk out on me like that again."

Miranda and Macie looked at him, surprised, and Miranda said, "I have no idea what you're talking about."

Before Jacob responded, I said in a calming voice, "Jacob, I saw you wave good night to us. I didn't realize wanted us to come over."

Jacob fumed. "You knew very well I wanted you to come over to my table. I will not put up with your disrespect. I am the governor of this state right now and will be appointed the president of Aarde in the near future."

We all looked at him like he was crazy as he continued his rant. "As governor. I have a lot of power. As president, I will have nearly unlimited power. As your governor, I have the power to change The Proposal rules. For instance, I can override a bid and choose who each of you gets married to. Think about that before you disrespect me again. I could easily marry the three of you off to men from different parts of Aarde, and you'll never see each other again." We all were shocked that he would even consider that.

Miranda said defiantly, "I would never go."

Jacob just laughed and said, "Have you forgotten what happened on the spaceship? I have even more power here than I did on that ship."

Miranda just glared at him while I said, "Jacob, we get your point."

He lowered his voice and said, "You will call me Governor or Mr. Verndari. I will not tolerate disrespect from you three."

All of us intoned, "Yes, Governor." Macie said it in a British accent, and we all started laughing. Jacob glared at us.

His glare turned into a smirk as he started talking again. "Madison, I am still deciding what to do with your sisters. Selling them in The Proposal would be a good option that would bring me a lot of money. I am Discover for all three of you, so I get sixty percent of the bid profits. As I mentioned before, I could choose their husbands and have them sent to different parts of Aarde. I could also keep them with me until they are of age and then sell them later in another Proposal. I could even let them live with you until they are of age.

"There is talk among the people to get rid of The Proposal and let people marry who they want. I don't think I will let that happen, though. I might even impose a tax so I get a cut of every bid. All that being said, here is what it boils down to for you three. Madison, you will be getting married in five days. What happens to your sisters is up to how you three treat me. Cross me, and I guarantee you will not like the result. If you do what I say and show me respect, it might not turn out too badly for you. But I will win either way."

We were quiet and stared at him for a few seconds before he turned and headed for the door, saying "think about it" as he left. We were all pretty tired from the day, so we didn't say much and went straight to bed. As tired as I was, it still took a while for me to get to sleep. I missed the rest of my family and said a prayer that we would all be back together again someday. It had been over a year since we had seen them. Morgan would be walking and talking by now. I knew in my heart that if my parents were not still in jail, they would be trying to find us.

I eventually fell asleep but awakened to someone shaking me. I looked up and saw it was the man who'd helped us to escape in New Mexico—the one I had seen on the spaceship. He was telling me to get up and get packed. I was too sleepy and bewildered to do anything but mumble, "What's happening?"

He said, "It's time to go if you don't want to be sold."

That jolted me awake, and I jumped out of bed. "What do I need to do?"

"As soon as you and your sisters get dressed and pack your bags, we will leave. Wear something warm because it's cool outside, and we will end up in the mountains before the trip is over."

He stepped out while I got dressed in jeans, a sweatshirt, and some boots. I told him he could come back in and then asked where we were going.

"We need to get you away from Metis to get you safe. There's no time for questions, so let me help you."

I kept quiet while the both of us stuffed all my clothes in my duffel bag. When we finished, I asked, "Can I know your name now?"

"Yes, my name is Xander. I will tell you the rest of the story when we get to where we are going." We left my room to go to the living room, and I saw Miranda sitting next to her bag. Not surprising since she hadn't even unpacked.

I looked in Macie's room. The boy we'd chased in Zero Grav on the space station was helping her pack her stuff. She was dressed similarly to me. They were almost finished. I asked Xander, "What's the boy's name? He wouldn't give it to us when we met him on the space station.

"His name is Edmond, and he is my son. Thank you for not trying to talk to us on the trip. It could have been very dangerous for all of us. Now that we're here, we have a group that's helping us."

"Really? How did they know we were coming?"

"We've been tracking you ever since you were taken from your home. Once we found out you were being sent here, we put together a plan to free you. I'll tell you more about it later, but now we need to leave."

Just then Macie came out of her room with Edmond following her, carrying her bag. It was very nice of him to help but not surprising that Macie would enlist help. Xander led the way out of our suite with Macie, Edmond, me, and Miranda following. Xander had offered to take Miranda's and my bag, but we had politely refused. It was awkward to carry, but it wasn't any heavier than the backpack stuffed with school books I used to carry in school.

We went down the stairs and out the back door of the hotel to the street. The whole town seemed deserted as we walked through it. I guess that's the nightlife of a small town. There were a few street lights, so we stayed in the shadows where we could. Xander told us to be quiet, so we didn't talk as we made our way. It took about twenty minutes to get to the edge of town where a man and seven horses were waiting. One of the horses was already loaded down with what looked like supplies. I guessed we were going to be traveling for quite a few days. Xander introduced the man as Philip Marshall. He didn't look very old, but it was tough to tell through his scruffy beard. He even said "hello, ma'am" with a twang. We all had ridden horses before, but Miranda had had a bad experience when we were younger and was afraid of them.

When she was about ten, we were on a trail ride in Palo Duro Canyon. Her horse stopped to eat some leaves off some bushes. The horse in front of her got way ahead, so by the time she was able to get her horse moving again, it took off at a gallop to catch up. When her horse caught up with the one in front of her, Miranda started to climb off, saying she was going to walk the rest of the way. It had taken Dad about fifteen minutes to calm her down enough so that she would stay on the horse and finish the ride. We hadn't been able to get her back on a horse since then.

When Miranda saw the horses and understood we were going to have to ride them, she said, "There is no way I'm riding a horse."

Xander just looked at her and asked, "Why not?"

Miranda didn't give a reason. She just stood there and said, "No way am I riding a horse."

Macie and I tried to encourage her. "Come on, Miranda, you can do it." Miranda just shook her head no.

Xander was starting to panic about what we were going to do when Macie suggested that Miranda ride with her or with me. Miranda said, "I've seen you ride, Macie, and there's no way I'll get on with you."

Xander spoke up. "Miranda, I've been riding since I was a little kid and know horses very well. We would make much better time and you would be more comfortable if you rode by yourself, but would you consider riding with me?" Miranda thought about it a few seconds and nodded yes—but everyone could tell she was terrified.

Philip, Xander, and Edmond tied our bags to a horse while Macie and I climbed onto our horses. Philip helped Miranda get on behind Xander, and then he and Edmond got on theirs. We started riding single file, away from Metis, down a trail wide enough for only one horse at a time. Philip was in the lead, followed by Macie, myself, Edmond with a pack horse, and Xander and Miranda with a final pack horse in tow. I really had no idea where we were going but didn't really care—as long as we were away from Jacob. Especially after that last outburst he'd had in our room.

We had to ride single file for a couple of miles until we intersected with a road. The road was more like a wide trail than a road back on Earth. It was quite overgrown with grass and flowers, but you could make out the ruts that cars would make. We were able to ride two abreast on the road which was a nice change. Macie was peppering Philip with questions about horses and where we were going. Xander and Miranda had pulled up even with me, and Edmond was riding behind me and next to the pack horse.

I asked Xander where we were headed. He said, "We're going to a house outside of Elara. It belongs to a friend and should be safe until we can move on. We'll only be there during the day tomorrow to rest."

Miranda said, "Do you think Jacob will come after us?"

"No doubt about it," said Xander. "He doesn't seem like the type of person to put up with you escaping. He was planning to make quite a bit of money off you three. He has a lot of power as governor, but he needs money to finance his ambitions to be President of Aarde."

"Who is the current president?" I asked.

Xander shook his head. "There isn't one. We don't need of a president. The governors and mayors have too much power as it is."

We rode another hour or so without talking much. Xander told us all to be very quiet as we rode through Elara. It was still dark outside, but from what I could see, it looked like one of those Wild West towns I had seen in history books. All the buildings were made of plain wood. It was much different from Metis. There were no street lights at all, but they weren't really needed because Jupiter was high overhead, and that made it more like twilight than real dark. It only took us about ten minutes to ride through, and then we were back on the road. Xander had mentioned that we were going north, but it was tough for me to tell because I had always been directionally challenged anyway.

About thirty minutes past Elara's outskirts, Philip turned into the trees just as the sun was coming up. I didn't even see a trail, and it was only wide enough for one horse at a time. We were back to single file riding again, same order as before. This trail seemed more like a walking trail than a riding because it was very winding and we had to keep ducking under branches. We finally emerged from the trees and saw a small two-story house in the center of a clearing. It looked more like a cabin than the houses I was used to seeing on Earth, but it did have a very pretty porch all the way around it.

We climbed off the horses and grabbed our bags to bring inside. I looked around as we walked up the steps to the porch. The wood on the porch was very clean and looked quite new. The area around the house must have been recently cleared because I could still see the stumps of cut trees. Inside, there was a very large living room furnished with a couple of couches and chairs — and a large, rustic fireplace. Off to the right was a small kitchen with a stove, unlike anything I had ever seen before. It was cast iron and had a bunch of wood on the bottom shelf. I was expecting the house it to be primitive, but wasn't prepared for how nicely furnished it was.

There were stairs on the left side of the room which led up to the second story. Xander motioned for us to take our stuff up to the far room upstairs. He and Edmond would take the other room upstairs, and Philip would use the small room off the living room downstairs. We lugged our bags up to the far room and glanced around. There were two sets of bunk beds on the right of the room and a desk to the left. Macie ran and threw her duffel bag onto one of the top bunks. Miranda did the same to the other top one. That just left me the choice of the bottom ones. I chose the one under Macie because Macie likes having someone close to her while Miranda likes to be left alone.

We looked around the room a bit and then out the windows. The room was plain—just a desk and the beds. There were a couple pipes between the bunk beds with some wooden hangers hanging from them. The view out the windows of the cleared field and trees was very pretty. I was tempted to get in bed because I was so exhausted from riding all night and getting very little sleep the day before when Xander woke me up. Miranda and Macie looked as tired as I felt. I was about to suggest a nap when Xander yelled for us to come downstairs. We slowly moved from our room to the stairs.

Xander motioned us to sit down at the dining table. I saw Philip busying himself in the kitchen, making what looked like bacon and eggs. My mouth started to water as I got a good whiff of the bacon, and it was only a couple more minutes before Philip set a huge stack of bacon and bowl of scrambled eggs in front of us. I dug into the eggs with a spoon and grabbed a handful of bacon right after Macie did. As we started to eat, Xander spoke up "We're only staying here today and will leave tonight for the town of Titania in the state of IO. If Jacob does find us there, he will have to work with Governor Henry Merric of IO to get you back and to punish Philip, Edmond, and myself. Philip has met Henry before, and he seems like a good governor who might help us. But first we must get there.

"After you finish eating, you need to get some sleep because we have another long night of riding ahead of us. From the looks of you three, you probably won't need much encouragement to sleep." I looked over at Macie and Miranda, watching as Macie's head kept nodding. Miranda's fork was moving slower and slower. I was barely able to hold my head up as I finished my breakfast.

Macie was the first one finished, and she asked, "Can I go up to bed now?"

"Yes," said Xander, "please do because we will have a long night traveling to Titania." Miranda and I dragged ourselves out of our chairs and followed our sister up the stairs to our room. None of us even undressed but just flopped down on the beds and were asleep immediately.

I must have slept the whole day because when I woke up, the sun was just going down. I could also smell the most wonderful aroma coming from downstairs. Miranda was still sleeping, but Macie was already gone. "Miranda," I said. "Time to get up. We need to get going soon." Miranda ignored me as usual, so I said it again. This time she stirred.

"Just five more minutes!" she begged.

I said, "Smell the air and you won't want to wait the five minutes!"

Miranda sniffed and then started to get out of bed, saying, "Please wait for me." I waited for her to get up, and then we went down.

The smell was just too good to be true as we walked down the stairs. Philip was sizzling steaks over an open flame on the stove. I almost ran down the stairs but noticed my legs weren't working as smoothly as I was used to. I walked stiff-legged down the stairs and up to the table. It slowly dawned on me that I was sore from riding that horse all night. I looked over and saw Miranda was walking funny, too. Macie got up and moved around the table to hand Miranda and me each a glass of orange juice and then she poured some powder into it.

I looked at her and asked, "What's that?"

"Kratom powder," she said. "Similar to aspirin but natural. And it works better. I took it thirty minutes ago and I feel great—no soreness from the horseback riding."

I took a sip and didn't notice any taste other than great-tasting orange juice, so I drank the rest and asked for more. Macie wasn't so accommodating after she'd had her moment of attention, so Philip came around and poured me another glass. He also poured Miranda a second glass as she had finished also.

We all had steaks, a baked potato, and beans to eat. It was the second best steak I'd ever had. My uncle still holds the title of "best steak ever." As we started to eat, I asked for a clearer idea of what we were going to do. "Now that we're not so sleepy, would you please tell us where we're going—and what we're going to do once we get there? Are we really free from Jacob?"

Xander sat for a few moments and then began. "We're leaving for Titania tonight to get you away from Jacob. I'm hoping that the governor of IO, Henry Merric, will be willing to protect you from Jacob. He has a great reputation for being fair and kind to the people of his state. We will stay at Bill Hickok's ranch outside of Titania." I remembered Bill was the one I had talked to at the orientation dinner. Xander continued, "He helped to plan your escape and volunteered his ranch as our destination. He's also very good friends with Governor Merric."

Bill Hickok had seemed very trustworthy, so I was glad we were going to be staying at his ranch. I had gotten along with him really well at the orientation dinner and was looking forward to seeing him again. I asked, "How far is it to Titania?"

"We should be there a couple hours after the sun comes up," Philip answered.

I was dreading another night of riding but didn't feel very sore because the Kraton was starting to work. We finished up eating and loaded up the horses again.

Macie and I climbed onto our horses, and Miranda got on with Xander again. It was an uneventful ride into the sunlight of the next day. We had to stop a few times for rest breaks and to eat some snacks and drink some water, but it was a really a boring ride. As we rode through Titania, I wondered if it was really big enough to qualify as a town. All it had was one street with buildings on either side—a grocery store, a building supply store, a saloon, a jail, a barber shop, a bank, a stable, and a few buildings without signs. Maybe buildings without signs were built expecting future expansion.

Once through the town, we rode a couple more miles on the road and then turned left onto a smaller road. It was well-maintained as far as the roads here went. Since the sun was up, we got to experience the beauty of our new world. Xander had told us we were in the mountains, and now I could see the peaks covered with snow off in the distance. We had on warm clothes, but the temperature was fairly moderate as we traveled.

We passed a few roads with signs showing some people's names. I remember seeing Jones, Smith, and Rumpelstiltskin. Hard to believe someone was actually named that, but it was right there on the sign. We went a few more miles and then passed under an arched sign that said *Hickok Ranch*. I looked ahead and saw a very large ranch style house sitting atop a hill overlooking a beautiful valley with many cattle grazing contentedly. As we approached the house, I saw a man standing on the porch.

He waved and started to walk toward us. I immediately recognized Bill Hickok, the man I met at the orientation. I felt like I was going to fall off the horse I was so tired, and I barely made it to him before he helped me down. I was a little wobbly but was able to give him a hug and tell him how thankful we were for him helping us. I saw that Macie and Miranda followed my lead and did the same. He just said, "You are very welcome. I have some great news to tell you as soon as we get inside."

I looked at him but didn't say anything because I was just so tired. Philip told us to go inside while he and Edmond unloaded and took care of the horses. I said a silent prayer, thanking the horses for taking us far away from Jacob. The animals looked to be almost as tired as I felt. As we went inside, Bill motioned us to have a seat on the couch. The couch was nice and soft so I knew it wouldn't take long to fall asleep in it if given a chance. Xander sat down in one of the chairs next to the couch.

Bill pulled up a chair in front of us and said, "I have great news. I've talked to Governor Merric, and he says that you three are not legally bound by The Proposal because it was not your choice. I explained to him how you were brought here against your will and that Jacob was going to sell all three of you." We all looked at him in surprise.

"How did you know all this?" I asked.

Bill just said, "I have my ways. Let's leave it at that. You three are free to make your own choices now. A governor only has jurisdiction in his state. If you do go back to Callisto, then Jacob could make some trouble for you. I'm not sure what he could do, but governors do control the government and can influence laws. You are best not going to Callisto for at least a few years just to be safe and are welcome to stay at this ranch as long as you would like."

Even though I was dead tired, I got up and gave him another hug from happiness. I was so relieved that my sisters and I did not have to get married and were going to be able to stay together. After a few minutes of us hugging and crying from our happiness, Bill spoke again. "I have other news for you—even better than not having to get married."

I couldn't even imagine what it could be and asked, "What could be better than not being sold and having to get married? Other than getting to go back to Earth, of course."

Bill became a bit somber and said, "I wish I could send you back to be with your family, but I have something close. I received a communication from Earth that your father is alive and will be coming to Aarde!"

Made in the USA
Charleston, SC
30 July 2015